# J. A. JACKSON

# Mistress of Desire & The Orchid Lover!

## *Book I*

IngramSpark

Lightning
Source™

an INGRAM Content company
More at lightningsource.com

*Dedication:*
*For Rossi V. Jackson Jr., who was with me when I wrote my first seven*
*novels. He was my editor, my best friend and my husband.*
*In loving memory of Rossi V. Jackson Jr. 1942 - 2015...*

"Better know your friends
 Or
you might get burned…"

~ JERREECE A JACKSON

# Contents

# Acknowledgement

**To my readers and fans, I am forever grateful. Thank you.**

Next, I'd like to give out a big endless gratitude of thanks and appreciation for the wonderful support and editorial guidance of my editor the very knowledgeable Mr. Rossi V. Jackson.

*I'd also like to say a special thanks to the incredible man in my life, my husband who believed in my writing and supported my dreams.*

**Also, a special thanks to my sisters Kay, Shelia and Marie. And my brothers Ray and Eric I thank you all for your wonderful support.**

*For Rossi, Daddy & Mommy always...*

# I

# Welcome!

# Prologue

**Eyes playing tricks...**

Camille Baptiste shook out her thoughts. She was dead tired, she realized as she made her way down the street toward her mother's house. It was then it happened. She saw the lights flash as if by magic, she stopped abruptly and turned her head.

Camille Baptiste's eyes widened in recognition. She stood staring spellbound. A ghostly white light glowed back at her. It raised the hairs on the back of her neck.

She gasped and took a step back. Disbelieving panic overtook her. "Desmond… Desmond… But you're dead. I saw them kill you."

Desmond's body floated like a vapor on the wind.

That was the last thing Camille remembered before the shock took her body and she fell hard to the ground.

The shrill shriek of a siren blaring imperiously was the next thing she remembered.

Someone was shining a flashlight into her face. She opened her eyes trying to see.

"Miss… Miss. Are you alright?" the policeman asked.

Camille recovered enough to answer. "Yes," she said, clasping his hand tightly.

# Chapter 1

**Present Day...**

Camille Baptiste wondered what her life would have been like if she had married Desmond Garcia and lived in this gigantic big house that resembled an enchanted home that she had seen in an old Hollywood movie. The home, nestled in the San Juan Bautista Valley, was an exact replica of a Spanish mission, complete with a giant wrought iron gate to protect the estate from unwanted intrusions.

*The quiet rural area would take some getting used to,* she thought as she stared off into the distance admiring a covered walkway alive with a yellow Bougainvillea, named California Gold.

She took a deep breath. It felt like her mind was drifting, being pulled away along with her thoughts, to no place in particular.

Camille was still staring off into space when she felt a hand touch her shoulder. She looked up into the face of Consuelo. She had been Desmond Garcia's housekeeper.

"It's real peaceful out here, isn't it Miss Camille?" Consuelo's soft voice hardly held an accent.

Startled back to reality, Camille shook out her thoughts. She glanced up with an insulting slowness. "Yes, it is," she looked anxiously about. "Maybe too peaceful," she hesitated. "So peaceful it might drive a sane person insane."

Consuelo's eyes glanced back at her with suspicion.

Camille regretted the words as soon as they left her mouth. She paused for a second and thought about how complex things were for her right now. "I didn't mean it the way it sounded."

Consuelo smiled softly. "I know what you meant to say. Anyway, this is a good place. Once you have lived out here long enough you get used to it. In fact, you come to cherish it. How are you, by the way?"

Camille wondered if Consuelo saw the fine tremor shaking her hands. She clasped her hands firmly behind her back. "I'm fine. I've just been putting in a lot of hours at work, keeping busy."

Consuelo silently nodded and studied Camille, never batting an eye. "That's good to hear, after such a shock…" Her voice trailed off. "Well, just so you know, I'm still worried about you."

Camille was grateful that she didn't question her more. Her eyes looked away.

"Thanks again for letting me come by and pick up my things. This sweater was given to me by my Nana," Camille said cradling it close.

"Yes, I know, Consuelo said. "I remember you're saying so over the phone."

The two women stood in silence by Camille's car, both deep in their own thoughts.

"Miss Camille I'd like to ask you to do me a favor."

At first, Consuelo had debated about whether or not to tell Camille about her unconventional therapist. She had a feeling Camille was a skeptic and she feared what Camille would think. She knew that sometimes the most skeptical people couldn't accept help from a regular therapist, let alone from an unconventional one.

Consuelo sighed. "Camille there is someone I want you to see. She is waiting for you in town."

"Why?"

"Because she can help you make peace with what has happened," Consuelo said.

Camille shrugged. "I am at peace with Desmond's death."

Consuelo ignored her. "You have to trust me Camille and go and see my friend. It is the right thing to do."

A dove flew overhead and screeched loudly as it crossed the sky. Camille shivered.

Consuelo looked up. "There is nothing to be afraid of. The Dove has long been admired as a symbol of peace, love and spirit. And it is thought to be a symbolic sign of a vision quest.

Camille stared back at her. "Are you serious?"

"Here," Consuelo said, taking her hand and placing a card in it. "Her address is on this card. She is waiting for you. Go now!"

Camille looked at the card in her hand. She knew the address.

# Chapter 2

**Off to see the Glenda D'Goodwrench…**

Camille checked the clock on her dash.  It was half past ten on a Saturday night as she headed west off the old highway 156.

The old town of San Juan Bautista loomed ahead.

Camille slowed her car speed and smiled pleasantly. The old town looked like she'd stepped back in time.

That evening was cold, too cold for September. The day had been a crisp autumn day. She stood at the street corner of Main right across from the old rustic building she was heading for. She looked up; a huge moon hung directly above it.

Camille walked quickly heading straight for the front door. She'd just placed her foot on the first step and grabbed the banister when she heard a loud blast, like a car engine backfiring.

She turned around quickly just in time to see a huge smoky cloud. It vaporized like an apparition, but she saw no sign of a car. She thought it was strange, as if she had summoned up the smoky apparition.

She looked around and noticed a soft array of lights from the moon, silver rays luminously cast as if by magic.

Camille's breath caught, and she straightened as her fingers encountered something strange as she held on the banister railing. Something came to life under her fingertips. She looked down and noted knotted twisting grapevines coming to life and crawling up the side of the walls of the building.

She gasped, clenching her fingers tight. The moment felt enchanting and surreal.The crawling vines bloomed into a kaleidoscope of colors that made her think about the old story her mother used to read to her as a child, of a magical building that if you walked through the door you walked back in time.

Her heart began to hammer as she walked up the steps. What if it were true? She didn't believe in legends or the old stories her grandmother Nana had told her, that there were people born with the gift. Second sight was what her mother Gabby Baptiste had called it. What if this woman really was some kind of psychic, she thought? What if she walked inside and the last five months hadn't happened?

A curious calm came over Camille as she shook her head to clear her thoughts. She always prided herself on her being logical, and that, coupled with her intelligence, she knew could explain anything. There was no use in dwelling on "what- *ifs*" she assured herself as she pushed open the heavy wooden doors and walked inside.

Tall high ceilings greeted her as she entered the building. A very long, highly polished, and ornately carved bar captured the eye. Tall cushioned bar stools lined the bar. An equally long, unique, custom made mirror hung behind the bar and caught the eye.

Inside the bar was dark, quiet and empty except for the bartender. The bartender looked up as she entered. His white brows lifted. He had an elfin bearded face and spiky white hair, and his mouth widened into a grin. "Welcome, come on in and sit for a while," he said, waving her over.

Camille smiled. She had the whole place to herself. She closed the distance between them and sat down at the bar.

He walked over cheerfully. "What can I get for you Miss?"

She immediately noticed his soft blue eyes sparkle.

"A *Cadillac Margarita* with an extra shot of tequila on the side."

The bartender didn't blink an eye as he said, "Coming right up. Anything else?"

"Yes, I'm supposed to meet a woman named Glenda here. Do you know her?"

"Yep, I know her. She ain't here," he nodded. "But that doesn't mean she ain't coming."

The bartender turned his back to her to make her drink. He wanted to ignore the sadness in her eyes. Part of him wished that she would just walk back out the door and get in her car and drive away. But he knew Glenda would want him to make her feel at home.

"Do you like fresh strawberries?" he asked her looking back over his shoulder.

Anxiously she looked up at him. "Yes, I do."

"They are really good. I'll bring you a bowl. No charge of course," he said, placing her drink in front of her.

Minutes later, the bartender proudly placed a large bowl of plump juicy red strawberries in front of Camille. "Do you want me to keep an open tab? For the drinks I mean."

"Yes," she said, wrapping her hands around the tequila. "And bring me another shot of tequila."

The bartender nodded and walked away.

She tossed back the tequila as soon as he turned away and then ate several strawberries. The berries tasted delicious she thought eating a couple more.

The bartender looked into the mirror. He knew just the angle to look back at his clients without them catching you watching. He watched her face twist in agony as the tequila hit the back of her throat. The lady was tormented about something. The beautiful ones normally were he thought, and then his eye caught something. The woman saw it too.

"Oh!" Camille sucked in her breath and yelped, as a strange black cat briskly strolled past her drink. "What is this place? A circus or a bar?"

The black cat sat down boldly and curiously stared.

Camille frowned back at the cat, but the cat didn't move. "Shoo!"

The bartender swore under his breath. "Pinky! You get down from there or I'll tell Glenda you weren't behaving," he said walking over to retrieve the cat.

"I'm sorry miss. That's my old lady's cat. Tell you what, the drinks on the house."

"Oh!" Camille shrugged. "Thanks, but you don't have to."

"No bother, besides Pinky seems to like you," he nodded. "Glenda should be by shortly, Pinky doesn't usually come out unless he knows she's near," he said as his soft eyes met hers.

"I admire a man that's willing to cat sit for his ah…Uh…A friend…" She hesitated. "By the way my name is Camille. Camille Baptiste. What's your name?"

The bartender refilled her shot of tequila. "My name is Scott Irishman-Jackson," he smiled warmly. "And the cat's name is Pinky."

"Nice to meet you Scott," she said in one breath. "What a strange name for a cat that is completely jet black," she said. "I'm sure Glenda must have had a special reason to name that cat Pinky."

Scott chuckled "Glenda named her right."

The bartender studied her. He didn't know her, but he saw the effects one shot of tequila had on her. Now she'd just swallowed a second shot. Truth serum he thought, now she was going to start talking a lot.

Camille bit into a large ripe strawberry. "Isn't Glenda's last name Jackson?"

"Yeah and that ain't a coincidence," he said, gently stroking Pinky the cat's back. "Glenda… Glenda D'Goodwrench-Jackson is my wife."

A laugh escaped her as if he'd said something funny. "Really? Let me get this straight. The cat's name is Pinky and I could have sworn you just said Glenda was the *Good Witch*. Whew. Scot Irishman-Jackson you are a funny man."

The bartender stared at her as his eyes twinkled. He said nothing as he stood there slowly caressing the cat's back.

Pinky purred loudly and gave her a mesmerizing stare.

"Give me a moment and I'll take Pinky upstairs and get her out of the way. I think she's about to feel one of her changes coming on and I wouldn't want the cat to spook you," he said reaching for the bottle of tequila and pouring her another shot."You know Camille; I don't mean to be nosy. But my Glenda has a real talent for fixing matters of the heart, and it looks like someone broke your heart. But don't worry. My Glenda will be here shortly."

Camille said nothing as she watched Jackson walk away with Pinky, the cat.What a night she was having, she thought as she turned her attention back to the bowl of fresh strawberries in front of her. There was only one left. She couldn't remember eating all of them. She threw back the shot of tequila and then picked up the last strawberry and popped it into her mouth.

The burst of strawberry favor seemed to calm her. She thought back. Remembering back to the day she first met Desmond Garcia. It all seemed like a dream.

A voice shrilled from out of nowhere. "I'm sorry I'm late," a woman called.

Camille looked up and watched as the woman approached. She must be Glenda she thought, and she was carrying another bowl of strawberries.

"Are you Glenda Goodwrench-Jackson?"

"That's Glenda D'Goodwrench-Jackson. Accent on the D it makes it sound of *"The"* when you say it right. And yes, that is the correct pronunciation," she said sitting down the bowl of strawberries. You look hungry, so I brought some fresh blueberries muffins too."

Camille shivered. Glenda D'Goodwrench-Jackson didn't look the way she thought she would look. She was slender, fine boned, and youthful in the face. But her eyes held wisdom. They looked ancient. She had what her Nana used to call a "rubber face" a face that didn't age.

Glenda's soft sparkling blue eyes looked Camille over and captured hers. Camille stared and then swallowed hard. Glenda's eyes were mysteriously looking as if they could look into your soul.

Silently Camille studied her until her attention eyed the tray she was carrying.

"Let's take a seat here by the table," Glenda said. "Those chairs are much more comfortable.

Camille watched as Glenda sat the tray down on the table. The tray held a pot of coffee, two cups, another bowl of strawberries and a basket of muffins, a crystal decanter with a golden liquid, and a small miniature translucent bag filled crystal bottle.

"Sorry I was late," Glenda began. "I took the old highway in and some farmer's cows were blocking the road, and I had to persuade them to move," she said. "Anyway, now that I'm here, what can I do for you?"

Camille couldn't take her eyes off the basket of blueberry muffins. She stared at them hard.

"Have a muffin," Glenda said. "Oh, and this gift bag is for you."

Camille grabbed a muffin in one hand and accepted the small gift bag with the other. The aroma of the blue muffins was irresistible, she quickly took a bite. It tasted like heaven and smelled like something from her childhood. She savored the moment and remembered the small gift bag. "What is this for?"

"Just a small token of appreciation," Glenda said. "I give one to everyone. Consider it like a business card."

Camille chewed her muffin as she held the tiny bottle to her eye and stared at it.

All at once Pinky the cat appeared out of nowhere and sat on Glenda's lap.

Camille shivered and shut her eyes. She thought she was seeing things. The cat's hair looked midnight purple.

"What's the matter with you?" Glenda asked. "You're not hung over, are you?"

Camille opened her eyes and stared back. Pinky the cat was still sitting on Glenda's lap.

She rubbed her eyes. "No...No," she lied. "Suddenly something exploded on her tongue. It burst with favors from the blueberry muffin. It was a taste she remembered. "I haven't tasted anything….," she hesitated. "This tastes and smells like the ones my Nana made me when I was a kid," Camille confessed. "It brings back sweet memories."

"Good!" Glenda said patting her hand. "Now Camille do you want to tell me why you're here?"

"How do you know my name?"

In an all-knowing tone Glenda nodded and said. "I've seen you coming."

Camille almost choked on her muffin.

"Don't be afraid," Glenda stated directly. It's my business to know about people. Besides don't you want to discover the truth. I thought you loved Desmond Garcia," she paused and let her words sink in. "Don't you want to have a good night's sleep?"

Glenda started to hum softly and stared off into the distance.

Camille stared back at Glenda wide eyed. Her rush of questions overwhelmed her. She didn't know which one of Glenda's questions to answer first. But one thing she did know was that Glenda had spoken the truth about her wanting a good night's sleep. She hadn't slept in days. Camille softly smiled and relaxed slightly. She couldn't let down her guard entirely.

Glenda waved her hand. "Here, have another muffin and tell me your story."

Camille took another bite of muffin. A dreamy look came into her eyes. "My story?" she mumbled taking another bite.

"Yes, your story," Glenda softly said before her voice lapsed backed into the soft hum.

Like a little child falling asleep at dinner Camille's rounded shoulders slumped. "My story…" her voice trailed off.

Glenda gently hummed. "Yes Camille, please tell me your story. About how you met Desmond Garcia, and start from the beginning…"

Camille yawned. "I met him at my birthday party. Sort of," she said faintly, as she slowly leaned her head back against the soft cushion shoulder of the chair. Her eyes started closing, as images came to her. Was she dreaming? She wondered as her mind traveled back in time. A face appeared. All at once her eyes widened at the shock at seeing the other man's face, she woke her instantly. It was time. The story must be told.

Glenda stared back at her and reached out her hand. "Camille is everything alright?"

Camille grabbed her hand. "Yes, but first I must first tell you about another man, and a woman," she exclaimed.

"Why of course sweetie, if you must," Glenda nodded patting her hand.

Tears beamed up on Camille's eyes. She was silent for a moment with her thoughts. "The man's name is Delmar Devereaux and he was a first-class crass pervert who had grand illusions about everything and everybody including me," she hesitated. "Maybe I shouldn't talk about this. I don't want to bore you."

Glenda studied her. "Camille sweetie-pie, from the look on your face I don't think this story will be boring at all now tell me."

They stared at each other a moment longer. Finally, Camille broke the ice.

"Well, Delmar Devereaux is an asshole and he carries a personal truck load of bullshit wherever he goes," she shuddered at her memories. "But then again so did the Mistress of Desire."

Glenda laughed. "The Mistress of Desire sounds like a woman with a nymphomaniac tendency."

"Yeah, she was just a wanton slut, but she was also a girl. A girl who had no idea the guy she had designs to marry, in reality he was still married to another woman," Camille muttered under her breath. She gave a wry smile. "Anyway, I don't personally like to call my best friend names. Let's just say they were both perfect for each other. And aren't conniving, manipulative and deceptive people always are?"

# Chapter 3

**Two years earlier...**
   **Champagne Anyone...**

Camille watched him from a well-hidden position in the corridor of the extravagant hotel. Every muscle in her body tightened, ready to do battle. She'd been planning to confront him the first time she'd had her suspicions.

The man was handsome, cold looking but handsome. The handsome distinguished model features of the man were known to turn the lady's heads.

She let her gaze take in the dark-haired young woman with the ample breasts, walking next to him. She stared back at the man as if he was God.

The man and woman made their way to their hotel room, entered and closed the door behind them.

Camille rose from her hiding place, walked over to the elevator and waited. It had been a long evening, she thought with impatience.

The elevator opened, and a hotel waiter dressed in a white jacket smiled at her, pushing his cart forward.

"It's extra if you want to use my white jacket," the waiter said.

"No thank you, but I'll take the cart from here," she said handing him a huge tip.

The hotel waiter smiled. "Okay, but remember lady, I didn't see a thing," he said walking back into the elevator.

Driven by fear, Camille pushed the cart to the door and stopped abruptly, lifting the bottle of champagne. She shook it violently and slowly positioned it back on the cart and then she knocked hard.

"Who is it?" A woman's cool feminine voice called.

"Hello, this is room service," Camille said disguising her voice with a heavy accent.

The woman opened the door clutching her unbuttoned blouse. Her full breasts were crushed into a bra too small. "You don't look like room service," the woman demanded.

Camille arched a brow and pushed the cart further into the room. "And you don't look like a slut Diana! Where's Delmar?"

The woman's dark eyes clouded with fear as she pulled her blouse tighter. Suspicion etched across the woman's face. "Say who are you? How do you know my name?"

Just at that moment Delmar Devereaux entered. "Camille baby, this isn't what you think!"

"Hello, Delmar Devereaux," she said smothering a giggle, staring back in the wide gap in his robe. He was naked. "Mmmm looks like I interrupted you're getting laid. Is Diana North your new girlfriend?"

"I'm not his girlfriend," Diana said with a tossed her long dark hair.

"Oh yeah, I forgot Delmar always did get a kick out of having sex with a total stranger," Camille countered, with an edge in her voice.

The edge in Camille's voice attracted Delmar's attention. "Say Diana, maybe you should go in the bathroom and get dressed."

"Yeah Diana give me a Delmar a moment to talk in private," Camille added. "Don't worry I won't take up a lot of his time. I know you're anxious to bet back to your little game of find the penis."

Diana's mouth firmed into a hard line. "Delmar would prefer I stay around for moral support."

"No Diana now is not the time," Delmar commanded, as he clasped his robe shut and stared at Camille's face for just a minute and then stared at his partner in crime as she went into the bathroom and shut the door.

Delmar strode across the room. The muscles in his face worked silently. "Look Camille, I can explain. You're making a mistake about Diana and me," he said closing the distance between them. "Baby, I'm sorry about all of this. But you and I were taking things slow. No sex for ninety days, remember?"

Camille laughed out dryly. "But Delmar…"

He interrupted. "You know I'm a decent enough man. Haven't I've done everything you wanted? I wooed you; I put you on a pedestal, I've shown the world what you mean to me. And the one time you catch me trying to get my needs met is because you weren't there for me…"

"Stop lying," Camille interrupted, her voice quivering. "We weren't building a relationship. As usual, that twisted manipulative mind of yours is trying to put a spin on this to make me feel guilty."

The muscle in Delmar's face worked silently. Normally he was excellent at making excuses. "Look baby, I'm sorry. Please, you've got to believe me…"

Camille grabbed the bottle of champagne and shook it hard. "Not this time Delmar," she said and took a step backward and at the precise moment the champagne cork popped.

"What the hell!"

Camille felt an adrenaline boost of power as the cork released. "Champagne anyone?"

The champagne blast hit Delmar directly in his face.

"Jesus Christ!" Delmar yelled.

Camille burst out laughing. "Or should I just say congratulations Delmar! You and Diana deserve each other," she yelled, as she threw the bottle at him and headed for the door.

"My eyes!" he yelled.

"Well I guess it's time for me to be leaving," Camille said as cold as ice. "Oh, and Delmar our relationship that wasn't, is now officially over," she yelled making her exit.

# Chapter 4

**Dreams, Schemes & Matchmakers...**

Almost a year had passed by since her disastrous breakup with Delmar and Camille's life settled into a normal routine. She stepped out of the tub and wondered if she'd ever find love. There hadn't been any romance in her life since Delmar.

She had heard through the grapevine that Delmar Devereaux sexual exploits were the stuff Hollywood movies were made of. He took and discarded women with no regards to their feelings. She knew that everyone had their own kind of loneliness, even Delmar.

Camille shook out her thoughts and noticed the time. She couldn't believe that her birthday had rolled around again. She was even more amazed that she'd let her two best friends throw a birthday party for her.

She finished her make-up and went to her closet and reached for the purple lame' gown with the mermaid styled bottom. She knew the dress fit her curves like a glove.

Two hours later, *The Palladium* Ballroom was filling up fast. Camille took a sip of her margarita. It felt good against her tongue. The Cadillac Margaritas were her favorite.

She took another swallow recalling the numerous stories she'd heard about who invented her favorite drink. Her favorite story was the one Eris had told her about the Margarita being concocted by a bartender at Hussong's Cantina in Ensenada, Mexico named Carlos

Orozco. While there was no solid proof that the story was true, it always brought a smile to her lips.

There was a loud burst of laughter from behind her. Her two best friends Eris and Tiara were holding court with a local magician name Harry Oz. She watched as the magician pulled coin after coin from behind Eris' ear.

The trick was childish, but it brought endless laughter from her friends.Eris and Tiara had spent over a month organizing this party and they deserved to have some fun.

Camille studied the ballroom and took another sip from her drink. A tall Geeky guy stood idly by the buffet table devouring the roast beef. The guy was handsome. She studied him. The man must really love his roast beef, she thought.

All at once he stared back at her with a happy expression on his face. There was a moment of silence as the two stared directly at each other. Their eyes locked with a sudden inevitability.

"Who are you staring at? Eris asked, breaking through the crowd and coming to stand beside her.

"No one Eris," Camille lied as she nervously turned away.

Eris Simeon was the daughter of a wealthy real-estate mogul, and she was one of Camille's dearest friends. She was also a romantic at heart.

Eris saw Camille glance up again. "Camille, I caught you staring at that guy by the buffet table again."

Camille pretended not to notice. "Eris, did I tell you how nice your hair looks? I really love the precision cut temple-to-temple fringe bangs you had styled."

"Cut the crap with the compliments. I saw you staring at that guy and you've gazed at him twice since I've been standing here."

Embarrassed, Camille gave a small laugh. "Okay, I'll admit it. But why should it matter to you?"

"Because I know he's single and available," Eris said.

"So, do you want a date?"

"Who's single?" Tiara Blake chimed in, closing the gap between them. "If he's single and rich I'll date him."

Eris shrugged. She felt uneasy with Tiara there. Tiara could feel desire for any man, especially if his bank account was large. "He's not for you Tiara. He's got morals and values. And he doesn't sleep with just anybody," she warned.

"What?" Tiara pretended surprise. "Come on Eris, he's a man. Don't you see the bulge between his legs? Boy that's some nice size eye candy," she joked. "It should pleasure up a woman really well, don't you think?"

"I beg your pardon Tiara," Camille shrugged. "Please don't take this conversation to the gutter. It is my birthday."

Tiara Blake ran her fingers through her custom bronze blonde streaked long hair. Over the years, she had spent large sums of money making sure her hair color was as real looking as possible. She adjusted her dress and felt the seductive dangerous curves of her tight toned body. "Okay I'm sorry ladies for going to *sluts-vale*. But you both know I'm right."

"Tiara it's so sad," Eris said with fake politeness. "You act all regal and refined and we all know you're no lady. You know you really just a sex-addict."

"You bet your ass I love having sex, and you're just jealous of me Eris, because I have way more sex than you ever will," Tiara responded.

"Oh please," Eris snorted, with a wave of her hand.

Tiara regarded her friend and knew how she could make her point. "Say Eris, an old boyfriend of yours told me to tell you hi. I saw him when I came out of the lady's room."

"Yeah who was it?"

"You know that old pimp looking guy. Oh, what's his name Robert Chandler? Boy that old pimp daddy is in love with you. You should have seen his face light up when I told him you were here."

"Tiara Mr. Chandler is just a nice old man, and you're such a bitch!"

"Cool it you two. You act like sisters more than best friends," Camille scolded, as she felt a need to put an end to their squabbling.

Just then a tall rugged looking man entered the ballroom.

Tiara's gaze shifted toward the main entrance door. She grinned wide. "Camille look!" She muddled under a scream. "Brandon Stone just came in."

Brandon Stone entered the room and people circled around him. The crowd was thick with well-wishers.

Tiara stopped smiling. "God how I wish somebody would introduce me to him."

Camille looked up it didn't take her long to spot Brandon.

Brandon Stone had been a successful actor turned director producer, and he was mega-successful.

"Look Eris," Camille nudged her softly with her elbow. "Why don't you introduce Tiara? You know she's Brandon's biggest fan."

"No and don't look at me like that Camille. Tiara shouldn't have talked bad about Mr. Chandler like she did," Eris spit out with laughter, walking a short distance away.

"Gosh that Eris can be a real witch sometimes," Tiara said, with a weary sigh.

"Don't worry Tiara, just ignore Eris. We'll figure out how to get you introduced to Brandon Stone," Camille said, staring across the room.

All at once Tiara's eyes caught what Camille was staring at standing beside the buffet table. "Oh Camille, you're not staring at that tall geeky guy standing by the buffet table?

You can do better than that!"

"Shhhhh! Tiara he might hear you," Camille warned in a tone that only she could use with Tiara when she was on the thinnest of edge.

As usual Tiara was being rude. Sometimes it made Camille want to scream.

"Tonight's my night. Remember Tiara?"

"Opps…I'm sorry," Tiara mumbled. "I didn't realize you laid eyes on your future baby's daddy," she chuckled softly.

There was a brief pause. Camille swayed. "A girl has to tread carefully with a handsome guy like that. He's the kind you want to keep long term. He's not the kind you want to do a one-night thrill ride with."

"I like thrill rides," Tiara told her. "A girl can be in charge and steer her ride to its full potential, if you get my drift," she retorted. "Anyway, how are you planning to snag that guy Camille?" she asked but didn't wait for a response. "If you ask me the only way to snag a guy like that is with my fool proof method of whips, hips, chains, and fingertips."

"Tiara you can be such a loud ill mannered…" Eris said, returning to their circle.

Tiara rolled her eyes. "Don't knock it Eris. Maybe if you tried some of my methods, you'd get a guy Eris."

"What's that supposed to mean?"

"It means that stupid matchmaker act of yours doesn't work for you, or for Camille. You both need my action-packed plan!"

"Stop it children," Camille scolded.

"By all means, mommy dearest," Tiara said. "I'll stop if Eris will."

"What's gotten into you Tiara?" Eris said. "You know Camille is using my formula for making it to matrimony bliss in one year or less. Besides Camille is a good girl as opposed to…"

"You mean a round away girl like me?" Tiara said ruefully.

"I was thinking of the word slut," Eris mumbled.

"If you both don't stop the mean girl talk, I'm suspending our friendship," Camille demanded.

"Sorry." Eris and Tiara said simultaneously.

A few feet away, Leah St. Gregory, a local piano player sat on the bench in front of the baby grand and waved to Eris.

Eris saw a quick escape. "Say Camille I'm going over to say hi to Leah, I'll be back in a second."

"Sure Eris," Camille called after her, noticing the heightened level of hostility between her two best friends she took the moment to speak to Tiara.

Camille touched Tiara lightly on the shoulder. "What's up with you and Eris, Tiara?

Tiara heard her words and froze. "Oh, she's just bent out of shape because when I met her for lunch last week the two of us caught Spencer Denton taking Raven Ahmed out for lunch."

"Oh no poor Eris, that must have been so embarrassing for her."

"I told her Spencer was a two-timing snake," Tiara said. "Anyway, Raven made a big stink out of openly fondling Spencer in public just to make Eris jealous."

"Are you serious?" Camille frowned. "That must have embarrassed Eris."

"Nay," Tiara said shaking her head. "Don't worry. I saw an old buddy from school, Quinn Rolandis. I spoke with him in private and told him what Spencer had done," she laughed softly. "Boy did he get even with Spencer. He walked over to where Raven and Spencer were sitting and told her he was sorry that he had to leave her alone that night at the hotel and that he was looking forward to making it up to her."

Camille laughed out loud. "What! You're not serious?"

"Oh yes and did I mention Quinn kissed Raven fully on the lips and she dared Spencer to stop him? Then turned around and winked at Eris and told her she was lucky she'd broken up with a wimp like Spencer."

Camille and Tiara laughed out openly.

"Well, Eris always said you were the one to count on to have your back in a situation like that," Camille assured her.

Slowly twirling and strutting a precise imitation of Eris. Tiara placed her hands confidently on her hips and said. "Tiara you have street smarts. You're conniving, and you know how to be a bitch. I like that about you," she mimicked in her best Eris accent.

Camille threw back her head and laughed at Tiara's imitation of Eris. It was perfect.

"Yep that is exactly what Eris said, she grinned. "You have Eris down perfectly. You know she cares about you. You're both my family," Camille said sternly. "And while you're fighting, I'm missing out on meeting that geeky, handsome guy standing by the buffet table."

"Yeah, and he's perfect for you," Tiara smiled as her eyes followed her friend's eyes.

Just at that moment Eris returned and leaned over and hissed at Tiara. "I heard you Tiara and you see I was right," she whispered, "The guy is perfect for Camille."

Tiara took another look at the guy and then looked back at Camille. She was grinning from ear to ear. "Yes, you are."

Eris waved her hand. *Oui! Oui!* Then let the matchmaker make her match."

"Don't start with the French Eris," Tiara laughed softly and touched her shoulder. "I guess I'll leave you with Camille. I'm sure you want to make introductions. That guy looks perfect for her and we both want her to be happy."

"Thanks Tiara," Eris said.

Just at that moment a photographer materialized, taking photos.

Eris knew him. "Hey, Colbert Lincoln, come here a second."

"Yes, Miss Eris?"

Eris leaned in and whispered. "Do me a favor and see to it that Tiara gets her picture taken with Brandon Stone."

"Sure thing," Colbert smiled.

Eris turned her attention back to Camille. She was still staring across the room at the tall geek.

"Come on Camille, let's go meet your geek!" she asked jauntily.

Camille fortified herself with a deep breath and adjusted the purple gown.

The dress clung seductively to Camille's breasts and hips and swirled out in mermaid style at mid-calf. She'd worn her hair piled high to emphasize the beauty of her cheekbones and the seductive display of her smoky eyes, which Tiara had done for her.

When she walked across the room Desmond's eyes held hers as if in a trance.

Ever since the sixth grade, when Eris went to her cousin Siena Simeon's wedding and introduced her cousin Amanda Simeon to her future husband, Robert Goldstone,

Eris had thought of herself as a matchmaker of sorts.

The two friends crossed the room.

Eris grinned wide and winked. "Hi, Desmond Garcia, this is my best friend Camille Baptiste, the girl I told you about?"

Up close Camille could see that Desmond Garcia was a tall man. With jet back wavy hair and slanted sleepy lidded eyes of coffee brown.

Eris placed Camille's hand in Desmond's. "Camille this is Desmond Garcia. He's been begging me to introduce the two of you for several months now and well I think tonight is the perfect time."

Eris looked between the two-shy people. She sensed a genuine fondness between the two. She laughed softly and joked. "Boy I've just introduced the perfect King Geek and to his perfect angel."

The moment was silent as Desmond Garcia pinned Camille with a mesmerizing gaze.

"Well I'll be damned," Eris said as she walked away from the couple.

As soon as Camille felt the touch of his hand, she felt warm all over as a jolt of energy coursed through her body. She looked up and politely and nervously smiled. He was tall, dark and dangerously handsome.

Desmond Garcia looked at her in disbelief. He couldn't believe his luck. She was perfect and beautiful.

"You can call me by my first name," Desmond said. "I mean I don't have a nickname or anything. Is it okay if I call you Camille?"

"Sure, Desmond and I don't have a nickname either," she said.

Desmond's dark eyes looked her over. "I just learned that this party was sort of your birthday party. I'm afraid I didn't bring you a gift."

Camille felt warm at the glare of his attention. "That was my intent. I made it clear to my best friends that they were not to stress to anyone that this was a birthday. It's a little quirk of mine."

"Oh, you don't like presents?" he asked.

"No, it's not that. I started saying no to presents at my birthday parties a long time ago. Really when I was a kid," she hesitated. "You see when I was a kid, I had a few friends who couldn't afford to buy presents for a birthday party. So, they didn't get invited to many parties. So, whenever it was my birthday, I wouldn't call it a birthday party just a party. That way all my friends would come and not worry about bringing me a gift."

"That was kind of you," Desmond said.

"Thanks," she said. "So, tell me Desmond is this your normal way of meeting women I mean… Do you often stand around buffet tables staring?"

He laughed. "Nope normally I just go the regular route. You know have a friend set me up on a blind date. You know like your matchmaker friend Eris does."

"Oh, really" Camille glanced at Eris sitting at the piano with Leah.

Desmond's handsome face stared back at her. He'd seen Camille almost two months ago at the convention center in San Francisco. It took him two months just to get one of her friends to agree to introduce her to him.

"In fact, we've met before, so this is actually our second blind date. We were both seated next to each other by Eris. But I'm sure you don't remember," he said.

"No not really"

His gaze swept over her admiringly. "It was at that charity play at the Montgomery Theater… Cinderella leaves OZ or something like that."

Camille softly laughed and shook her head. "Oh yes, now I remember. Eris sat me next to you. You were the guy that kept staring at me all night, but you never got up the nerve to say a word."

He chuckled. "Guilty as charged."

Desmond's mesmerizing smile caught her off guard. "So, what do you do for a living Desmond?"

Smiling broadly, he leaned back and gave her his full attention. He could tell she had no idea who he was, or his family connections were. "I'm a sort of a science-professor businessman."

Grinning from ear to ear Camille said. "Yeah you do sound all scientific. But you look too prosperous to be a professor. Most professors I know can't afford Armani suits."

"Thank you," he shyly said but didn't offer an explanation.

The DJ played a slow song.

His voice was deep and distinctive. "Would you like to dance?"

"Yes," she nodded, letting him lead her to the dance floor.

Desmond pulled her into his arms.

At his warm touch Camille felt a surge of warmth. She looked up into his eyes. His eyes told her she was beautiful. Slowly she rested her head on his shoulder as the music wafted through the air. She breathed deeply and instantly knew she'd fallen in love with the fresh scent of his aftershave. Being in Desmond's arms was heaven. She enjoyed the comforting touch of the man's strong arms wrapped around her.

He felt perfect, she thought, standing there with her arms wrapped around him.

The music finally ended.

"Can we go someplace where we can talk?" Desmond asked.

"Yes," she said gripping his hand and tugging free of the throng of people on the dance floor.

They walked to a quiet place at the far end of the room.

Standing close, hidden in the secluded area, they chitchatted for what seemed like hours.

Camille nervously adjusted her dress while chitchatting about nothing. She abruptly stopped talking and stared at Desmond. She really wanted to get to know him better.

Desmond's eyes traveled over Camille's face. He stared at her with intensity. "Would you like for me to go and get us a couple of drinks?"

"Oh no, she said abruptly. She didn't want him to run off. Her thoughts raced as she tried to think of a line of dialogue to keep him talking. "Desmond are you seeing anyone?"

Speaking softly, he leaned over and whispered into her ear. Desmond said, "No, why?"

"Well, a good-looking guy like you who's still single, well, he must like to go out for dinner sometimes, right?"

Desmond looked at her. "Are you asking me out to dinner?"

"Well yes," Camille said with a composed tone. "You see I just figure that I'd better break the ice and ask the hard question now, so to speak…" she hesitated. "Well, because you and I met months ago and, as I recall, you didn't ask me out on a date back then," she gave him her most charming smile.

"You've got me there," he laughed and stumbled against her. His arms closed around her steadying her. She barely reached his shoulder. All at once she stared into his eyes. "And yes, I'd love to go out to dinner with you."

Hot and bothered by the closeness of the man Camille composed herself. This man was lethal. She could feel her body responding to him.

"Wait a minute. I haven't asked you anything yet. Do you have a boyfriend?"

"Yes, she does!" A man's voice coldly sliced the air. "Damn Camille every time I leave you alone you find some guy to cozy up with. I'd consider your behavior slutty if I didn't love you so much," he chuckled.

Instantly Desmond turned around ready to do battle.

Camille looked disoriented for a moment as the three of them stood there staring at each other. Finally, she woke out of her fog and realized Delmar Devereaux, the attention needing drama king, had arrived and was trying to ruin her evening.

"Don't insult me Delmar! You are not my boyfriend," Camille angrily scolded. She sighed heavily wishing she had a saw to cut her way out of there.

Delmar Devereaux swooped in close and kissed Camille right on the lips."Camille, you know I'm just joking. By the way, happy birthday!"

Camille tried to hide her embarrassment as her eyes darted between Desmond and Delmar.

Desmond flashed Delmar an angry cold stare. It was apparent he didn't find Delmar's behavior funny.

As if on cue from across the room Eris eyed the situation, located Tiara instantly and tapped her on the shoulder.

"Come on Tiara, I need your help," Eris yelled quickly.

Tiara grunted, "Oh Eris, I was just about to get another glass of champagne."

"Please Tiara, I promised Brandon Stone I'd bring Desmond Garcia over to talk with him as soon as I could, and

I think the time is right."

"Brandon Stone," Tiara gushed. "Why didn't you say so?"

Tiara followed Eris as she made her way quickly to where Desmond, Camille and Delmar were standing.

"Desmond darling," Eris' fake politeness floated on the air. She took his hand and laced it with Tiara's. "Brandon Stone, the movie producer asked me to make sure he was introduced to you tonight," she spoke quickly, as she propelled them out of distance. "Tiara's going to take you over and introduce the two of you."

"Come on Desmond darling, we don't want to make Brandon Stone wait," Tiara said as she gripped Desmond's hand and lead him away.

Immediately Eris turned around and clasped her arms around Camille and Delmar in a huddle.

"Delmar Devereaux you filthy son-of-a-bitch bastard!" Eris hissed leaning in close. "How dare you show up and try to ruin Camille's birthday party."

Delmar loudly cleared his throat. "Eris darling, I've missed you too. Can't I have one dance with the birthday girl?"

"No!" Eris declared, wrinkling her nose and looking upset.

"Look Eris don't get your thong all twisted and bent out of shape,

Camille wants me here," Delmar said.

"What? Who told you that Delmar?" Camille said with a tilt of her head looking up at him.

Delmar cocked a smile. "Come on Camille, I heard through the grapevine how you've been so distraught over our break-up all those months ago. And looks like I arrived just in time, before you made some stupid decision to hook up with that tacky looking fellow there," he said glancing in Desmond Garcia's direction.

"For your information Delmar, Desmond isn't tacky," Camille said defiantly.

Delmar looked across the room at Desmond. He was the kind of man that was easy for him to hate, he thought.

Desmond's face was expressionless as Tiara Blake made mindless chatter with Brandon Stone. Quietly he shoved his hands in his pockets as the rage inside him kept building.

All at once Tiara Blake threw back her head and laughed openly at something Brandon Stone said.

Delmar watched Desmond smugly from across the room. It was apparent Desmond was annoyed.

Like an animal caught in a trap, Desmond Garcia followed his instinct and looked up. Delmar's attentive gaze stared boldly back at him. He made it a point to put a menacing angry scowl on his face that would put him ill-at-ease.

Their eyes leveled challenging as they both stared back at each other.

Then Delmar reached out a hand and smoothed away a strand of hair from Camille's face. He let his hand slowly stroll down and caress softly against Camille's breast, as his lips curled up into a sinister smile.

The gesture wasn't lost on Desmond. He pulled his hands out of his pants pocket, adjusted his jacket and headed for the exit.

His face twisted into a sinister grin. "Camille darling, it looks like your friend Desmond has just left the party. And since that is the case, I believe you should have this dance with me."

"What?" Camille asked turning around just in time to see Desmond's back as he walked through the main entrance.

31

# Chapter 5

**Lunch is spoiled...**

Days later, Eris Simeon hurried down the sidewalk on First Street in downtown San Jose. She was late as usual. She knew Camille and Tiara were waiting for her.

Looking ahead, she breathed out a long sigh of relief as the giant white chef's hat painted on the window of the Bistro Café came into view. She smiled and reached for the door handle and pushed.

Instantly a tall and handsome man wearing a dark pair of shades pulled from the other side of the door. His rush of action flung Eris into his arms.

He looked down at her from his tall frame. "Hello gorgeous woman of my dreams, you're late for our lunch date?" The man playfully said.

Eris pulled back out of his arms and looked up at him. "Say, why don't you watch where you're going."

"Please accept my apology for bumping into you," he said taking off his shades. He held out his hand. He gave her an irresistible smile. Soft dark eyes stared back at her. "By the way, I'm Ethan Armand of the Sonoma Armand Family."

Eris hesitated, and then recognition hit her. "Say, aren't you…." she hesitated

He smiled. "That charming news guy from television."

"Charming, you think you're charming?  With a huge ego," she laughed out.

He surprised her by saying.  "I believe in positive thinking and declaring what you want to be or have. Just like I believe you're the future mother of my children. By the way I love the precision cut temple-to-temple fringe bangs thing you've got going. I always dreamed my dream girl would wear her hair exactly like you do. Soft sexy bangs," he softly murmured with a curious gazed overlook.

"Damn Ethan you do lay that charm stuff on real strong in real life too. I thought you just oozed that sex appeal stuff for your viewers on TV," she said, trying to ignore the man standing in front of her. She swallowed hard and tried not to stare.

"Actually, I only ooze this way when someone matters. On TV I just read some lines some writer wrote for me. Just so you know I'm serious, I want to take you out for lunch," he said. "But, not today because I bet, you're running late for lunch with those two lonely ladies I saw sitting at the table in the back with a place setting for three."

Eris looked across the room at her two friends. "You're good," she said with a smile. "Those are my friends. How did you know?"

He shrugged. "I know, it's just a knack we folks in the journalism business have," he said blatantly staring at her. His entire personality changed as he flashed a cool mesmerizing smile. "By the way what's your name?"

"Eris… Eris Simeon."

Ethan nodded. His eyes held a polite irresistible coolness as he said, "Well Eris Simeon would you do me the honor of going out with me?"

Eris felt her face flush. The man was good. "Sure…."

"Good here's my business card with my cell phone number. Call me," he smiled again.

"No… I mean yes," she swallowed hard. "I mean, I will be giving you a call," she said as sweetly as she could.

He held the door open wide. "Good and I'll be looking forward to hearing from you Eris Simeon."

Minutes later, "She is here! Finally," Tiara Blake said rolling her eyes as Eris reached their table. "God, I hope you know Camille and I have been waiting here for almost half an hour for you, Eris?"

Tiara took a gulp of her wine. She needed it to deal with the total princess package known as Eris Simeon. It was fair she thought, that one woman had been blessed with not just good looks but a father with money. Eris was like her and Camille. They worked hard for everything they got. For once she'd like to see that smug confidence of hers torn to shreds.

"Well, I'm here now," Eris said, smoothing a stray strand of hair. "Boy they're cooking something good in that kitchen. My mouth is watering. Have you guys ordered?" Eris asked.

"Yes, Tiara said with a wave of her hand.  She got the waiter's attention.

"Would you like for me to bring out your order now?" The waiter asked.

"Yes," Tiara said.

The waiter walked away.

Eris turned her gaze. "I hope one of you ordered my usual."

"Our usual," Camille said. 'Eris honey, we are way ahead of you. Here comes the waiter now with our orders."

Their waiter brought over their order.

He placed three steaming hot bowls of toast crusted French Onion soup in front of each of them. And then three full grilled chicken salads.

Camille took a whiff of soup. "Everything smells so good."

The three friends were quiet as they shared their meal.

The constant clanging of forks hitting plates jarred Camille's attention as she looked between her two best friends and noted how quiet they were.

Minutes later, Camille glanced between her two best friends. Neither had asked anything about that awkward moment that night at her birthday party. Nor had they inquired about Desmond Garcia. In fact, she was a bit annoyed that not one of them had asked her if she liked the guy.

Impatient for one of them to bring up the subject, she loudly cleared her throat. "I can't believe neither one of you has asked me whether not I liked Desmond Garcia. Or if I had a nice time at my birthday party, or a bad time, or something."

Eris gave a small shrug. "I know you like him. I'm the matchmaker. I arranged everything remember. Desmond is perfect for you."

"Yes, but does Camille want him, you know, feel that sexual desire thing for him. You know like that wild mad passion stuff," Tiara piped in cooling, raising an eyebrow.

Eris' mouth was open for the next protest. "Hello Tiara! Yes, Camille does. Didn't you see the way she looked at him, or for that matter how he looked at her, like she was so irresistible he was going to pounce on her like a tiger and have his way with her right in the middle of the dance floor."

Tiara maintained a quiet silence before throwing both her friends a cursory glance. "Eris don't you think Desmond is so typical and Geeky? I know he's Camille's type, but will he fuel her mind for sexual satisfaction? Can he make her body writhed in ecstasy? Can he rouse her to heights of passion?

Will he give her that inner glow of pure ecstasy?"

Camille and Eris stared back at Tiara in a state of shock and then their voice's erupted simultaneously with laughter.

Finally, Camille broke the ice and said. "That was very funny Tiara. Oh, and thanks for the advice," she said sarcastically. "But at the end of the day I'm not into the bad boy types that only want to screw you for a night or maybe two, and then you find out you're not in a committed relationship, when you catch him out with his latest girlfriend."

"Camille's right," Eris said.

A wicked expression lit Tiara's eyes. "Good, then that leaves more bad boys for me to screw. And you know I can be one greedy bitch when it comes to f..."

"Tiara!" Camille cried. "We are in a public place."

"I'm calling a truce," Eris chimed in. "Ladies let's change the subject."

Tiara waived her hand at them.  "Oh alright, well anyway I was annoyed that Desmond had the nerve to leave. And while we were talking to Brandon Stone," she said pushing back her empty salad plate. "How rude was that."

Eris threw Tiara a look.  Tiara could be so self-absorbed sometimes."Correction Tiara," while you were talking with Brandon Stone. From where I stood, I don't think Desmond managed to get a word in edgewise."

Tiara shrugged. "Well anyway, Desmond was rude."

"So, what if he was, you don't have to like him, Camille does."

"And I do like him Tiara," Camille began angrily. "And I don't care if…"

"Camille!" a familiar voice exclaimed interrupting her, as he closed the distance to their table and came to a halt right in front of Camille.

"Good afternoon ladies."

"Oh my God!  Delmar, I haven't seen you since the party," Tiara squealed flipping her hair back.

"Uh… Delmar what are you doing here?" Camille nervously asked.

Eris stared back at in steely silence.

Delmar Devereaux smoothed his moustache and studied Camille. He was wearing a classic dark charcoal grey suit.

Only Tiara looked happy to see him. "Delmar, you look handsome in that suit," she said with smile.

"Thank you, Tiara, as always you have good taste," he said with a nod.

"Camille," he said enthused. "It's wonderful to see you again. Oh, and you also Eris," he added.

Tiara watched Delmar intensely as he greeted them.  He was handsome. The kind of handsome she liked, rich handsome. "Don't be unfriendly Camille and Eris, say hello," Tiara grinned.

Delmar threw Tiara a cursory glance and then ignored her.

Camille weakly smiled at him, noticing the way that he had slighted Tiara.She hated it when Delmar did things like that; it showed exactly what he was.  He felt elitist.  "Hello Delmar, forgive me for my rudeness," she said, hoping he took her hint.

"Hi Delmar," Eris muffled out, ignoring him as if he was non-existing.

Still in a state of mild shock Camille nodded. "Hello Delmar," she said in a flat tone.

Delmar's eyes continued to lavish their attention on Camille. He was not concealing his desire for her. The truth was, he was in love with her. "I'm so happy to see you here Camille. It seems like a coincidence that we keep seeing each other like this."

Camille didn't want to meet his gaze. She gave her friend Eris a pleading look.

Someone cleared their throat loudly interrupting them.

As if by magic, Delmar stepped aside and somehow magically produced a small petite older woman. She wore a double-breasted, pink and navy trim collared Chanel wool suit with a matching pink pill-box hat. Her hair was dyed with a purple rinse.

Before Camille could open her mouth the petite purpled-haired woman approached their table.

"Camille my dear, I thought that was you," the blue-haired old lady smiled.

"Forgive me Aunt Vie. I forgot you were with me," Delmar smiled.

"Hello Camille, Aunt vie said. "It's good to see you again."

Camille, you remember Aunt Vie?" he asked.

"Yes of course, hello Aunt Vie," Camille answered. "Please let me introduce you to my two best friends, Eris Simeon and Tiara Blake."

"Hello ladies," Aunt Vie said with a wave of her hand as if dismissing them."Bless my heart. Camille, you look wonderful," Aunt Vie said, extending a hand covered in a navy blue kid-glove.

"You look wonderful too," Camille returned the compliment. She'd always had a warm spot in her heart for good old Aunt Vie.

Aunt Vie blinked several times. "Camille, I've heard so much about how well you are doing at your job. Delmar tells me you've been working as an agent for a small firm. Too bad you had to sell your father's business."

Silence followed.

Camille felt a knot tightening in the pit of her stomach. She gazed between Delmar and his Aunt Vie. She could tell he'd filled her in on the goings-on in her life. "Yes… Yes, I am working at a small firm. It's a title company. *Lipton Escrow*, perhaps you heard of

it. I really do like my job," she rambled out without knowing why.

Aunt Vie sighed and shook her head in disapproval. "Yes, but it's not the same as owning your own business now is it? I bet your father would turn over in his grave if he knew you'd sold his business. Wade Baptiste really built that business up."

Annoyed, Camille lifted her chin and smiled tensely. "It was my father's decision that his business be sold," she said defiantly. "And because I respected my father, I honored his wishes."

Chagrin and dismay covered Auntie Vie's face. "Well, I hope you haven't given up your dream of owning your own Tea Shop, one day? Even you have to admit everyone should cherish their dream and pursue it," she stated directly. "It has been my experience in life to learn that we are happiest when we do the thing we love."

"Don't worry Aunt Vie I haven't given up on my dream," she said softly. "That's why I'm working; I'm saving up for it."

"Really?" Aunt Vie said in disbelief. "Camille, you don't have to work to get the money to open your own tea shop. I'm sure Delmar would love to give you the money. Wouldn't you Delmar?"

Camille gave Delmar a sideways glance as she slanted her eyes in silent warning.

Delmar's smile faded as he pretended not to notice. He knew Camille was annoyed.

"Camille, if I were you, I'd take the money," Tiara murmured low.

"But you're not me, Tiara" Camille interrupted, giving her friend a shrewd stare to stay out of her business.

"Ouch!" Eris giggled.

Camille turned her attention back to Delmar and folded her arms and gave him a serious look. "Delmar don't you have someplace to go?"

Her gesture wasn't lost on him.

Delmar cleared his throat. "See Aunt Vie, I told you Camille wouldn't think of letting me help her open her business. Now look what you've done. You've upset Camille and we must leave." he said fixing Camille a dazzling smile.

"If we must," Aunt Vie shrugged. "Delmar, I'd better run to the lady's room before the valet pulls your car around."

Aunt Vie paused. "Camille, it was so nice seeing you again and meeting your friends," she said making her exit.

"Have some good lunch ladies," Delmar said, walking off.

Seconds later Tiara rose. "I think I need to go to the lady's room too, and you know, I need to make that call and check and see if my car is ready," she quickly said and then she was gone.

Eris waited a few moments and then made her excuse with Camille before rushing off. She didn't waste time making her way to the hallway separating the kitchen from the seating area. Few people knew it held a back way leading to the rest room. Instantly she veered around the corner. Just in time to see Tiara talking with Delmar.

Frantically she looked for a hiding place. A ménage of plants and a wrought iron trellis loaded with climbing vines provided the perfect hiding place. They concealed her well, as she watched Tiara talking with Delmar. She leaned over and could just hear their conversation.

Delmar weakly smiled. "Tiara where did you come from?"

Tiara looked around nervously. "I was looking for you Delmar."

"Why?"

"I thought maybe you and I could have a drink sometimes and maybe talk and share. You might find we like the same things," she said.

He grinned wide with his thoughts catching her meaning. Tiara was one person that could be easily used. "Yes, I think I do know what you mean," he said slipping her his business card. "My number is on this card. Use it," he said to her in a matter of fact tone. "Oh, and as soon as you leave here, I expect to hear from you," he demanded before putting some distance between them.

Tiara blinked rapidly with her thoughts. Her instincts told her to jump in and see what happen. She hurried after him. "Better yet, I came today by taxi. Maybe you could offer me a ride."

"Your friends," he said weakly.

Tiara shrugged. "I'll call them from your car on my cell and tell them I got a ride."

"Good, "he said taking her arm in his. "Let's go. The valet should have brought my car around."

Eris watched the two of them leave out of the front door. She stayed in her hiding place even though the coast was clear. "That conniving bitch!" she whispered under her breath.

She made her way toward the lady's room.

A voice sliced the air. "Eris? It's so good to see you again. I was just thinking of giving you a call."

Startled Eris recognized the voice. "Desmond Garcia – how are you? Are you having lunch here?"

"Yes, I have a business lunch with a good friend of mine."

"Oh?" she asked curiously.

"Yes, and before he gets here, I need to ask you a big favor?"

Eris smiled softly. Things were looking promising. He wasn't meeting a female for lunch. "Sure, If I can, but first tell me what it is…"

Desmond breathed out a sigh of relief. "Oh, thank God. For a moment I thought you were going to say no. Look I know you have rules about matching, but you are Camille's best friend and that's why I'm asking. You've got to get your friend to go out on a date with me somehow."

"Oh, is that all. For a minute I didn't know what you were going to ask me," Eris laughed out. Fate was obviously on her side. In her matchmaker's world these were moments you'd live for. "Sure, I can arrange that. In fact, if you have a moment, please follow me," she said pulling him behind her.

Seconds later Eris walked briskly ahead of Desmond and reached her table. "Camille," she softly called.

Camille had just raised her spoon taking her last bite of soup. Slowly a perplexed expression crept over her face. "Yes Eris?"

Eris kept her cool. "Camille, look who I found?"

A whimper of surprise escaped her lips as she glanced up. "Desmond, what are you doing here?"

Eris smiled wide. "Like I said the other night Camille meet Desmond."

Camille looked up and smiled at the tall Geeky handsome guy standing before her. His jet back wavy hair made him look like the Geek King of her dreams.

Desmond smiled warmly back at Camille. It was obvious they had eyes only for each other.

Eris cleared her throat. "It's good to see you two are happy to see each other. Desmond, you can have my seat.So now I'm going to leave you two alone," her words tumbled out. "But before I do, might I suggest that you two go on a date? The Rosicrucian Egyptian Museum is fun, and Camille, you love that place."

Eris stared between them. Neither one acknowledged her presence. She sighed loudly. "Good, then I'll just leave you two to work out the details," she said making her exit.

Camille calmed herself. "Desmond what are you mumbling?"

"I guess I'm thanking God that I dodged going out with a girl that can eat that much food," he said playfully.

Camille laughed nervously, waived her hand and placed it on the table. "I didn't eat all of this. If I had, I'd be big as a house. Are you here for lunch?"

Desmond was enjoying watching her laugh. "I came here for a business lunch when I spotted Eris. I hope you don't mind that she brought me over," he said, taking her hand in his.

His hand was warm she noted. She liked the feel of his touch. "No, in fact I want to apologize for the other night."

"Oh?" he asked arching a brow. He'd made it a point to do his research on Delmar Devereaux. He knew the man had once dated Camille, briefly. He knew he wasn't her boyfriend.

"Delmar isn't anything to me. Not my boyfriend or

anything. I dated him briefly almost two years ago. And I'm sorry I didn't get a chance to tell you the other night."

Desmond touched her hand. "I'm so happy to hear that. I'm just so happy to see you again."

He grinned, leaned over close and then seriously got to the point. "Well, will you?"

"Will I what?"

"Will you go on a date with me to the Rosicrucian Egyptian Museum? I hear it's your favorite place."

"Yes," she breathed out slowly enjoying his holding her hand. "I would love to go on a date with you."

He looked into her eyes and then kissed her hand again.

"Will tomorrow at 2:00 be alright for you?" he asked.

"Sure."

A second later a man's voice interrupted. "Hey Desmond, are we having our meeting?"

"Hey Dre, yes we are," Desmond said releasing Camille's hand.

"Camille this is a good friend and a business partner of mine, Dre Stoneman. Say hello to Camille Dre."

"Hello Camille."

Desmond turned his attention back to Camille. "Well, it looks like my business lunch needs to get started," he said reaching into his jacket pocket and handing her his business card. "Here's my number. Please give me a call and let me know where to pick you up."

# Chapter 6

**Getting to Know Each Other...**

Camille knew she'd always remember the magic of her first date with Desmond. The image of the fuchsia and white cymbidium Orchid he'd given her would forever hold a magical place in her heart and mind for the rest of her life.

She admired the way the orchid looked, elegantly pinned into the side of her hair as she stared back at herself in the mirror.

Desmond flicked an appreciative gaze at the Orchid nestled in Camille's hair. A fantasy snuck up on him and he wondered what she would look like, naked, lying on a bed of Orchid petals. Warmth spread through him as he devoured her with his gaze.

He grinned wide staring back at her. "The orchid looks beautiful in your hair. I'm so glad you wore it that way."

Camille felt herself blushing from the warmth of his smile. Her heart skipped a beat. He awoke something in her heart. Something she hadn't felt in a long time; the stuff dreams were made of she thought."Thanks for the compliment."

Desmond cleared his suddenly dry throat. "And thank you for being a great listener. Not many women would find the topic of bioengineering interesting."

"And what a fascinating topic," she joked.

He smiled back and laughed and grabbed her hand.

The two walked silently hand in hand together.

Abruptly, Camille came to a halt, as a nervous expression etched on her face. "I have a confession. I didn't think this date would go so well."

Desmond looked back into Camille's clear gold flecked hazel eyes and started laughing. "You didn't," he hesitated. "But I did," he said putting his hand on her shoulder and turning her to face him. His finger traced her face and then his mouth slowly lowered to hers. The kiss was soft and gentle.

Camille felt frozen to the spot. She'd forgotten that there was so much to feel. She could feel the heat moving up from her toes. God the man was lethal, she thought, pulling out of his embrace.

Their conversation slipped off topic. Camille quickly tried to steer it back on course, as she walked on.

"So, Desmond you didn't tell me where you went to school?" she asked. "I'm guessing Stanford or maybe Berkley."

"Good guess, I attended Berkley University for my undergraduate and did my master's degree at MIT."

Camille listened intently. The man was gorgeous, she thought, as she stole glances at him as they kept walking. Seeing him at her birthday party had seemed like a dream come true. He'd brought up emotions in her that she'd thought had long since died. He made her feel warm with pleasure inside, a happy feeling that she had denied herself for too long.

At that moment Desmond took off his jacket. He was tall, his body was hard and muscled toned. Camille stared back at him astonished. He looked more handsome in the light of day. He had a high cheek-boned face and a chiseled chin with a cleft in it. His body was tight like the body of a boxer. She said the first thing that popped into her mind. "Whew! How often do you work out to keep your body so tight and sexy? I mean you are a pretty gorgeous man," she blurted out and then hated herself as soon as the words escaped her lips.

Desmond was stunned by Camille's words. Nobody had ever thought he was sexy, nor gorgeous.

"I didn't know men could be gorgeous," he jokingly smiled.

Panic set in. He must think I'm a woman obsess with men's bodies. Quickly she thought of something to say. "Did you know that the Rosicrucian Egyptian Museum is architecturally inspired by the Temple of Amon at Karnak?" she asked but didn't wait for him to answer. "I read that in ancient Egypt unmarried women were free to choose their sex partners, as they so desired?"

Desmond shook his head and wondered if she had any idea how desirable she looked all flustered like she was. The really big question that ran through his mind was what he should do about what she had just said. He moved in close. "You think I'm gorgeous. Well, what if I told you I think you're beautiful and that you've been running though my dreams so long I'm not sure if we are safe standing here in front of this museum?"

Oddly Camille slowly giggled. Her emotions were running high. There was something about him that sent twinges of sparks running through her. She'd waited a long time for someone to look at her the way he did. She wondered about what she was going to do about them.

"Come on Camille, let's go get something to eat," Desmond softly said while pulling her close. "I know a great restaurant not far from here."


An hour later, they sat eating at a new Italian restaurant not far from museum. Alone with Desmond in an intimate cozy booth, Camille felt uncomfortable.

Excitedly she said, "This place looks just like a Travel Book on Italy."

The restaurant held a nostalgic atmosphere of old-world Italy. It felt like they had stepped back in time.

Desmond looked around the room. "Yes, they capture the feel of Italy."

He waved and got their waiter's attention. "Bring us a bottle of Château Charmail," he commandingly said.

"Right away sir," the waiter nodded.

"You ordered a French wine...."

"In an Italian restaurant," he said finishing her sentence. "Believe it or not the wine menu here has a great selection of French and Italian wines."

Shortly, two glasses were placed in front of them and the waiter poured.

Absentmindedly, Camille sipped her wine and softly swayed to the rhythm of Tony Renis singing the hauntingly romantic *Quando, Quando, Quando*. The old song made the room come alive with enchantment and romance.

"So, tell me about your life," Desmond said.

Camille took a sip of the wine. It went down smoothly. "My life is kind of boring. By the way, this wine tastes really nice."

Instantly, her eyes held his and something flashed behind them. Camille could have sworn she saw a deep hunger within them. "Well, just like you, I grew up an only child too. I have a few cousins. But mainly, since the death of my father, when I was nineteen, it's just been me and my mother, Gabby Baptiste. My mother has a fondness, or a habit I should say for Bingo," she threw back her head and laughed passionately. "She plays it with such an intensity, you would think they had a million dollars in every jackpot"

Desmond stared back at her with intensity. Any other woman wouldn't have allowed herself to be so spontaneous with her laugh. That was one of the things he liked about her. He was a man of instincts. There was something about Camille. She had a quality that touched him in his soul.

He shrugged. "Oh, it sounds like playing bingo really makes her happy."

Camille joked out. "Oh yeah, it makes her and her posse of friends happy. So happy, that they all go every week."

He nodded. "Maybe your mother is just lonely and going to Bingo may fill a void.

Camille froze with her thoughts. Desmond was on target. Her

mother and her father, Wade Baptiste, had been devoted to each other. Since he'd died, her mother had been devoted to bingo.

"I hadn't thought about it like that. My mother did start going regularly after my father died."

He smiled and looked into her eyes with intensity. "Interesting, it sounds like your parents were the lucky ones. They found that true love."

"I guess I never thought about it like that," she said as she stared into her glass and the words *"true love"* echoed through her mind. When she finally looked up, Desmond's eyes were silently consuming hers.

A powerful, raw, animal, sexual aura radiated from him as he stared back at her. He wanted her. She was the kind of women you'd wait for, all of your life.

Camille could feel her heart beating in short, sharp strokes.

Gently he leaned over. His voice was deep and distinctive. "Do you want to know what I want out of life Camille?"

He was so close. Camille could feel the warmth of his breath against the side of her face.

Spellbound she tilted her head and looked deep into his eyes. "No… What?"

"The fairytale," he said.

Camille bursts into a grin. "What?"

He gave her a smile that seared her. "It's not a joke. When I was a kid my mother read a fairytale story to me every night. So, I grew up believing in happy endings."

"Are you serious?"

"I kid you not," he said. "Okay maybe I fudge just a little bit," he joked. "You see my mother only read the fairytale stories to make me stop asking her questions about things I read in my science books."

She laughed. "Now that sounds like the truth. I'd love to hear more stories about you growing up."

Desmond looked into Camille's eyes. They beamed with tenderness and understanding. "And I would love to spend the rest of my life telling you all of them."

Camille was overwhelmed as a sense of panic ran through her. The small voice of caution raised itself. She turned over thoughts in her mind back to a time when she had been too trusting of a man.

Desmond noticed the change in her mood.

His arm wrapped around her body and drew her close. "I'm sorry if you think I'm moving too fast, but several months ago I sat beside you at that play and I haven't been able to get you off my mind. The only thing I can say is a fact is that I've never felt this way about anyone. When I'm around you I can't seem to keep my hands off of you and when I dream about tomorrow, I see you in it."

Camille's stomach flipped flopped as if she was a teenager again. She felt warm inside.

Desmond laughed softly then leaned back and looked at her. "And you won't believe this one," he said. "I've even had a crazy fairytale dream with you in it.We had two beautiful children, a boy for me and a girl for you, and you were my wife of course, and to live the happy ever after life."

Suddenly as if cold water had been thrown on her, Camille's fantasy of Desmond being the perfect man dissolved. Men didn't fantasize and dream about living happily ever after. Women did those things. Obviously, Desmond Garcia had mistaken her for being a fool. Instantly, she pulled out of his embrace.

An awkward silence hung in the air.

He rubbed his chin. "I guess I touched upon a nerve with you. What's wrong?"

"How many women have you've got to go to bed with you with a story like that?"

Desmond gave her an apologetic look. "It's not a story or a pickup line. I'm not trying to play you for a fool. Do you really want me to give you an honest answer?"

This wasn't the comeback that she had expected. She looked at him oddly and studied him. "Yes, in fact I demand that you give me an honest answer."

Desmond realized he was moving too fast for her. He made a mental note that he needed to take things slow.

"Believe me Camille; you don't know your worth. You're the only woman I've ever dreamed about in my happy ever after life. But I can see I've been moving too fast. Don't worry I'll slow things down and woo you the right way.After all, when a man finds the woman, he wants to spend the rest of his life with, he's willing to take his time."

He gave her a wide grin, and then reached out his hand. "So, Miss Camille Baptiste, would you like to give me a second chance and go out on another date with me?"

Slowly Camille placed her hand in his and let out a long breathe. "Deal."

He enclosed his hand around hers and squeezed tight. He didn't realize he had been holding his breath. "The choice is yours Camille where would you like to go?"

She smiled an idea came to mind.

# Chapter 7

**Guilty Pleasure...**

Tiara was good at keeping secrets. For the past few weeks she called and cancelled all her social engagements with both Camille and Eris, telling them her work schedule had increased.

At twenty-seven years of age Tiara Blake was a year and a half older than both Camille and Eris. Neither of them had any idea about the difference in their ages. She'd managed to keep that secret from them as well.

Tiara thought back. It had been mother's fault that she'd been held out of school for a full year. She remembered that year well. It was the year that her mother filed for divorce from her father. Her mother had hidden them out in a small town just outside of the Mojave Desert, until her father met her demands in their divorce settlement.

Her mother, Lana Blake, was a selfish, manipulative, skinny woman with an abundant cleavage that got men's attention.

Growing up her mother Lana always cautioned her against one thing. "Never be a man's whore for free living life daily had its expenses."

Tiara held no illusions about what she wanted out of life. She had learned over the years from watching her mother's life experiences to be sensible about love. After all, she'd thought, if you really looked at what love was, it was just the commodities and exchange business.As a woman you exchanged sex for the money you needed to live on.

The *Eves' Hideaway Inn* which was located off highway one just past

Half Moon Bay, didn't look like a hotel at all, but a rustic old mansion sitting on a cliff overlooking the ocean.

The evening ocean breeze was chilly as Tiara got out of her car. She pulled her coat tighter as she quickly walked across the parking lot, ignoring the stares of several men as she walked by.

The lobby was scarcely populated as she made her way to the elevator. She couldn't believe her luck. She was finally in a relationship with a rich man.

She knocked hard on the door. It opened quickly.

"Tiara you sure took your time driving here," Delmar said. "Here, let me take your coat. I have a fire going in the fireplace."

She smiled and wafted into the room in a haze of expensive perfume. "I took the scenic route, highway one all the way," she said giving a throaty, seductive laugh.

She'd been seeing Delmar exclusively ever since that day she ditched Camille and Eris at lunch. Tiara felt she was the most consummate actress that ever lived. Neither of her two best friends had a clue that she was seeing Delmar. Not to mention the fact, she thought, that she really didn't want Camille to know because she knew that Camille and Delmar had dated briefly.

Tiara sighed heavily, enjoying her secret.

Delmar walked over to a side table and poured a drink. "I hope you are in the mood for champagne," Delmar said, "Because I ordered us a magnum of *Dom Pérignon*."

*Tiara's laugh was easy and light as she took her glass of champagne, he handed her.*

*She took a sip. "It tastes excellent."*

*"I know how to please. Here try this," he held up the tray of chocolate dipped strawberries.*

*"Oh, these are my favorites," she said, as s*he walked further into the room and admired the ambience.

Delmar walked over and handed her a drink.

The room was lavish in velvet curtains in an elegant deep burgundy with elaborate gold fringed trim. It reminded her of a boudoir in an old west hotel.

Tiara swayed her hips in a sensual manner before coming to a halt in front of the mirror. She thrust her hand in the bustier of her dress, adjusting one of her breasts. She had no inhibitions. She turned on the charm. "Delmar I've missed you. Have you missed me?"

The effect of her purposeful sway wasn't lost on Delmar as he watched her in the mirror. "You know I did," he said, smiling softly. God what a woman he thought, already he could feel an erection.

"Delmar, I haven't forgotten that you made me a promise."

"Yes, I said I would do something special for you and I always keep my promise," he said, as his eyes looked straight into hers making her melt with desire.

Tiara stared back at him spellbound by the expression on his face. Everything was going as she planned.

Delmar Devereaux was used to using women. His dark handsome good looks and ruthless nature had gotten him more women than he could handle. Tiara was no different as far as he was concerned, but for now she interested him and kept his mind off of he woman he really wanted. *My God, he thought, Tiara was a sexy woman.*

His thoughts raced thinking of his ideal woman, Camille. Unlike Tiara, Camille would never sleep with a man on the first date. He loved that about her.

But at the moment he didn't want to waste the energy needed to chase Camille. He just wanted to have his guilty pleasure. That's what he called Tiara secretly his guilty pleasure. He prayed Camille would never find out that he'd been sleeping with her best friend.

Tiara walked over and handed him her empty glass. "Another refill please."

"I'm here to please," he said turning his back to her as he refilled her glass.

Tiara walked over and checked out the view from the hotel window, before she sat down on the sofa.

He handed her the drink and gulped his back as he watched her.

Tiara followed his lead. Her drink went down smoothly. Instantly she felt like her inhibitions were gone. She crossed her legs letting the deep split of her dress expose the sensual curve of her bare thigh. She traced her hand up the curve of her thigh and caressed her crotch.

Delmar silently walked over studying her. "I love it when you do that."

"Ohhhh Delmar," she sensually cooed. "Would you like to see what color panties I'm wearing?"

Delmar flinched out of his trance like he'd been slapped. He eyed her for a moment as some compartment in his brain clicked on. He felt the hardening of an erection. "You're not wearing panties."

Tiara giggled. She liked the way Delmar was looking at her; his face was flush with desire. She stood up quickly. "Let me help you take off your clothes," she cooed, reaching and undressing him quickly.

Delmar stood there. "Mmmm, I love it when you undress me."

Tiara laughed softly as she held his gaze. "So, Delmar, what's your pleasure?" She asked as she undid the zipper at the back of her dress.

Delmar's excitement mounted as he stared back at her naked perfect full breasts. He moaned softly. They always gave him an erection. He grinned wide. "You of course, I need you really bad."

Tiara giggled seductively and crawled back against the pillows of the sofa. "You know what Delmar I think you put something in my drink," she said spreading her legs wide and looked back at his erection and ran her hand along the length of her inner thigh.

Delmar caressed his erection watching her. He quickly walked over and grabbed a condom.

She grinned back at him as he slid his body next to hers.

"All my pretties are not free," she giggled.

"Baby I can pay your price," he said as his hands feverishly touch her breasts. He kissed her for a long time, his tongue filling her mouth as his hands played roughly with her breasts.

A jolt of pleasure coursed through Tiara's body as Delmar's fingers found her warm spot. It shouldn't be long now she thought. I should have everything I ever wanted. Money, a closet full of Jimmy Choo shoes, homes, furs and cars she dreamed as she felt Delmar straddle her and in one fluid move rammed hard into her. She jerked in response concentrating harder on her dream.

Hours later, "Damn you were good!" Delmar exclaimed as he lay recuperating, tracing his hand over her firm breasts.

Tiara smiled softly back at him. Now had to be the time she thought, she cleared her throat. "Delmar about that something special you promised."

"Oh yeah, I almost forgot," he interrupted and leaned over and reached to retrieve something from the table beside her. "Here it is."

"What?" she asked at a loss for words. Her heart sank as Delmar placed the box in her hand. A deep despair gripped her. Her thoughts and Delmar's weren't on the same page.

Delmar looked at her. "Well? Aren't you going to open it?"

Tiara's face darkened with sadness only for a moment as she sat with her thoughts. She had a will to overcome whatever happened in her life. Slowly she opened the box.

Something electrical charged the air as Tiara stared back at the exquisite string of pearls.

# Chapter 8

**Alone, what's a girl to do...**

Eris Simeon was starting to get used to spending her Saturdays alone. Camille was off spending the day with Desmond and Tiara had called a few days before and cancelled on their monthly Saturday shopping day.Friendships needed a little distance every now and then she thought as she looked over the long wall of shoes. She tilted her head and that's when she caught sight of the shiny pair of black leather pumps. Instantly her hand reached for them as she waved over the salesclerk.

"Miss, are you sure you only want to try on these twelve pairs of shoes?" The pimpled faced sales associate condescendingly asked.

Eris frowned.  "You know you are so lucky I've become a better person. The old me would be yelling for your manager, trying to get you fired."

The salesclerk glanced at his watch and walked away.

Eris smiled and glanced at herself in the mirror. At twenty-five she was a permanent fixture in Silicon Valley society. Her father's wealthy real-estate business meant that she knew the who's who in the élites of money makers in the valley. Still, a girl had to have a hobby and Eris' was shopping for shoes.

A few minutes later, Eris tried on the last pair of shoes. It was the black patent leather pumps that she'd seen earlier. She stood in front of the mirror and admired the shiny black patent leather pumps. They were the perfect height. She crossed and uncrossed her legs, admiring how the four-inch height of the shoes emphasized the sexy curve of her calf muscles.Slowly she pulled her skirt higher revealing her slender thighs.

"Those shoes become you," a familiar masculine voice called out.

"Ethan," Eris stood there frozen.

Ethan moved in closer and looked back at her admiringly. "If you were trying to go for sexy, you've achieved it. Those shoes have got I want to be your sex slave written all over them."

"Whoopi! That's not what I was going for," Eris hissed sarcastically.

"Yeah well if you wear those pumps, any man, and especially this one, would be a content man for life."

Eris looked up into the soft dark sexy eyes of Ethan Armand as he stood behind her. She felt the heat climb into her cheeks.

"No shirt and tie today?" she asked.

He wore a black *Alfani* t-shirt that made his bulging biceps protrude seductively.  He looked casual and cool and sexy in a pair of stonewashed jeans.

He grinned softly and crossed his arms. "No, just like you I'm dress down for casual Saturdays. But you look beautiful no matter what you're wearing."

Eris snapped to attention and thought back to the brief first time they'd met. He'd been everything she abhorred, self-centered, overly confident and arrogant. She took a deep breath.

Their eyes met and held a second too long.  The earlier tension she'd felt the first time meeting him seemed to dissolve. Maybe it was because he sounded so sincere. "Thanks for the compliment Ethan. But as I remember, you're full of compliments," she said with a sneer on her face.

He decided to ignore her mean-spirited comment.  His eyes skimmed down and admired the pumps she wore.  Then his eyes slowly caressed up to study her face. "My mamma always said that black patent leather pumps made a woman look classy and elegant no matter what else she was wearing. And you know, I agree with my mother's opinion."

Eris turned and leveled her eyes at him. "I can't picture your mother saying such a thing. I bet you made that up," she declared.

"For once that son of mine is telling the truth," a petite pretty brunette woman said while walking deliberately toward Eris.

The woman laughed. "He's sickening isn't he, with those phony compliments of his," she smiled, extending her hand. "Hi, I'm Adria Armand, and believe it or not, I'm Ethan's mother. And who are you my pretty lady?"

"I'm Eris Simeon."

Adria stared back at her. "Not only are you gorgeous but I can tell by the feel of your hand that you are a romantic at heart. In fact, you have a match-maker's heart and that's a good thing," she said with a naughty twinkle in her eye. "I can see why my son likes you very much. You're a very pretty woman inside and out. So tell me, are you single?"

Eris flushed deeply. Just like her son, Adria's words could melt butter, and she was direct and to the point. For some reason Eris found she couldn't lie to her. "Yes, I'm single."

She stared back at Adria Armand and studied her. She didn't look like she could be Ethan's mother. Her hair was styled into an exemplary chignon that made her look regal and elegant and her eyes, which were luminously dark brown, held a commanding gleam.

Eris glanced back at Ethan. She could see he had inherited his mother's brooding dark eyes. Slowly she shook her head. "I can't believe you are Ethan's mother you look so young."

"My goodness, I like you even better, your compliments are sincere," Adria announced tilting her head with a knowing smile she jabbed Ethan playfully in the rib.

Adria turned her intent gaze back to Eric. "Do you like tea Eris? I mean like the afternoon high tea *hoity toity* stuff."

Eris wondered where this conversation was going. "Yes of course I like afternoon tea."

"Well of course you do. I should have known. You are a girly girly woman just like me. I can tell. What about charity events?" Aria asked sizing her up.

"Yes, I like charity events too," Eris said.

Adria paused as if remembering something. "Good, then Eris please promise me you won't move from this spot. I want to speak with my son a moment in private."

Adria quickly pulled Ethan out of distance. "Ethan, I like Eris. She is quite unique and perfect for you darling. And I can tell you've got a thing for her," she presses her lips together to stifle a giggle. "But you're not going to get her with that I think I'm God's gift to woman attitude. You need to work on your approach with her.

"Aw mother, you and your jokes get to be annoying sometimes," Ethan responded.

Adria laughed. "Yes, I know that's what mothers are good at," she said glancing back at Eris. "Now look son, normally I wouldn't mind sticking around and trying to help you get Eris' telephone number because this one I can honestly say would be worth my doing so. But I'm in sort of in a hurry. I need to run to the perfume counter and pick up a bottle of Chanel No 5. And get back home. Do you want me to just get her number or can you ask for her number yourself?"

Ethan grimaced with a sigh. "Mother, I can get her telephone number myself."

Adria shrugged. "Suit yourself, I know how you've been moping around because the girl hasn't called you."

With a big smile Adria waved and got Eris' attention. "Eris sweetheart, it was lovely meeting you. Oh, and do give my son your telephone number. I'd like to invite you to a charity event that I'm hosting," she said turning and walking away.

Embarrassed, Ethan pushed his hands in his pocket and strolled over to Eris.

"I thought you were leaving with your mommy Ethan."

"Very funny Eris. I see you do have jokes."

He lifted a brow studying her. They stared between each other. The silent seconds seemed like hours as they stood there.

Ethan glanced back at her. "You know you promised to call me, and you never did," he said nervously pushing his hands further into his pockets. "So, are you going to give me your telephone number?" he hesitated and quickly added. "So that my mother can call and invite you to that thing she was telling you about?"

Eris folded her arms in an aggressive stance. "You've got some nerve."

"What?" he innocently said.

"You know Ethan that's just low, using your mother to help you pick up women. Go away Ethan," she hissed angrily dismissing him and turning to walk away.

"Miss, are you going to buy those pumps?" The pimple faced sales associate asked.

Eris reached down, took the pumps too off and handed them to him.

"No!"

# Chapter 9

**You Touch My Soul...**
 **Camille's Surprise...**

A week later the remote beach just south of Carmel seemed like an island, as Camille stood silently in the sand and watched the blue sky turn orange and red. She closed her eyes enjoying the feel of the sun against her eyelids, she felt like the sun rays were touching her soul.

Desmond waited patiently watching her, believing she needed to be alone. It gave him a chance to notice the way the sun rays made her hair glisten with cinnamon red highlights.

All at once Camille stretched out her arms. He walked in close. "You look happy. I hope I'm not intruding, am I?"

"No, of course not, you're the one that brought me to this beautiful place.This is the first time I've ever experienced the sun setting against the ocean."

Nervously, she clasped her hands together not knowing what to do with them and then quickly stole a glance at him. His chest was ripped tight with muscles. The dark shades were bookworm and Geeky but couldn't hide the attractiveness of his face.

The moment seemed too good to be true. Like so many things in life. Awkwardly, she turned away from him and thought of Delmar and his betrayal. But that was in the past. It was over and done with. It was time to move on, if she wanted to.

He hated when she turned away. He noted her smile had faded from her face. "Camille, are you alright?" He asked, resting a hand on her shoulder.

She tilted her head and looked back at him. Her eyes held the shadows of the sun setting. She breathed out slowly. "I'm alright. But I had no idea this beach was so remote and so incredibly chilly."

"I know it is starting to get cold," he said, reaching up and touching a long flowing hair. "Hold on a minute. I brought a blanket."

Quickly, he grabbed the blanket. "This should warm you up," he said wrapping it snug around her shoulders

Camille turned and faced him. "You thought of everything, I'm glad I came here with you."

"Yeah, you should be. I was a youth scout. I learned to be prepared for anything," he playfully joked. "Come, I also brought hot coffee," he said as they sat down on the beach and grabbed his thermos.

Camille sat down on the beach and wrapped her hands around the cup of coffee Desmond handed her. "So tell me again. You said you were a writer?"

"In high school everybody was a writer," he joked. "But seriously, I did get a chance to write for our local County weekly newspaper."

She sipped her coffee. "The county weekly news, now that sounds exciting. I bet you cover some big stories."

Desmond put the cap back on his thermos and glanced at Camille. She had no idea how small the town he grew up in was.

"So, tell me about your biggest story," she said.

"I never got an occasion to write about drug dealers or neighbors who were addicts, or but I did write a great story about our local priest being caught hosting crap games in a cellar under the old mission. But my teacher pulled the newspaper before distribution stating that Father John was actually using the money from the crap games to keep local families in need fed."

By the rhythm of his voice, Camille knew he'd been upset that his story was not told. "You sound like you were a little angry at your teacher for not letting your story get told."

"Yeah, I was," he shrugged. "But I got over it after Father John showed me firsthand the good his ill-gotten games did in the community."

Camille sighed. "So, let me get this straight. Not only were you one of those Geeky scientist types in high school who loved math and science, but you were on the school's local county newspaper. Wow, you really kept busy," she said blowing out a breath. "I'm curious. Did you date much in high school?

Desmond laughed. "Yes, I did. But enough about me. Now it's my turn for questions. What about you. Did you date much in high school?"

She shook her head. "Nope, not really just your normal dates to prom and I did get to go to the winter ball and a couple of dances. But my father kind of ran guys away. He had a no-nonsense attitude about guys I went to high school with. In fact, he would ask them point blank if they had any ambition, and if they didn't, they couldn't date his daughter."

He chuckled. "Your father sounded tough?"

She looked up. "In some ways, I guess so. Anyway, emotionally and financially my father was there. But now that I look back, he's wasn't that tough in his business." She trailed off; her voice laced with pain. She glanced down and studied the cup of coffee she was holding.

Desmond reached out and touched her hand. "It sounds like the topic of your father has hit a bad note. We don't have to talk about it if you don't want to?"

"No, I'm okay with it, and since you've been truthful," she paused. "It's just that I remember one summer this boy named Spencer, who lived down the street from us, kept asking me out to the movies and I kept saying yes, but the only thing, he was also asking me to pay for the both of us. Which I did," her eyes held his. "I guess I paid because I was just happy to go to the movies. When my father found out that I was the one paying he confronted Spencer and embarrassed him and me. Later my father told me, Spencer was using me, and that in life, I had to look out for the hustlers like Spencer. I accused my father of being mean and labeling Spencer something that he wasn't," she took a deep breath. "My father said he knew what Spencer was because he was a user too. After my father died, I found out he'd had told me the truth. He was a user. He had used up my mother's inheritance and never told her."

She grew silent.

His hand reached out and touched hers at the sadness etched on her face. They came from different worlds. Still he could tell by her voice she loved her father. "I can't let this date end with your telling me that. Now tell me a good memory that you have of your father."

Her lips curved into a smile "I...I..." she hesitated, and then nervously said. "Well, when I was six years old. My father took me to have tea at a place called *Mia's Tea Treasures*. I fell in love with the place. I told my father when I grew up, I would own a string of my own Tea House's and I would call them Camille's Tea Shop & Treasures," her words died on her lips as she bowed her head. "My father said that was a wonderful dream to have and to never forget it. He encouraged me that day, and he told me I could do anything and own any place I wanted. I remember that day like it was yesterday. What a stupid kid's dream."

Desmond reached out and touched her chin. Camille tilted her head and stared back at him. "There is no such thing as a stupid kid's dreams Camille. Your dream sounds wonderful to me too."

The man was too good to be true, she thought.

A sound brought her back to reality. The landscape had darkened.

Nervous, Camille sat up straight. "Which direction is the car from here?"

Desmond laughed and pinned her with a mesmerizing gaze."North, it's that way," he pointed. "Don't worry I know how to get us back," he paused. "Unless of course, if you're nervous to be alone on the beach after dark with me, we can go," he said.

Camille shivered. "No, I just worry that it might get even colder than it already is."

"Here, share your blanket with me," he said pulling her close.

As his arms circled around her, she nudged in closer. She relaxed and savored the heat of his body.

"There, are you warmer now?" Desmond asked.

Camille tilted her head back and stared back at him. "I'm still a little chilly," she softly murmured.

He kissed her lips softly. "I will warm you."

His moves were smooth, unexpected, and incredible.

Camille felt her body sliding down blindly against the sand.  Instantly the surprise chill of the cold night air startled her. She pushed back and rolled from under him.

As she stared back at him, she caught an expression in his eye. She knew that look; it was a warning.

"Ah! Whew! It's cold!" She spoke quickly, rising. "I think we should go."

Desmond looked up at the dark sky. "Mmmm, yes I think you're right."

# Chapter 10

**Grand Illusions**

The morning sun penetrated through the window and Tiara grinned wide determined that today would be the day she made her move and pressed Delmar for her special gift.

She watched him dozing softly, his hand resting on her hip. She smiled remembering what his hands had done to her.Earlier those were like a master guitar player who was expert at bring her body to a climax. Softly she skimmed her hand over his body remembering.

He dozed softly and let out a moan.

Her voice purred out low, "Delmar, it's been a couple months since we started seeing each other and since you promised me, I could pick the next special gift."

Groggy Delmar murmured, "Mmmm, you're right, I did."

"Oh, thank you Delmar," she excitedly said. "I want you to take me out to dinner."

"Fine," he yawned.

She scooted in close and ran her hands down his body. "I can't wait to introduce you to my friends at dinner."

Delmar sat up in bed. "Damn, I'm fully awake now."

Frustrated, he got out of bed, walked across the room and sat down in a glove-leather armchair. He ran his hands through his hair. Tiara was trying to complicate matters, he thought. They discussed this subject before. A relationship wasn't what he wanted or needed. He glanced back at her. A muscle worked in his jaw and suddenly his face changed.

The last reaction Tiara had expected had been his silence.

"Delmar, you said I could choose the surprise this time," she nervously laughed.

"And dinner with your friends was the only idea you could come up with?"

Automatically she laughed out amazed at how calm her voice was. "Delmar listen, it doesn't have to be a lavish dinner or anything like that…."

Anger flashed in Delmar's eyes. "Damn Tiara, what is this, some kind of test? "Where is this coming from?" he angrily demanded.

Confused Tiara froze. She hadn't expected this outburst. Things had been going well between them. Before she could get any words out….

"I asked you a question Tiara! What put this grand illusion in your head?"

"I thought …" she said calmly.

He grinned maliciously at her. "Who asked you to think? Besides, we had this conversation before in the beginning. I told you then what this thing we do was all about!"

Tiara was sacred. He looked angry enough to leave. She watched as he ran his hands through his hair. She kept her cool. "Look Delmar …

He eyed her for a moment. He stood in silence with his thoughts. Camille would never pull a foolish stunt like this with him. But then again, Tiara wasn't the level-headed woman Camille was.

"What is up with you Tiara? Do you think that if I go out to dinner with you and your friends, it puts us on the path to a relationship or marriage or something?"

Tiara softened her voice and calmly said. "No, it was just a suggestion to have dinner that's all."

Breathing heavily, Delmar watched her like a hawk. "I told you this was just about sex and you said you wanted the same thing. I thought we had an understanding. But I guess we didn't.

Anxiously he glanced between her and the door. "Well I guess since we don't have an understanding one of us should leave and since I'm paying for the room..."

The moment was tense.

Tiara's thoughts raced as she wondered how she had forgotten that underneath all that charm Delmar was a ruthless, arrogant, and cold-hearted man.

Calculatingly she thought for a moment and then she looked back at him with innocent eyes, as she crawled up on the pillows and spread her legs wide. She laid there quiet and very naked.

The movement had the effect she needed, as Delmar stared at her bare breasts. It was obvious that his brain was shifting gears.

He felt his body awaken at the sight of her naked breasts. He licked his dry lips. His voice was cool when he said, "Well Tiara, what is it going to be? Do you want to leave? Or are we finished having this conversation?"

She could tell his anger had pretty much worked out of his system, she cooed, "I'm here for the same thing you are sugar," she said resting her eyes on the swelling mass of his full erection.

Tiara watched as his temper subsided and was replaced with lust, as he rose up out of the chair like a lion that finds its prey. He crossed the room and got back into bed with her.

His eyes locked with hers. "So, we have an understanding?" he asked, kissing her softly.

"Oh yes baby," she quickly said"

Delmar made a low moaning sound as he straddled her and in one swift movement thrust deep inside her hot wet walls.

Tiara moaned softly as she pushed her body against his in urgency joining the rhythm of his groove.

A half hour later, Tiara pushed from under Delmar just in time to see a fiercely intent look of pleasure shadow Delmar's features.

"Wow you were amazing Tiara," he said rising off of her. "Now about that gift, I have my own surprise for you. Do you want it?"

"Yes," she anxiously nodded.

He got out of bed and walked over to his jacket and pulled out a long jewelry box. He walked back to the bed and opened it. A sapphire and diamond bracelet caught the light. He put it on her wrist.

"Here is my surprise. Do you like it?"

Tiara felt a surge of excitement as she examined the bracelet. She traced her fingers over it. Her eyes glistened, mystified by heavy weight of the sapphires and diamonds. There had to be at least twenty carats in sapphires alone on the bracelet, they weren't too small she thought. "Of course, I do. In fact, I love it."

Would you like to order room service?" He asked feeling like things were getting back to normal between them.

"Not right now" she said, as her eyes appraised the bracelet on her wrist. The bracelet was expensive. He'd chosen well, she said to herself. Well enough for me to screw his brains out again, she thought with a smile.

Tiara pulled him back into bed and rolled on top of him. She positioned herself over him and felt the intense heat of pleasure as he filled her.

Delmar looked back at her like a teenager who'd gotten his first taste of pleasure. He pulled back and looked at her grinning like a like a wolf. "Oh God you are!" he said, his voice strangled with pleasure. "You are so good."

# Chapter 11

**Camille & Desmond...**

A week later, as Camille busily rushed through the Santa Clara Convention center; she was heading out earlier from the *Northern California Networking conference.*She checked her watch. It was just past noon…almost time to meet Desmond Garcia for their lunch date.

Quickly she navigated her car through the mid-day traffic down Tasman Avenue. Luckily the restaurant they picked wasn't far.

*The Cajun French Waiter* restaurant was a local hot spot for celebrities, and it was known to have some excellent food and private dining rooms.

Camille checked her appearance in the glass front door as she walked up. Her hair was styled in a classic French twist that accented the high cheekbones of her face. She adjusted the cherry red suit with the heart shaped neckline. The red color made her feel radiant.

A distinguished-looking waiter greeted her. "Do you have reservations Miss?"

"No…I mean yes I'm meeting Desmond Garcia," she said.

The waiter's eyes flashed knowingly. "Right this way," he said, leading the way down a long corridor behind the main dining area.

She knew they were headed to the covered stone path where the chestnut colored French doors lined the atrium and hid the private dining rooms.

The waiter stopped abruptly in front of a chestnut colored door and knocked softly before he entered.

Mr. Garcia, your guest has arrived. Shall I open the wine for you now?"

"No thank you. I can do that," Desmond said.

Silently the waiter closed the door behind him.

Desmond's expressive coffee brown eyes captured Camille's. He smiled softly at the woman of his dreams.

Her breath caught in the back of her throat at the sight of him. The classic dark navy-blue suit, white shirt and red power tie he wore made him look very handsome. "Desmond," she said flustered. "I hope you weren't waiting long."

"No Camille, I'm so glad to see you," Desmond said, closing the distance, giving her a hug.

At the feel of his touch Camille thought she'd died and gone to heaven. His body was hard and powerful. She took a deep breath, inhaling the intoxicating scent of his cologne. Christ, she thought. She could visualize his hard body on top of hers making love to her. She pulled out of his embrace and stared back at him.

"I'd better take my seat," she said. Nervously she studied her menu. "Shall we order?"

"Yes, I'll summon the waiter," Desmond said pressing a button.

Twenty minutes later, their waiter placed streaming plates of seafood jambalaya in front of them.

"So, you love golf? And it sounds like you've played golf at a lot of exciting places. I can't believe you played golf at Pebble Beach," Camille said excitedly. "Did you see any celebrities?"

"If I did, I probably didn't recognize them. You know I only played there once," he said, taking a sip of his wine.

Camille wasn't listening to a word he said as she sat staring at him talk and remembering how well his arms fit around her.

"Do you play golf," he asked.

Camille shook out her thoughts. "What, oh golf, me? No," she said apologetically shaking her head. "Unless you count miniature golf," she smiled. "I did want to learn how but I just never got around to taking lessons."

"Then I'll teach you. Besides, it's a great way to get in a lot of long walks together."

For an instant their eyes held. He made her feel special and something else.

She glanced back at her empty plate and tried to change the subject. "My Nana used to make seafood jambalaya for me. This was almost as good as hers."

"I bet you're a good cook just like your Nana was."

Camille's unexpected laugher rang out. "Oh, you do, and I bet you were also a prankster when you were a kid."

Desmond laughed with her and then paused for a moment with his thoughts. "Yes, and I bet you have a lot of your Nana's qualities. I can tell she raised you. When I hear you talk about her, she seems to have made sure you had a good upbringing and she sounds like she was a very caring woman. Just like you are.

She looked back into his clear brown eyes. They were bright with understanding. "You are an unusual man Desmond.

"Thanks for the compliment. Now I have a question for you. What if you had the chance to pursue your dream of opening your own string of tea shops, would you do it?"

She laughed out again. "Of course, I would, and I will do it just as soon as I win the lottery," she joked. "Right along with buying my dream home in the suburbs and buying my mother a brand-new Honda Civic loaded with everything."

Desmond smile she'd didn't have a clue about who he was. He didn't want the moment to end.

Instantly his cell phone rang. He checked the number. It was Nona his secretary. If she was calling it was urgent. He checked the time. It was after three thirty pm.

"Camille," he said with urgency. "It's my secretary Nona. I have an urgent meeting I can't seem to get out of within the hour."

She investigated his face with a quiet serenity, knowing he told her the truth. "I understand."

"Could I see you again?"

She smiled at him and without thinking said. "You mean after your meeting, tonight.

Her answer caught him off guard. "Yes, I would love to see you tonight."

Later, that night, Camille was glad Desmond had suggested the quaint little ice cream parlor nestled in the lobby in of the *Millennium Hotel*. The ice cream tasted rich and smooth she thought, as she devoured her chocolate ice cream.

Desmond knew he was in love, watching her as she devoured the ice cream cone.

"I bought you something," he said as they sat together at a small table. When I saw it I thought of you," he said placing a box on the table.

Their hands touched, and an electric charge rushed between them.

Camille opened the box and was taken by surprise. An elegant gold necklace held a miniature Orchid bloom with a carat size diamond nestled in the center, stared back at her.

"Desmond, it's beautiful."

"Allow me," Desmond said, picking up the necklace and slipping it around her neck.

His hands slipped up to caress her face. "Gosh, I'm so lucky, you're beautiful, classy and everything I ever wanted."

Feeling a demanding hunger for him mounting and mounting she looked back at him and whispered. "Desmond, you make me want to break all of my dating rules. If I wasn't afraid, we might run into my mother if I took you home, I'd suggest that we go to my place."

She couldn't control herself any longer she leaned over and kissed him softly on the lips.

Nothing prepared her for Desmond's kiss as she felt an onrush of pleasure until he released her.

"Let's get out of here," he said. "I know just the place where we can go."

Minutes later, Camille stood in wide eyed in wonder staring back at the Silicon Valley Skyline as it shimmered under the afternoon sun. The penthouse suite of the *Millennium Hotel* held five thousand square feet of supreme extravagant luxury.

The crisp jet white bedroom was a room that Camille felt she would never forget as she stared around the room trying to memorize every inch of it.

"Camille," Desmond said softly, removing his jacket. "Did you hear me?"

"Yes," she said shaking out her thoughts, turning to face him. "You asked if I'd mind if she took my clothes off and no, I don't mind," she purred. "In fact, I do believe I'll find it very simulating to my senses seeing your gratification in doing so."

Camille slowly lifted her arms up as Desmond closed the distance between them.

He fingered the buttons of her jacket, removed it and then took his time letting his eyes drink her in. Slowly pools or cherry red fabric floated to the floor as he removed every item of her clothing.

Camille stood there naked in her stockings and heels and slipped her hands on his chest and peeled off his shirt.

"Keep the heels on," he said, as they stood facing each other free of clothes.

Then taking her hand, he kissed the palm of it and made his way up her arm. He groaned as his lips swooping in brushing her shoulders, then her breast.

Camille moaned as he brought her to quivering life.

He felt the heat of her. "You see Camille, my needs are very simple," he said easing her back on the bed.

He watched her as she watched him and then exhaled when he

slipped inside her.

# Chapter 12

**Help is on the way ...**

"Dammit... Dammit!... Dammit!" Camille yelled inside her car as the blasted the radio. Why was highway 680 heading to Pleasanton so slow that Sunday evening?  Everybody knew that all the weekend travelers were going home on the south side of the highway.

Her mind switched gears as she thought about Desmond Garcia. The man was handsome and a great kisser that made her heart go flip flop. She bet he was an excellent lover she wondered if he went in for the kinky and erotic sex stuff.

She was so wrapped up in her daydream about Desmond that she almost missed seeing the white Honda Civic on the side of the road with the hood up.

Quickly she took the Sunol exit and got back on the southbound side of the highway. She knew the moment her mother called and didn't want her to call the car service. She would drop everything and come to help. She never denied her mother anything, especially after she'd learned that her father had spent her mother's inheritance.

Soon she spotted the white Honda.Cautiously she wheeled her Cadillac directly behind the Honda.

Her mother Gabby Baptiste got out of the Honda.

"What took you so long Camille?  I could have died of thirst out here."

"No, you couldn't mother. You have a cooler full of water in the trunk," Camille said, popping the trunk and retrieving a bottle of water and handing it to her mother. "Perhaps, if you took the time to check your car's radiator like you do that cooler, your car would still be running."

"Oh, hush up," Gabby said accepting the bottle of water.

Camille walked and stood in front of the opened hood Honda. "This is the last time this radiator overheats on you. We're getting it replaced."

Gabby toke a gulp of water. "Do you have replacement funds in your budget? You know I can't be touching the money I budget for bingo."

Camille rubbed her forehead, suddenly weary from the drive. "Mother don't worry, you don't have to deal with the radiator. I will."

Sighing, Gabby studied her. "Camille, have you ever thought about taking Delmar Devereaux up on his offer to buy me a new Honda? A new one is less than twenty thousand dollars. Why that's nothing to a man like Delmar and he even offered to loan you the money if you wouldn't take it as a gift."

Camille studied her and saw the desperation in her eyes. "Mom don't worry. I'll get your car fixed and I won't touch your bingo money.

A moment later the tow truck pulled in front of Gabby's car and a pudgy waist driver in oily overalls walked over and said, "Which one of you ladies called me for a tow?"

# Chapter 13

**Visitation...**

A week later at work, Camille rose from her desk and walked to the filing cabinet.

Moments later, a heavy knock on her door drew her attention away from the reports she was looking through.

"Come in, the doors open," she yelled, thinking it was Eris early for their lunch date.

The door to her office opened and a man stepped in and closed the door.

Out of the corner of her eye she could tell a man was standing there in an authoritative stance, his legs apart.

Camille looked up puzzled. "Delmar? What are you doing here?"

Delmar Devereaux stood there wearing a dark steel grey suit and donning mirrored sunglasses.

He watched the curve of her backside as she stood over the filing cabinet. He quickly closed the distance between them walked over and gave her a peck on the cheek.

*Camille, my love,* he thought, but didn't say it. "Don't you look beautiful today? How are you and that lovely mother of yours doing?"

She paused. She'd wondered if Gabby had told him about her car. "I'm fine and mother is good. Thanks for asking."

He walked around her office, examining the place. "So, this is the famous *Lipton Escrow* Company you work for?" He asked but didn't wait for an answer. "You have a nice little office here."

She smiled pleasantly. "Are you here on business Delmar?

Before he could answer, a soft knock urgently hammered out before the door was opened.

Bob Madden, the owner of Lipton Escrow appeared with his usual pinched expression like he'd just bit into something sour. He walked forward and clasped Delmar's hand.

"Mr. Devereaux, this is a great honor. Forgive me if I was late. I thought our meeting wasn't until noon.

Camille sighed with relief; Delmar wasn't' there about Gabby's car. She glanced up at him.

The corners of Delmar's lips curved up as he removed his shades.He was annoyed his plan wasn't working as it should. He hadn't even had time to invite Camille to lunch with them.

For once in her life Camille was glad that her boss, Bob Madden, was a former lawyer. She was lost in admiration of the way he commanded Delmar's attention, bombarding him with question after question.

"Hey, Camille, are you in there?" Instantly the atmosphere was shattered by Eris' loud voice.

Delmar flinched as Eris's form stood in the frame of the opened door. Today wasn't going as he planned.

Eris Simeon studied Delmar as she moved in closer into the room.She stopped directly in front of him. "Delmar what are you doing here?"

A frown crossed Delmar's face. *What a disastrous day,* he thought. Eris Simeon was the last person he'd wanted to have a confrontation with.

He cleared his throat. "Mr. Madden and I have a lunch meeting."

Bob nodded enthusiastically. "Yes, we do."

Eris Simeon nodded evasively. "That's good, because Camille and I made lunch plans also and I hope they won't interfere with your plans Mr. Madden?"

Bob nodded his understanding. "That's fine by me."

Eris oozed composure as she coolly said, "Oh Bob, you can't speak for Mr. Devereaux, maybe he wanted a pretty face at lunch with him today."

Reluctantly Delmar nodded. "No of course not my appointment was with Bob."

Bob smiled. "Okay that's all settled let me grab the reports off my desk," he hesitated. "In fact, Mr. Devereaux, I can show you the title record I found on that Carmel property you requested."

Grudgingly Delmar followed behind Bob. "Yes of course."

Eris waited until Bob closed his office door. "Camille what was that all about?"

Camille shrugged. She didn't have the heart to tell Eris her suspicion that her mother, Gabby, had called Delmar after her car broke down."I don't know," she said innocently."Come on let's go to lunch."

# Chapter 14

**Desmond Garcia...**

The next morning, Desmond Garcia stared out of the window of his downtown San Jose Office and saw the massive Adobe Towers, out of the corner of his eye. Within the last seven years he watched those massive towers just as he'd watched his business grow into a multimillion-dollar conglomerate. At first, he'd thought that was what he had wanted, now he realized how incomplete his life really was. His thoughts went back to Camille Baptiste. She was everything he'd ever wanted. He smiled.

He turned back and looked around his office. It was way too big for just one man. It was an eclectic mixture of postmodern and classic with a double pedestal antique desk with leather insert panels and his favorite piece, a large overstuffed leather executive chair that looked like it belonged in a museum. He smiled softly. It was his most prized possession. Tall ceiling to floor windows covered one wall. While the other walls were painted in a neutral soft tan, standing on a wall all by itself hung a huge painting of the San Juan Bautista Valley.

Absentmindedly, he touched the soft leather on the chair and smiled as his thoughts went back to Camille. His fingers caressed the soft leather as if he was caressing her. He sat down in the soft leather chair, his thoughts still on her. He remembered back to how soft Camille's kiss was and how it tasted uniquely like her.

A soft knock sounded from the door of his office and woke him from his daydream.

The heavy door swung open. His secretary Nona Allen walked in.

"Here are the reports you wanted. And here is the package you've been waiting for from Maui," Nona said, placing them both on his desk.

Desmond's coffee brown eyes glittered like crystals as he smiled excitedly as he scanned the placed *FEDEX* envelope she'd placed on his desk.

Nona smiled. "It must be good news, because Fredrick Chiu called from Maui personally to check and see if it had arrived."

"If Fredrick called it must be good news. Did he say anything else?" he asked.

"He said he understand you are busy right now and can't take the time to visit the lab. He said to tell you not to worry. Everything is fine and maturing normally like they should. He said everything is on schedule at the lab," she said.

Desmond nodded. "I'm glad Fredrick understands I just can't get away right now."

Nona walked with a quick step toward the door. "Yes, he does and he did say on your next visit to Maui he'll show you the results personally," she said turning and looking back over her shoulder. "Oh, he did say you should plan to stay at least a couple of weeks when you make your visit to Maui because he has lots to show you."

Desmond grew silent as he watched Nona close his office door. His fingers tapped the envelope. There was no way he was leaving on a business trip right now. He didn't think he could stay away from Camille that long.

He stood and walked back to the window calmly, deep in thought.

The telephone on his desk rang, and he quickly walked over, catching it before the second ring. He checked the caller ID before picking it up and smiled with surprise.

"Hello old friend, it's been a long time," Desmond said.

"Hey Desmond, I didn't think you'd pick up I figured Nona would answer and then I'd try again to ask her out on a date," Ethan Armand said.

"Nona has too much good taste to date someone like you Ethan."

"Ouch!" Ethan chuckled. "Now that was a low blow Desmond, albeit truthful, but low."

Desmond gave a light chuckle of amusement. "Besides, my secretary has been happily married for over twenty-five years."

Ethan's voice became serious. "Yeah, I know, and don't think that doesn't make me sad, because I'm not in a relationship. Speaking of which that's why I called and what I need to speak to you about can't be told over the telephone."

"Well Ethan it sounds like you want me to meet you for lunch and you're paying, right?"

An hour later Ethan Armand was anxious when he saw Desmond Garcia arrive at Il Fornaio restaurant for lunch. He sat up and checked his watch. He was on his second martini.

"Damn, what took you so long?"

"Hello to you too Ethan, I can tell you have been drinking on an empty stomach, no more liquor for you."

Desmond caught the attention of the waiter. "Bring us two strong coffees and two orders of Pollo Toscano."

Ethan looked at his empty martini glass and made a face. "Okay Doctor Desmond, if you insist, I'll stop drinking but only if you tell me."

The waiter interrupted and brought the coffee and two large glasses of ice and water.

Desmond took a sip of coffee and grinned. "Mmmm, this is good coffee."

Ethan shook his head. "Come on the suspense is killing me. Did you finally go out with that Brazilian girl with beautiful big breasts? You remember the one that gave you her number at the CBE Convention in San Francisco?"

Desmond merely raised and lowered his brows and shook his head.

"Okay…Okay that one was more my type than yours," Ethan chuckled. "But man, think about all the fun time you could have had playing with her two full breasted friends?"

Desmond shook his head in confusion. "Ethan you've got sex on the brain again. I take it you're not dating anyone at this time?"

"No, I'm not, nor am I getting any sex regularly."

"Tough break," Desmond said shaking his head. "What's wrong? Are you in a slump? It's not like you to be without female companionship."

"Something weird happened to me. I can't figure it out. I met this girl or rather I've seen this girl a couple times out in public. But she won't give me her number or call me or anything."

The waiter placed their food in front of them.

Desmond sliced into his chicken. "Mmmm… The Pollo Toscano is excellent," he said silently watching Ethan eat his food.He thought for a moment. It wasn't like Ethan to be so quiet.

Ethan looked confused at his plate.

"Eat your food Ethan. You'll get over her."

Ethan stared back at him. The two were distant cousins who had grown up together.They shared a strong bond, stronger than brothers. "Desmond, your big brother trait is showing. But you don't understand, I can't stop thinking about her."

Desmond took a drink of coffee. "She's an anonymous lady that won't call you back. Either hire a private detective to find her or move on."

Ethan took a swallow of his coffee. "I guess I could hire a private detective …"

Desmond shook his head. "It was a joke Ethan. Get a grip."

"Who said she was anonymous? I know her name."

"Look Ethan have you thought that maybe she's not interested or she's seeing someone? What's her name anyway?"

Ethan never got to answer as his eyes stared fiercely in the distance.

"Damn, there's Raven Channing."

Desmond's smile faded. "What?

Raven's head shot in their direction as if summoned by her woman's intuition. She quickly walked over.

"Good afternoon boys, enjoying lunch?"

Both Desmond and Ethan looked up in confusion.

Raven walked closer and placed an attention gaze at her prey. "Hi Desmond, how are you doing?"

Desmond shook his head. "I don't know but I think I'm having a really bad nightmare in the middle of the daytime."

"Ouch," Ethan coughed out. "Raven, hello to you too."

Raven's eyes flashed instantly, and she regained her composure. "There's no need to get mean Desmond. I came to offer an olive branch."

An astonished expression crossed Desmond's face. "Really?"

Raven nodded and turned her attention. "Ethan … Do you think I could speak to Desmond in private?"

Ethan shrugged. "No way! Anything you have to say to Desmond you can say to me."

"Desmond," Raven's eyes pleaded.

"You heard the man Raven," Desmond said. "You're no longer like a wife up in my presence. Anything you want to say. Say it."

Ethan gave a humorous laugh. "Desmond is not feeling your vibe anymore Raven."

"Suit yourself Desmond…" Raven paused and sized him up and continued. Flattery was always a good way to start, she thought. "You're a good man Desmond and I've been feeling pretty guilty about the way I behaved toward you."

Her revelation caused a shared silence.

Raven leveled her eyes with his. "I've been thinking about you a lot lately Desmond. I know I messed up and I was wrong. I apologize, and I think we should give each other another chance."

"You must be broke," Ethan coughed out under his breath.

"Shut-up Ethan, I was talking to Desmond."

Desmond said not a word.

Raven stood there a second longer thinking about Desmond. One of these days she thought silently, when you least expect it, I'm going to catch you totally off guard. That's when I'll show you what you have been missing, she said to only herself.

She cleared her throat. "Well like I said before, I'm sorry if I've done anything in the past to hurt you Desmond. I've embarrassed myself enough for one day," Raven breathed out slowly. "But don't get me wrong. It was worth it Desmond. You were worth it. I meant every word I said. Too bad I didn't realize what a good man you were until I lost you."

"Gold-digger!" Ethan muddled out under a chuckle.

Raven snapped her head around and gave Ethan a look that could kill.

She took a deep breath and turned her gaze. "Well Desmond, I'll take my leave," she said softly. "You and Ethan have a nice lunch."

Ethan laughed out as she walked away. "What's her problem?"

Desmond frowned. Lunch was over as far as he was concerned. Every time Raven Channing came around him. He felt like he'd entered the last shade of midnight.His instincts told him Raven wasn't finished having the last word. "You know Raven. She has her own special way of spinning the truth to suit her. But I have a private investigator's report, which says different."

"Yeah, I know you do. But why can't she get along without you?" Ethan asked but didn't wait for as response. "Oh yeah, I almost forgot. You always did have a way with the ladies. You shouldn't have been sprinkling all that love dust on her so fiercely Desmond."

"Love dust? Ethan, what are you talking about?"

Ethan chuckled. "You know, love dust, the green stuff called money."

Desmond grimaced. "Yeah, I see what you mean," he said thinking back to the short time he'd dated Raven. She did love for him to spend money on her.

# Chapter 15

**Camille & Tiara**

Days later, Camille Baptiste was seated at the sidewalk table at the restaurant on Main and Angela Street in downtown Pleasanton. She got the waiter's attention and ordered a glass of wine.

It was just like Tiara, she mused, to be a half hour late. Her thoughts turned to Desmond while she waited. She visualized Desmond sitting on the beach with her that day in Carmel. His muscles were the stuff dreams were made of. She smiled softly, remembering how good he looked when he got out of bed naked after they finished making love. Boy was Desmond good looking naked. – *Stop it!* She told herself.

"Camille you're talking to yourself. Are you okay?"

"Tiara! Yes, I'm fine."

Tiara leaned over and gave Camille a hug. She noticed how good Camille looked wearing the dark Chartreuse satin blouse. She was always dressed flawlessly. But today she looked elegant and chic. No woman should be so beautiful; she thought as she watched as Camille fidgeted with a strand of loose hair and tucked it neatly behind the orchid, she wore it her hair.

Tiara took the seat across from Camille and felt a pain of envy knowing this was the woman that Delmar Devereaux wanted. Life wasn't fair, she thought before putting on her best fake smile. "Sorry I was late. I was running errands. You look nice. When did you start wearing flowers in your hair?"

Camille thoughtfully looked at her and said. "Since Desmond

started giving me orchids. I call him the orchid lover."

"Terrific. You're dating an orchid lover. I thought that breed died out in the last war. Well, there is hope for me yet," Tiara jokingly said. "Oh, and I do love the way you're wearing that orchid in your hair. It makes you look very sophisticated."

"Uh oh, you're paying compliments?" Camille asked staring back with suspicion. "What do you want Tiara, a favor?"

"Who me? Never!" She said innocently. "Right now, I just want to order and get a drink," she said catching the attention the waiter.

"Sir, please bring me whatever my friend is drinking."

Camille glanced up at the waiter. "I'm ready to order. I'm hungry. I'll take the Chicken Picatta."

"Yeah me too," Tiara muttered. "And I'll have a glass of water also."

"Make those two glasses of water," Camille added.

The waiter took their menus and hurried away.


Twenty minutes later, the waiter placed their food in front of them.

Tiara looked at the Chicken Picatta placed in front of her and inhaled. The food smelled delicious. She cut off a piece and savored the first bite and grinned. "This Chicken Picatta is excellent," she said glancing up.

"So, Camille, from what you told me. Desmond sounds romantic. Are you two getting serious?"

Camille laughed. "I don't know how romantic the museum was but our date on the beach. Now that was romantic!"

Tiara looked at her quizzically. "Am I hearing right that Desmond has taken you on a romantic date to the beach, as well as, he's given you orchids."

Camille nodded. "You've got it right so far."

"I thought the guy looked like a Geek when I first met him," Tiara said. "But from what you've told me, Desmond can't be a true Geek; there must be a bad boy hidden underneath that exterior if he knew a romantic beach to take you to," she said, dabbing at her lips with a napkin. "Be careful Camille, don't let him take too much control or the next thing you know the bad boy will come out and

he's trying to get in the panties and run."

Frustrated, Camille adjusted the orchid in her hair. Tiara could always make her feel lacking in the managing your sexual relationship department. "Don't worry, Desmond was and always will be the perfect gentleman."

Tiara condescendingly smiled. "Never say the word always, especially if you're not taking control over running things with your man. And it sounds like you're not. Look Camille I'm just saying, be careful. You don't handle the casual sex thing well," she said. "And Desmond sounds like he's an undercover bad boy that needs a woman like me to handle him. You know I wear the big girl panties between us and I know how to handle a man like that."

Camille froze. It was just like Tiara to say something mean.

The silence at the table as unnerving. Tiara sensed Camille's discontent and looked up. Her voice was almost a whisper. "I'm joking. I didn't mean it."

Camille took a sip of her wine and felt a mean girl streak of her own. She spoke up. "You don't wear big girl panties. You wear big girl drawers," she corrected, rolling her eyes. "Anyway, you need to get some more sleep Tiara. I'm starting to see bags under your eyes."

"Ouch!" Tiara said glancing back at her. "Okay you got me back," she said, taking a sip of her wine. "Do you think I could ask you now?"

"What about that small favor you wanted?"

"Yes," Tiara said letting her finger toy with her glass of wine as she considered telling Camille the truth, but at the last moment her years of keeping secrets prevailed. "I know you think my life is perfect but it's not."

Camille let out a sigh. Tiara's mind was back on its favorite subject herself.

"First off, I want to say thank you for not including Eris today for lunch," Tiara said, taking a sip of her wine. "I love Eris, but she gets on my last nerve sometimes."

Camille knew that her two best friends sometimes didn't get alone. She studied Tiara's face. She looked worried about something.She had a knack for knowing when something had Tiara down. "What's wrong, do you need to talk?"

"Yeah I'm just a little confused about why Eris treats me like she does. I think she's still mad at me about something and well…" she said timorously with a shrug.

"Don't worry, you and Eris, you've two been at each other's throat before. You always forgive and make up."

"This time it's different. I can feel it," Tiara shrugged. "I mean don't you ever just feel a little jealous of Eris and all that wealth she has?"

Camille knew where this was going. Every time Eris and Tiara had a falling out, Tiara would pester her for days that the two of them needed to find rich husbands who could buy them mansions as big as Eris' daddy's someday.

"Here we go again," Camille announced in a crisped tone. "I won't lie to you Tiara. Sure, I get a little jealous of Eris' wealth. Especially now with my mother trying to twist my arm to buy her a new car."

Tiara chuckled. "It sounds like mother Gabby is up to her old tricks."

"Yeah, she is, but back to your picking on Eris for being rich. When you talk like that it sounds like you're picking at an old scab and keeping the sore from healing."

"Ha! No, I'm not Camille," she hesitated. "Look I know sometimes I can make stupid comments like the one I made earlier about Desmond, that you know I didn't mean. But Eris holds grudges against me fiercely and forever. Did you know she won't even use her match making business to help me?"

Camille shrugged. "I know."

Tiara leaned in close. "See now that's just childish and petty. The least Eris could do is find me a rich guy to marry. Maybe then I wouldn't be so jealous of her and all her wealth."

"Oh Tiara, how I wish that would happen," Camille sighed. "Maybe then it would solve all the discord between the two of you."

"See you admit it too," Tiara said polishing off her Chicken Picatta. "But what I can't figure out is, how you of all people never get jealous of Eris and all that wealth. I mean, don't you ever dream about someday owning a mansion bigger and finer than the one Eris grew up in?"

"Of course, I do. But Tiara, money has never been as important to me as being in…"

"Being in love with a man who loves me," Tiara interrupted and finished her sentence. "Christ, I wish I had a million dollars for every time you said that line. I'd be rich by now."

Camille studied her friend and then reached into her purse and pull out a crisp bill. "Here, this is for you. I pay my debt."

"What's this?"

"A million-dollar bill, now what are you going to do with all that money?"

"Very funny Camille, this bill isn't real, it's fake. Where'd you get it, from the local joke shop?"

"Yep, and I thought of you when I bought it. Good joke huh? Now stop chasing money Tiara and start looking for love."

"That's the problem with you Camille. You believe all that happy ever after bull. Don't you know true love is just a cruel hoax somebody made up to feed woman's fantasies? You need to start thinking like a man when it comes to love and make sure the guy's got a big bank account to afford to take care of you and all the kids, he thinks he wants to have and a big penis."

Camille grinned jokingly. "You don't believe that."

"Be serious Camille," Tiara voice softened. "You know what I'm saying is right," she said waiving her hand. "Maybe I am a little jealous of you because you've never given up on that love thing. And after listening to you talk about Desmond, I think that maybe you've found the right Geeky guy that's perfect for you," she paused. "And I'll be the first to admit, I'll always be jealous of Eris because well she's rich." She shook her head. "Anyway, you both have a piece of happiness while I'm still stuck out here with all the ogres and the rejects, in *single land*."

Camille looked over and noticed the sad expression on Tiara's face. She remembered the little girl that came to her rescue that long-ago day at school when Tiara stood up with her against the school bully. Her father always said people came into your life to help you when you need them most. Tiara had been there for her. She would never forget that. "Tiara I apologize for being mean earlier."

Tiara hesitated and bowed her head. "You're never mean Camille even when you think you are being mean. Anyway, I wish Eris would just put in a good word for me with Brandon Stone."

Camille hesitated and thought for a moment. "Tell you what Tiara; I'll see what I can do to persuade Eris to help you with her match making business. But no promises on Brandon Stone, deal?"

"Okay deal," Tiara smiled. "Boy does that make me happy."

Camille laughed. "Good then, I'm happy if you're happy."

Tiara saw her chance. She blurted. "Do you ever regret it?"

"Regret what?"

Tiara gasped. "That you picked Desmond Garcia over Delmar Devereaux?"

The moment was awkward.

"I'm just saying just looking at the surface, I think Delmar is way more handsome than Desmond. He's taller and he's wealthier."

Camille was completely taken aback for a few seconds. She sat up straight in her chair. She checked to see how serious she was. *Tiara always was one for speaking her mind,* she thought. "Tiara, that's your opinion, but I happen to know for a fact that Desmond is three inches taller than Delmar," she snapped. "And no, I don't regret my breaking up with Delmar Devereaux."

"Maybe you're right on the height thing. But I'm sure Delmar is way wealthier than Desmond."

"How do you know that Tiara?" Camille took a deep breath and calmed herself. Tiara was crossing boundaries.

"Oh, I don't, I'm just guessing. Delmar looks like he's way wealthier than Desmond," she shrugged. "Do you know how much Desmond is worth?"

"No," Camille murmured. "I never ask questions like that. Anyway, I'm not dating Desmond for how much money he has. I don't care about stuff like that Tiara and in the future, don't ask me questions like this."

Tiara snorted thinking out loud.

Camille wondered about Tiara's strange fascination with Delmar Devereaux. She took a deep breath and thought out her question before she asked.

"Tiara, you're not interested in Delmar Devereaux because he's rich, are you?'

Tiara shrugged. "Of course not, what makes you think that?"

Camille paused. "Oh, I don't know. I guess, like you, I just took advantage of the moment to ask a really dumb question," she shrugged. "Anyway, if we're talking about Delmar verses Desmond.

You should know that Delmar Devereaux is an arrogant, bossy, power driven and self-absorbed person. And oh, the jury hasn't returned a verdict on how cold hearted he truly is."

Tiara said in a breath of sarcasm. "Whew, I take it that your love affair with Delmar is completely over."

"Yeah, it was over before it began. Anyway, you know what I feel like doing right now Tiara?" she asked and didn't wait for a response. "I feel like making a toast to Delmar."

"What?" Tiara asked with a startled expression.

Camille held her glass high. "Here's to Delmar's finding his next diversion."

"Diversion?" Tiara asked curiously. "Camille don't you mean true love?"

"Girlfriend, please!" Camille tried to smoother a laugh. "Delmar's heart is too cold to love anyone but himself."

Nervously Tiara smiled and hid her feelings. She could feel her hand balling up into a fist. *Who did Camille think she was,* she thought?

Camille didn't know a thing about satisfying a powerful man like Delmar Devereaux. One thing was for sure, she definitely wanted Delmar and she was willing to do whatever it took to have him. She'd show Camille when she had Delmar put a ring on her finger. The corners of her lips turned up. Oh, how sweet revenge would be when Camille saw that she was the only woman able to tame Delmar Devereaux.

Camille saw the cool smile on Tiara's lips and the strange way her eyes stared into space. She leaned over and whispered. "Tiara let me give you a word of advice. Some women who like thugs, hustlers, and players sadly mistake them for being the stuff true love is made of. Don't make that mistake."

# Chapter 16

**The Book Barn...**

A week passed. At the bookstore on Stevens Creek Camille made her way to the self-help section near the café at the back of the store. The store was crowded with boisterous shoppers.

"Here's that new novel I told you about Eris," she said passing the book to her.

Eris frowned. "You've got to be joking, *Matchmaking for the Matchmaker*? I don't need this crap!"

"If you're not going to buy it, I'll take it," a woman's voice said. "That's the last copy."

Camille and Eris turned toward the voice. A middle-aged woman with jet black hair that was strategically streaked with the whitest platinum color, stood in front of them. The streaks of her hair framed her and made her skin look deathly white. She wore yellow striped black cat's-eyeglasses, with matching yellow striped tights that made her look like a cast-off from a witch's coven.

The two friends looked at the woman, then back at each other.

Silently, Eris gripped the book tighter. She didn't want it, but the thought that it was the last copy gave her pause.

"So, are you going to let me have the book?" the woman wearing the cat's-eyeglasses asked, pushing them back on her nose.

Slowly she studied Eris and shot a glance at Camille. "By the way, I'm not a witch, even though I might look like one. I have a few friends who are though," she nodded. "I'm Clairvoyant."

Camille cleared her throat loudly. "You don't say."

Eris flipped back her hair. Her temple-to-temple fringe bangs fell right back in place as she stared hard with a doubtful stance. "Well alrighty then, looks like you do need this book more than I do."

The woman leveled her cat's-eyeglasses at Eris and then peeped over the yellow stripped rim. Her slanted eyes were cat green."Honey relax, I'm for real. I'm a professional. I pick up on people's thoughts and I know what they're thinking," she said, and paused. "Right now, I'm picking up that you really don't need this book. In fact, your mister right is coming your way very soon. You just need to relax and let go of your constant need to control your life and others and let the man walk in," she stifled a giggle.

Eris gazed back at the woman with a confused expression.

The woman giggled. "Oh, and honey, do stop giving off that bad energy vibe. You wear it like bad perfume. The next time you see your *mister right;* don't act like he's a pile of shit; just because he's in the movie business. Being on TV doesn't make him a bad guy."

The woman quickly reached out and took the book out of Eris' surprised hands. The woman threw back her long hair, turned and dashed toward the checkout stand.

Eris turned and looked at Camille. "Okay so let me get this straight. Some weirdo in a witch's costume, who says she is clairvoyant, just told me I'm a complete control freak and that I'm going to meet a movie star," she shrugged. "I can't believe the distance some people will go to just to buy the last copy of a book."

"Oh, forget about her," Camille shrugged. "Shall we go to lunch now?"

Eris paused. "What happened to Tiara? I thought she was meeting us here."

Camille inclined her head. She could already feel a headache coming on. "Tiara can't make it." "What? I don't believe it. She's the one who suggested we pick up that stupid book today. We're supposed to all have lunch!"

Camille shrugged. "Okay so she called me and cancelled."

"When did she cancel?"

"Tiara called me on my cell phone just before we arrived. She said she was called out of town, on an urgent meeting."

"An urgent meeting my ass. She's off screwing some man," Eris responded. "I wonder who it is this time."

"This time?"

Eris shrugged. "I bet you it's a different guy each time. I just wonder how she does it. How does she get men to whisk her off someplace and seduce her? Gosh I need to take lessons from Tiara."

Camille glanced at her watch. She rolled her eyes as she brushed past her. "Speaking of men whisking you off, I have a date tonight with Desmond and I want to be rested."

"You have a date with Desmond, in the middle of the week?" Eris asked in one breath. "I swear everybody's got a man but me. So where are you going?"

Camille looked thoughtful. "We're going to that new play at the Montgomery Theater. I think."

"What do you mean you think?"

"Well Desmond said I should wear an evening gown.I'm going to wear my black georgette gown with the crystal halter collar."

"Whew, the one with the thigh high split? Eris asked but didn't wait for an answer. "You'll be a knockout for sure."

"Thanks," Camille grinned, heading for the parking lot.

Eris rushed to keep pace with her friend. "I don't suppose you guys need me to tag alone and keep you company?"

"No," Camille said dryly and realized how harsh she must have sounded. "Sorry, I was kind of rude with you Eris."

"No problem."

"Eris do you think I can borrow...?"

"My 1920's vintage, art deco black crystal earrings?" Eris interrupted with a grin. "I was going to suggest them as soon as you told me you were going to wear that blinged-out black dress."

# Chapter 17

Tiara's eyes opened as the sunlight hit her face. She tilted her head and saw Delmar leaning on his elbow gazing back at her.

She softly smiled back. Delmar Devereaux wasn't a prince, but he was rich. Long ago she had learned to hide her true feelings behind a smile that promised much, especially when she was lying naked next to a man.

"Good morning Delmar," she purred.

"I need you again," he murmured. "You were sleeping so peacefully I didn't want to wake you."

Tiara felt his hard erection as he climbed on top of her, then she felt his warm breath against her neck as he made little groaning noises.

At first, she laid there and watched Delmar pumping away at her and then she thought about her plan to make him need her and want her. Instantly she picked up the rhythm of the up and down motion he made and rode the sensual pleasure wave again and again until suddenly Delmar climaxed with a desperate cry.

"That was amazing," he said rolling off of her, self-centered and assured, he chuckled contently. "I bet it was the best lovemaking you've ever had."

"Yes, it was. You were great," she purred, hoping he didn't see that she lied.

"And you have more skills than a porn star," he exclaimed. "That's why were so perfect for each other," he said with a callous sneer. "You use me for sex, and I use you."

Tiara forced herself to laugh. Her resentfulness at Delmar's colossal ego smoldered like a volcano about to erupt.  She propped up on her elbow and gazed back at him feeling insulted. Her lips quivered, trying to hide her resentment. "I won't always be available

to have sex with you Delmar."

Nothing seemed to faze Delmar. "What kind of fun would you have in life without me banging your brains out whenever you needed it?"

Tiara frowned at him. His response wasn't what she expected. A tiny voice in her head told her to say it. "One of these days some guy is going to come along and sweep me off my feet and marry me. And you yourself have said many times that marriage Etiquette dictates that the wife be faithful to her husband."

Delmar let out an up roaring laugh. "I meant what I said before. I expect my wife to be faithful to me. But after you're married to your prince charming Tiara, you and I can still have sex anytime you can get away from him the bastard." His tone was sinister. "Your prince charming needs never know you're playing the whore and sleeping around on him. I will make sure we are discreet."

A deep resentment crease marred her brow. "Don't you dare call me a whore Delmar? You know you make me mad when you say stuff like that Delmar," she said clearly offended. "I'm not a whore. And you don't know what your little dream wife will do if you ever find her and marry her," she said, yanking the sheet around her.

"Okay… Okay I screwed up calling you a whore. I'm sorry," he softly chuckled. "It's just that parents shouldn't feed their daughters that load of fairytale bull shit.  Then leave them to grow up in a world where none of that fairytale mess exists," he said gruffly.

Tiara said nothing as she stared back at him and lifted her brows.

Delmar chuckled and shook his head.

"In fact, if I ran this country, I would make it mandatory that every sex education class taught that the notion of love is ludicrous and then show a power point presentation on the correct way to give a man a blow job that results in his complete satisfaction."

Tiara looking back at Delmar as if he'd grown horns said, "Sometimes you can really act like an asshole Delmar. Maybe we shouldn't sleep together anymore then I'd have much more time to go out and try and find my prince charming and show you that two people can be faithful and happy together."

Delmar realized he'd hit a nerve. "Christ I'm starved," he said walking past her giving her a nudge and a smile. "Okay I apologize. Come on Tiara what say we get a shower and see what we can have for breakfast, and then I'll look for those couple of presents I have hidden around here somewhere for you. You know they are very expensive."

Tiara stared after him a long second as her brain raced, she couldn't wait to find another man and move on. A few minutes later she dutifully rose off of the bed and followed behind him.

# Chapter 18

**Camille, Desmond & Eris**

A week later, Camille and Desmond sat in the packed restaurant waiting for their order.

Desmond looked up. Out of the corner of his eye he spotted someone.

"What are you staring at?" Camille asked.

"I believe it's your friend Eris. She looks kind of lonely. Maybe we should invite her over to join us," Desmond suggested.

Camille smiled at his suggestion.

Desmond waved for their waiter; a guy named Lou. But before he could get his attention, Eris spotted them and sauntered over.

"Hello, Camille and Desmond," Eris said as she stopped in front of their table. "Mind if I join the two of you? I hate eating alone."

Camille smiled then glanced at Desmond. He winked at her.

"Sure, as a matter of fact, Desmond spotted you and was just going to alert our waiter," she said, squeezing closer to Desmond in their booth.

Desmond beckoned to the waiter. "Lou, bring us another menu please."

Eris stared between Camille and Desmond. They looked so happy together. She envied them. "Gosh, it feels we haven't had lunch together in ages. Don't get me wrong Desmond, I'm happy I hooked you two up. But I've missed my best friend."

Eris was always the happy matchmaker. She lived for matching up friends and knowing which person was right for whom. But Eris had a stubborn streak a mile long when it came to meeting men herself. She always found something wrong with them.

The waiter brought their food.

Eris continued chatting away without paying attention. She picked up a fork full of mashed potatoes and gravy and it spilled down the front of her dress.

"Oh, dear me," Eris said biting her lip. "I hope this comes out. Will you two please excuse me while I run to the lady's room and try and rinse this out?"

"Sure," Camille said, watching her leave.

Camille looked at Desmond to see if he was annoyed.

"I'm sorry about Eris talking so much," she said.

He softly smiled. "She misses you and no she's not bothering me. Besides, I think I have an idea," he smiled warmly. "How about we invite her to dinner, and I ask a good friend of mine to join us. I can just say that an old friend of mine dropped by unexpectedly and I brought him alone. Then I'll introduce him to Eris, and we'll see what happens. That way we have four at dinner instead of three."

Camille glanced at him. "Hmmm, sounds like a plan. But I'll tell you what. Let's do the dinner thing privately. How about, I cook dinner for the four of us at my place? I'll arrange a date that's good for Eris and you can maybe bring your friend."

Desmond smiled. "Sounds like a perfect plan."

# Chapter 19

**The Bingo Queen Spoils Dinner**

Friday Camille left work early. The door to the elevator in her building opened and she squeezed between several men wearing dark suits. When the elevator made it to the first floor her feet quickly strode across the marble lobby floor making her way to the exit.

She found her Ford Mustang and got into it and started the engine. Slowly she made her way through traffic.

She arrived home and dropped her purse down on the bed in her bedroom. She quickly changed into a pair of jeans and an oversized faded denim shirt and headed for the kitchen.

Camille turned on the double oven wall unit. Then walked over to the refrigerator and retrieved the prime rib roast and placed it in her bottom oven. The four-ribbed roast could feed at least six people and would cook in under an hour. But Eris loved her roast chicken so much that she prepared it too. She placed the baking dish holding the roasted chicken in the top oven on a lower heat.

She turned from the ovens to the chrome double sink, and quickly peeled some small potatoes and placed them in the stove with the chicken. Next, she quickly sautéed some green beans and placed them in her favorite serving dish. She cleaned a head of lettuce. She strained it well and began tearing it apart into a salad bowl.

A half hour later, the table was set, and dinner was just about done. She checked the clock. It was quarter after six. She toyed with the idea of changing her clothes and twenty minutes later, she put the finishing touches on her makeup and gave her attire the once over. She decided to wear a soft black sweater with a soft rhinestone sweetheart neckline that looked simple and elegant.

Back in the dining room, she finished setting up the buffet table with her chafing dishes and looked over her setting. With the centerpiece of miniature pumpkins and dried leaves befitting the fall season, it looked warm and inviting.

At ten minutes to seven her doorbell rang and when she opened it. Desmond Garcia stood their holding four bottles of wine.

"Hi," he whistled. "You look sweet and delicious."

"Thanks, that's the look I was going for," she shyly laughed. "Here, let me help you with those wine bottles. Do you think you have enough?"

Desmond gave her an apologetic look. "I wasn't sure what Eris likes to drink and, so I guess I got a little carried away."

"No problem, I'll put a bottle of Chardonnay and a white Zinfandel in the crystal ice bucket on the buffet table in the dining room. They'll be chilled before you know it. If you fill up that third ice bucket in the kitchen on the counter and bring it to the dining room, we can put a bottle of red wine in it and put that bottle on the table. I know you like your red wine chilled," she said.

"My woman does know me," Desmond grinned.

At exactly seven o'clock Eris Simeon arrived.

"Something smells wonderful. Camille, you cooked. Good I'm starving," Eris said, giving Camille a quick hug and then peeling off her faux fur cheetah walking jacket and handing it to Camille.

Eris turned and looked Desmond up and down. "Well Desmond, since Camille invited her two best friends over I guess you are officially Camille's boyfriend or should I say man?"

Desmond chuckled puzzled. "Ah, her two best friends? Here for dinner tonight?"

Camille inwardly cringed and stepped on Desmond's foot to get his attention. "Tell you what, let's all three of us have some salad," Camille said nudging Desmond.

He caught her understanding as he looked back into her mesmerizing hazel eyes. "Oh yeah, I forgot. I'm looking forward to dining with Camille's two best friends," he softly said. "In fact, I'll go and open the wine."

A half hour later they sat discussing issues of the day and had almost finished the first bottle of wine.

Eris looked up and caught Camille's hazel eyes watching her. "Camille you've got to face it," she said all at once.

"Face what?" Camille asked with a perplexed expression.

"That Tiara isn't coming for dinner tonight. So, we might as well eat," Eris said with a wave of her hand. "I wouldn't have set a place for her if I were you. You know how Tiara has been cancelling on us lately."

"Yeah, you are so right, Eris. I don't know what I was thinking about when I sat that extra place setting," Camille nervously shook her head and eyed Desmond as she inwardly cringed. It looked like Desmond's friend was a no show.

He shrugged and took a sip of his wine. "Yeah, He hasn't... I... I mean she hasn't called or anything," he said raising his glass. "I agree with Eris. We should just start eating."

Silently, Camille agreed as well. "I'll bring in the main course," she said, heading for the kitchen.

"And don't forget the roast chicken," Eris suggested. "You know my nose knows when it smells your roast chicken Camille."

"Yes, I'll bring the roast chicken too," Camille nodded.

Minutes later they were all enjoying the meal and chitchatting about nothing when the front door suddenly opened and closed.

"Hellooooooo?" a woman's voice called. "Anybody home?"

"Oh my God," Camille moaned.

"Yes, Mother Gabby, we're in the dining room," Eris yelled, laughing hard. "This is getting good. Bingo must have let out early."

"What's so funny?" Desmond asked.

Camille turned and grabbed Desmond's hand. "Well Desmond

darling, dinner is now officially spoiled by the Bingo Queen. I'm so sorry but you're about to meet my mother, Gabriela Baptiste. Everyone calls her Gabby and you are about to find out why."

Seconds later, Gabby Baptiste walked into the dining room, walked over and swapped air kisses on each of Camille's cheeks.

Gabby was a tiny woman in her early sixties. She was an attractive woman. A frizzle of soft graying strands lightly highlighted her temples. She was wearing a red hat cocked over one eye with a large purple plume. The feather was so large it made her look funny. She sported her favorite bright yellow jumpsuit with a purple jacket.

Camille thought her mother looked ridiculous."Mother, I take it bingo night is over?"

Her mother frowned. "I wore my lucky yellow jumpsuit for nothing. That Mildred Lane ruined the whole evening. She won the grand jackpot. It was five thousand dollars. And instead of just taking the money and going home, like I would have done. That old cow had the nerve to buy a bunch of Instant poppers."

"What are instant poppers?" Desmond asked out loud.

"Instant bingo tickets," Gabby grinned, and looked at him like he just arrived on planet earth. "Let me finish what I was saying young man before you start asking some dumb questions. Anyway, that Mildred won another fifteen hundred dollars, from the poppers and the thirty-two-inch flat screen television from the night's raffle," she said in one breath. "That heifer went to Madame Zenobia's and got herself a good luck Mojo. I just know it."

Eris laughed.

Camille threw up her hands. "Mother please don't curse. We have a guest."

Gabby grew silent as she looked around. The spread of food on the table caught her attention. "Oh, my goodness, there is enough food her to feed an army."

Camille knew it wasn't good seeing the excitement gathering in her mother's face.

Her mother headed for the telephone.

"Mom what are you doing?" Camille asked curiously.

"I'm going to call Myrtle Duncan on her cell phone and tell her to turn that car of hers around and bring the ladies back to have a bite to eat. There's enough food here to feed an army."

Camille rose quickly and closed the distance between them. She grabbed the telephone. "Mother please come over to the table and have a seat."

Startled, Gabby looked curiously at her daughter. "Oh, my goodness, you called me mother, again. This must be serious."

Gabby gave Eris a calculative glance as she sat down. "Eris what's going on? Who's your friend?"

Eris shrugged. "It's not my place to say. But he's not my friend."

"Mother I need to introduce you to someone," Camille said.

Gabby nodded politely and stared.

Camille took a deep breath. "Mother this is Desmond Garcia. Desmond this is my mother Gabriela Baptiste."

"I beg your pardon. Is Desmond someone I need to know?"

"Desmond is not only someone you need to know. He is dating your daughter," Eris added.

Gabriela stared open mouthed.

Eris added. "Yes, mother Gabby our Camille has gotten herself a handsome man."

Grabby began to grab her chest and cough violently. She swooned.

Desmond rose quickly and rushed to her side.

Camille's eyes widened like plates as she reached out. "Mommy! Mommy! Are you okay? Here, have a drink of water."

Gabby laughed out and grabbed Desmond's hand. She winked at him. "Now you see my daughter was putting on airs calling me mother. But let her think I'm about to have a heart attack and I'm plain old mommy, just like I like. Welcome to the family Desmond. By the way, I love bingo, so please feel free to add to my bingo funds anytime."

Eris laughed out. "That's mother Gabby."

Camille gasped, "Oh my God mother, don't start begging for bingo money."

Desmond shook his head with laughter and winked at Camille.

"Somebody please pour me a drink," Gabby commanded, grabbing an empty glass.

Camille leaned over and poured wine into her mother's glass.

Gabby took a big gulp. "Hmmm… what kind of expensive wine is this? It tastes high society and French."

"It's Château Charmail," Camille said.

"Figures," Gabby said, greedily gulping down the rest of her wine. "Here gal fill it up. My glass is empty."

Camille rolled her eyes. It was going to be a long night.

Slowly, she took a swallow of her wine and then emptied her glass.

# Chapter 20

**Casa Grande,**
 **San Juan Bautista …**

That Saturday afternoon, Camille and Desmond hit the road in his Jaguar, for a drive in the country.

For a few minutes the two sat on the side of the road, near a cluster of trees and watched the Sun. Camille was still smiling madly. She felt happy and content sitting in Desmond's Jaguar after their long drive.

"Desmond, I think this is a beautiful part of California," Camille said with a pause. "But do you know where we are?" she asked, checking the car mirror and replacing a loose strand of her hair snuggly behind the orchid she wore in her hair.

Desmond chuckled softly as he steered the car back onto the unmarked road. "We're not lost, if that's what you're asking."

The Jaguar handled the curving country road with ease. A cluster of trees loomed in the distance as the Jaguar closed the distance and climbed as the country road grew narrower. A succession of small hills gave way to a mountain.

Finally, the road ended at enormous ornate wrought iron. Behind it, down a canyon road, stood a majestic estate overlooking a hilltop.

Desmond stopped the car and opened the moon-roof before he turned off the engine.

An eagle screeched overhead, and Camille looked up at the clear brilliant blue sky above. Then her eyes stared at the estate as it sat majestic on the mountain. The plaque on the gate read *Casa Grande*.

Camille breathed out slowly. "Will you look at that? That home looks just like a villa in old Mexico. The place glows like its being sprayed with light from the sun."

She stared mystified at the huge estate that sat on several acres. It was massive and beautiful, complete with compound walls, court yards, gardens, and fountains.

Desmond nodded. "You know I think you're right."

"Hey look there. They even have an airplane runway," Camille pointed. "

Desmond tried to stop himself from laughing. Camille sounded surprised like a child on Christmas morning. "Well, what would you say if I can get us in for the grand tour? Would you like to see if?" he asked.

"Yes, I would," she yelled loudly. "The place looks pretty secured Desmond. I don't think they'll just let anyone in," Camille softly said. "The small plaque says it is a historic home built in 1874. You know I read somewhere that a lot of these old historic houses were once nunneries. Do you think this was some kind of a nunnery?"

Desmond shook his head and laughed. "I don't think so."

"You should get a picture of me standing in front of the gate so that I can show Eris and Tiara that we were here."

He chuckled. "Not right now. The gates opening."

Camille glanced out of the window. Rows of tall Italian cypress trees lined the road. Her eyes widened in a mixture of anticipation and excitement as they drove on.

Silently Desmond brought his jaguar to a halt behind a shiny black Aston Martin parked in the driveway. The license plate read Dessie007.

He got out of the car and opened the door for Camille. "Welcome to the Casa Grande Camille," he said proudly. "This is my home."

"What did you say?" she asked looking up in surprise, as she sat in the car another moment.

He watched anxiously as she took it all in. "Come on, get out of the car," he said offering his hand.

Thunderstruck, Camille got of the car and got her bearings. She spun around looking at her surroundings and back at him. "Desmond, you just parked behind an Aston Marin with a personalized license plate that says Dessi007 are you telling me that's your car?"

"Dessie is a nickname, and like any man, I always dreamed of being the famous spy 007," he grinned.

He felt something twist deep inside him as she gazed thunderstruck back at him.He reached for her and gave her a hug. "All of this is real and I'm real. You're not dreaming. I'm sorry I never told you about all of this. But I wanted you to get to know me first."

From the moment he pulled her into his embrace she felt the sweet sensation of his touch. Camille pulled back and looked up at him. She opened her mouth to speak.

"Let me finish what I have to say," he said tenderly. "From the first time I met you I knew that you were different and special to me," he said with a distinct edge to his voice. "And, well, for a while now I've been concerned about these feelings, I have for you and I didn't want the sight of my home to confuse you about my feelings and those I think you have for me."

At that moment Desmond looked nerdish and serious, standing before her. She saw the concerned expression on his face and a thought occurred to her. He wanted to be loved for the man that he was, not for the man that owned a property the size of this.

"My feelings are true and real too," she breathed out slowly.

He nodded. "I felt that they were, and I just want you to know I've never felt like this about anyone. From the first moment I met you I haven't been able to get you out of my thoughts."

For an instant her eyes met and held his. Her heart was filled with so much emotion that she could hardly stand it. "We are both lucky we found each other to love," Camille said reaching up and gently kissing him quickly.

"You love me too? Like I love you?"

"Yes," she said smiling wide.

"And you're not angry that I didn't tell you about this place or who I was?"

She shook her head. "No, I'm not angry that you didn't tell me about all of this. In fact, after seeing all this, I can understand why you didn't," she said as she gazed around. "Anyway, you are really good at keeping secrets. The secret about Casa Grande I mean."

Desmond grinned softly as his lips found hers. The kiss was powerful as his arms encircled her waist and pulled her closer as she surrendered to his kiss.

All at once Camille felt the presence of someone staring. She opened her eyes and then stopped kissing Desmond. She abruptly pulled out of his embrace. She turned her head swiftly and caught sight of a gray-haired woman standing watching them. "Desmond who is that? Your grandmother?"

He laughed. "No Camille, that kind-hearted beautiful soul is like a mother to me, but she is my housekeeper Consuelo."

Camille pulled out of Desmond's embrace and straightened her dress. She was glad she took the time that morning to make sure she was immaculately dressed in her favorite, below the knee, A-line styled Denim Peplum Dress. "Good evening Senora Consuelo," she excitedly said.

"You may call me Consuelo. I like your dress. It is very modest and respectable for this day and age. Now please come inside so that Desmond can show you the rest of the house," the housekeeper said waving her hands for them to go inside.

Desmond chuckled. "Oh, by the way Camille, Consuelo has been known to say out loud whatever is on her mind?"

Hours later, Camille learned the house had been left to Desmond by his great grandmother *Theresa Diaz Galindo* who was *a* direct descendant of the early California settlers from what is today Mexico.

"My great grandmother married my great grandfather Gustavo Galvez; he was a Creole from New Orleans Louisiana. Their only daughter was my grand-mother Rosalita Galvez and she married my grandfather Gravois Garcia," Desmond said proudly walking her past the family portraits.

Camille soon learned Desmond was proud of his mixed ancestry, the Spanish, Native American, African American and Creole background that made him.

"So, you see Camille," Desmond said. "I have African American ancestry on both my mother's side and my father's side of the family. I am very proud."

"Wow, you have such a rich heritage," Camille said with interest. "So, tell me, what was it like living here? There are so many rooms and so much to do on so many acres."

Desmond laughed. "Many acres mean there was always much work to do. My father made sure I grew up knowing the land surrounding us and that I shared his love for growing things," he hesitated. "But sometimes having many rooms can also mean there were many places a small child can be lonely. You see I was an only child."

Camille looked up at Desmond, her eyes shown with an expression of sadness.

"Don't be sad for me Camille. I had a wonderful childhood. Come, I want to show you my favorite place in the whole house," he said taking her hand and leading the way.

They reached a hallway leading to huge glass doorway. The room was an in-door garden conservatory.

Desmond stopped abruptly at the entrance to the conservatory. "Close your eyes Camille and breathe deeply."

She did as she was told. The fragrant sweet heavenly scent of the roses kissed her nostrils. She took another breath. "I smell roses. They smell wonderful. What kind are they?" she asked opening her eyes.

The climate controlled in-door garden conservatory was nothing like she'd ever expected. It looked like a tropical paradise with its lush ferns and numerous tables of potted plants. Across the room a comfortable cushion wicker ensemble of sofas, chairs and table sat. The table held a romantic setting for two complete with chilled wine and two covered dinner plates.

"I see Consuelo has been busy arranging things, he said, grinning and leading her over to the table.

"What is that fragrant smell? I bet it is coming from the roses."

"Yes, and right now you smell a very old variety called the Bourbon Rose. It dates back to the nineteenth century."

Camille wrinkled her nose. "Whew! What is that pungent smell?"

Desmond smiled softly. "Oh, now you are inhaling the Asian Tea Rose and, as your nose is telling you, it is a little different."

"Yes, it is," she said. "What is over there in that closed off room?"

Desmond led Camille over and pushed open the heavy door. "The door has a spring action. It closes right behind you but doesn't lock. It does that because this is the hothouse."

"These look like more tropical type plants," Camille said taking in the scents. A long table held rows of neat trays that looked like ice trays that held dirt. "You're growing something from seeds I take it."

"Those trays are exclusively for my Orchids. The ones in there now are just seedlings but one day they will be blooming orchids as far as the eye can see."

"Wow, you really do have a gift for growing all kinds of plants."

"Yes, I do," he said. "Come; let's go back into the other room. In case you didn't notice there is seating and dining area. I believe Consuelo has prepared something for us to eat."

"Good, I'm starving," she said.

When they were seated Desmond removed the cover from Camille's plate and poured them both a glass of wine.

Camille tried not to smile too wide as she eyed the lobster on her plate. It looked delicious. She took her first bite and closed her eyes savoring the sweet taste. It made her want to pull off all her clothes and make love to Desmond as soon as she was finished with the last bite. She opened her eyes and looked across the table.

Desmond was staring at her with desire in his eyes.

During dinner they chatted easily. She found herself laughing at his stories about growing up at Casa Grande. Desmond looked so happy surrounded by the things he loved.

All at once they stopped and stared at each other, smiling.

"You make this house feel like a home again with your being here Camille. Please come back as often as you like. In fact, I think it would be great if you moved in to see if you could like to live here."

It was a strange proposition Camille thought, but she didn't want to seem too eager to accept. She sipped her glass of wine and then looked up at the clock. It was getting late. She stood up all at once and her eyes flashed with a worried expression as she walked and looked out of a window. She closed her eyes for a moment. "Looking out at all of this made me just realize something, Desmond."

"What?" he asked with deep concern.

The moment was silent.

Her head was buzzing with a million conflicting thoughts about Desmond and all of this wealth. The most obvious to her was what if things didn't work out between them and she told her mother about all of this or her best two friends. Eris wouldn't blink an eye but tell her not to move in until she was sure it was what she wanted. But not her mother Gabby or Tiara, she thought. She knew one thing for sure her mother Gabby and Tiara would have thought she had won the jackpot and they would tell her to take Desmond up on his proposition right away, before he changed his mind. But what if loving Desmond wasn't enough. What if she wasn't what really made him happy and worst of all, what if he didn't love her enough to marry her. How could she face her mother or Tiara if that happened? She looked out of the window at the surrounding grounds and mulled over what she had to do?

"All of this is a lot to take in," she said wryly. "But first I have a favor to ask. You've met my mother and you know who my best friends are," she hesitated. "Well, at least one of them and I won't say which one would love the idea of our maybe living together. But…," she said with a worried troubled expression on her face.

Desmond moved closer beside her. His fingers trembled, aching to touch her.

Her eyes were sad as she gazed back at him. "I hope you won't mind if I ask you not to tell them about you and that you own all of this, at least not for a while."

He nodded. "Sure, I can do that," he said touching her arm. His fingers reached out and touched her chin. "Like I said earlier, its' a lot to take in, I'll respect your wishes."

Standing so close to him she could smell his aftershave. She breathed in deep the earthy scent of him.

Desmond reached for a remote and he hit a button. Hidden shades descended out of the ceiling and closed over the glass entry door of the conservatory.

He drew her against him. "You smell delicious,"

"I smell like lobster and butter," she laughed.

He kissed her softly. "You taste like an aphrodisiac."

She laughed against his mouth. "Do I really?

"Will you sleep with me?"

Camille drew her head back and looked at him. "There's no bed in here."

She looked over at the wicker ensemble and hurried over and propped a couple of overstuffed cushions together. "But then again this wicker sofa looks very comfortable to me."

"Yes, it does," Desmond said, closing the distance between them and unzipping her dress.

Camille turned and eagerly her hands reached out and unfastened the buttons of his shirt.

In unison they groped for buttons and snaps until clothing lay scattered on the floor around them.

They stood naked, face to face, in the climate-controlled room.

Gently Desmond brought his hands to her breasts flicking her nipples with his fingertips until they were erect. "I don't know how slowly I can do this," his eyes glazed up at her tenderly.

The moment he gave her that look Camille was lost in her desire to satisfy him. She came on strong. She pushed him back against the cushioned pillows and swung astride him her fingers found his penis and imprisoned him inside her. Her voice was sensual and hoarse. "I never said I wanted you to go slow with me Desmond," she purred matching his tempo until they climaxed surrendering together.

# Chapter 21

**Second Thoughts...**

That Sunday evening Camille found herself thinking about Desmond Garcia.She couldn't believe he owned a home as regal as *Casa Grande*. Once again, she let her mind drift to daydreams about her living there. She saw herself serving tea on the stately back porch with Eris and Tiara in attendance and she smiled as she repotted a houseplant at the worktable in the backyard. She dusted off her hands and suddenly her mind filled with problems.

Camille sat down on a stool beside the worktable distracted by her thoughts. The distraction was her mother, Gabby Baptiste.

Her mother had been born into money but didn't marry it.She'd always thought her own father's fortune would come to her upon his demise but learned sadly after his death that there was nothing left.

As if that wasn't bad enough, things became really complicated for Gabby after her beloved Wade Baptiste died. As the widow of Camille's father, Wade Baptiste, Gabby Baptiste had been devastated to learn that though Wade had provided for her. He had not left her a wealthy woman.

The past had taught her that she had to be cautious with her mother Gabby. Too much information wasn't always a good thing and in life it didn't change the responsibilities or duties a person had, it only complicated things. Instantly, Camille knew she had to keep Desmond's grand home a secret from her mother.

She gave the carefully potted plant a soft pat before lifting it carefully and caring it back inside. Gently she returned it to its new spot in the hallway.

"You're pretty good at that," a familiar voice said.

"Tiara, when did you get here?" Camille asked.

"I've been here for a while. I didn't want to interrupt. Your Mom let me in. She and I were just sitting in the living room chatting."

Camille shrugged. "I was wondering what happened to my mother. She wanted her plants repotted and the next thing I knew she had disappeared."

"Whew, you're sort of dirty," Tiara said giving her the once over. "I thought I'd drop by and see what you've been up to. I see you were playing in dirt."

"Very funny," Camille laughed.

"Do you need some help?"

"No, that was the last houseplant and the last pot that needed repotting," Camille said. "Come into the kitchen so that I can clean up and get us a couple of drinks. I made some mango iced tea," she said turning and leading the way.

Tiara grinned as she followed her. "Great, I'd love a glass. Do you have something to go with it?"

"How does a tuna sandwich sound?"

"Positively marvelous, I'm famished."

Thirty minutes later, Camille and Tiara chitchatted about the changes in the weather and they finished off tuna sandwiches with their mango iced tea.

"God Camille, I don't know how you do it but you even manage to eat a tuna sandwich like a lady. While I on the other hand inhaled mine like I haven't eaten in weeks."

"I'm sure I didn't, but thanks for the compliment."

Tiara shrugged. "By the way, you still make a great tuna sandwich and I'd forgotten how much I missed sitting with you at the kitchen table and chatting about nothing," she said sitting her empty glass down. "Anyway, earlier, when I was talking to your mother, she mentioned you were thinking about getting her a new Honda."

"Oh, did she?" Camille asked with a genuine look of surprise. "Did she tell you where I would get the money for the down payment?"

Tiara had second thoughts about seeing Delmar Devereaux. Camille had been right. Delmar was a cold mean man. The only people she had ever seen Delmar nice to were Camille and Gabby. Besides, Tiara knew that she wasn't as cold hearted as she appeared to everyone. She had a soft spot in her heart for Camille's mother Gabby. Gabby had been like a second mother to her. She hated knowing Gabby was driving back and forth to bingo or the casino in that twenty-year-old Honda. She sighed with her thoughts, if she wasn't so readily available to be Delmar's pleasure toy. Then he would be checking in regularly to see how Camille and Gabby were doing.

I suppose, Tiara thought. I should tell Delmar about Gabby's car situation.And then she had an idea. She needed to tell Camille that she'd made a mistake dumping a wealthy man like Delmar.Camille had a duty and a responsibility to take care of her mother Gabby.

"Ah...," Tiara nodded. "You know Camille; I was just talking to Gabby about how bad that old Honda of hers is running. And I kind of agree with your mother right now. Maybe you should stop seeing Desmond and go back to seeing Delmar. You know Delmar did keep Gabby's old car up in repairs. Not to mention he did buy this old house a new roof."

"Yes, Delmar did," Gabby said, stepping into the kitchen.

"Mother you were eavesdropping," Camille yelled.

Gabby shook her head "No I wasn't!"

"Damn mother Gabby, couldn't you have waited until Camille and I finished talking?"

Camille's brows lifted. "Don't curse at my mother."

Tiara paused in alarm. "I didn't..."

"Camille honey, you need to calm down. Tiara was just trying to make you see logic," Gabby said, looking between her daughter and her best friend. The situation was getting out of hand. "How about I fix us all a pot of chamomile tea?"

"We don't need any more tea mother," Camille flashed a defiant stare.

Tiara glanced at her. "Camille don't be rude to Gabby. She's just trying to help."

"Yeah right," Camille said defensively sitting up straight. "Oh, and by the way Tiara," she said curtly. "I paid Delmar back for fixing the roof. And I paid him in cash and not with my ass!"

Tiara was shocked by her outburst. "What is that supposed to mean? Are you trying to imply something with that remark?"

"If it fits," Camille smirked.

Tiara froze, taken aback with vengeance. "You're taking our friendship for granted. I'm out of here!"

# Chapter 22

**Things in life are not how we really want it...**

*It was going to be a beautiful day*, Camille thought, as she made her way downstairs, dressed and ready to go to work.

The heavy aroma of fresh baked scones, cinnamon toast and fresh brewed coffee filled the air.

She tossed back a strand of loose hair as she made her way toward the kitchen.

"Morning," Gabby muttered, standing in her robe

The kitchen table was set with white tablecloth, napkins, and cups and saucers and her grandmother Nana's sterling silver tea service.

"Mom, I apologize again for yesterday. You didn't have to do all of this, she said waiving her hand.

"Yes, I did," her mother said placing an omelet on a plate. "Here I made your favorite. A Denver omelet and I've got some cinnamon toast and a fresh pot of hot coffee."

Gabby placed the plate down on the table. "Sit Camille and eat."

Camille sat down. "Mom, I feel bad you went to all this trouble. I guess I'll have to do something nice for you," she said taking a mouth full of omelet.

Her mother pulled her robe snuggly around her and watched her eat. "Well, I am going to hold you to it and you know what I want?"

A new car, Camille thought but didn't say it as she swallowed another bite and prayed her mother couldn't read her mind.

Gabby touched her hand. "I feel guilty for causing a rift between you and Tiara. And Camille I want you to call and make up with

Tiara," she said patting her hand. "Tiara didn't have a loving father figure in her life like you did. And that's why she's always associating with the wrong sort of men."

"What?"

Her mother had caught her off guard with her statement. "I don't have all the answers Camille, but sometimes nothing in life is how we really want it or expect it. It's the same with Tiara. Maybe it's the men that make Tiara do the things she does but that don't make her bad. You know what I mean?"

Camille managed a weak laugh and did a double take. Sometimes at moments like these she caught glimpses of the real Gabriela Baptiste. Not the self-absorbed, selfish, deceptive woman who was angry at the world for the hand it dealt her. But the caring woman, that was standing in front of her now.She recalled her mother always saying that underneath at the core of every human was just a small child looking to be loved. She cleared her throat. "Yeah, I know what you mean. Look Mom, you didn't have to fix me this nice breakfast. I was going to apologize to Tiara anyway."

# Chapter 23

**That was a long time ago...**

Camille left work early and stopped off at the grocery store. She arrived home and pulled into her driveway, got out of her car. She was glad to be home. She grabbed the bags of groceries and fumbled with her keys as she made her way to the front door.

Camille stood at the front door struggling with her keys and the bags of groceries before losing control when suddenly.

"Let me help you with those," he said, leaning in and kissing her on the cheek.

Baffled Camille turned around. "Delmar, where did you come from?"

"Gabby's car broke down. She called me and I gave her a lift."

Gabby quickly closed the distance. "That's right Camille and I promised Delmar we'd fix him a meal. I glad you stopped off at the market," she said leading the way.

Camille followed close behind her mother Gabby and said, "Let me guess he's the reason why you phoned me at work and wanted me to stop off at the store and pick up some steaks for dinner?"

Her mother Gabby avoided her gaze and acted innocent as they walked into the house.

At almost midnight after dining on steaks, baked potatoes and salad and watching and watching Gabby favorite old movie, *Sullivan's Travels*, Delmar helped Camille clean up the dishes.

And come to think of it, Camille thought as she recalled how her mother, Gabby had put on her pajamas just before the movie started. She also remembered how her mother had drank a whole bottle of California cabernet all by herself during the movie. No wonder she excused herself a half hour ago and went to bed.

She only hoped the movie would end soon and Delmar would go home.

Camille was just putting away the last of the salad into the refrigerator when she felt Delmar drop a kiss on her bare skin on the back of her neck.

"Remember when you used to love for me to kiss your neck like this?"

She turned around instantly.

"That kiss used to make your clothes drop off spontaneously when she was younger."

"That was a long time ago Delmar," she said as her throat tightened with the memory of his words.

Suddenly Delmar drew her tightly in an embrace and kissed her hard. His tongue was in her mouth hungry with desire.

Panic coursed through her as she felt his hands roam her body."Delmar don't," she said angrily pulling out of his embrace as she to stare back at him.

His predatory eyes capture hers. "Why not are you dating someone?"

She didn't want to tell him about Desmond. She didn't want him to know anything about the two of them. "My private life is just that private," she shrugged. "You know what I don't have to have this conversation with you.Thank you for bringing my mother home. We've feed you for your trouble. Now you need to go home, now! Or…."

Delmar snorted out a laugh. "Or what you'll make a scene? Gabby is sleeping."

Her anger grew at that moment and then she thought of something. "No, I think I'll just go outside and scream loudly. You know at around this time every night a police squad car cruises down our street, ever since that East Coast Mafia kingpin's mother moved in down the street," she lied and hope he couldn't see through it.

In an instant Delmar's smirk faded. "You used to be so nice," he said making his way to the front door.

Delmar stepped into the open front door and then stopped abruptly. Reached over and quickly pulled her close and kissed her hard and possessive.He kissed her breathlessly.

And then gave a mirthless laugh. "I bet he doesn't kiss as well as me."

Camille stood there and watched as Delmar started his car and drive off. She had an odd feeling she was being watched.

# Chapter 24

**A little distance**

Miles away, at *Casa Grande* San Juan Bautista, Desmond Garcia tossed and turned as the flames shot higher. He looked into the flames and he saw her. He could smell the stench of burning cordite and for a horrifying moment he was frozen to the spot. The moment seemed to stretch into infinity, and then finally he felt his body being released and he ran into the hot flames and felt its roar of heat burn against his skin. Suddenly he awoke from the terrible nightmare. His heart pounding hard as he looked at the clock beside his bed. It was only three a.m., the bewitching hour. The devil was riding him, he thought, inching back the comforter and getting out of bed.

He felt that old knot of despair. The dream was always the same. He ran to save the woman and then he ran for his life. He sat up on the side of the bed and shook his head, puzzled over his dream. He knew he was having the dream because he was getting close to her.

He knew what he needed to do. He needed to put some distance between himself and Camille, until he could figure things out. Now was the time to make that trip to Maui. Taking care of business always cleared his head.

Desmond walked over to his computer and turned it on.

The first thing he did was to email Fredrick Chiu, in Maui and let him know he was coming to meet with him.

An hour later, Desmond had taken care of several reports and rearranged his schedule. He then emailed his secretary Nona, to arrange the first flight that afternoon to Maui. He then got up out of his chair and headed for the bathroom. He needed a shower.

At six am promptly, he was dressed and satisfied with his appearance. The silence in his bedroom stretched thin as he dialed the number.

The phone ringing in the wee hours of the morning startled Camille. It was her cell phone.

"Hello," she mumbled.

"Hi beautiful, I hope I didn't wake you," Desmond's said, the tone of his voice was miserable.

Camille could sense something was wrong. She sat up in bed. "No, I'm awake. I don't need that much beauty sleep," she joked.

Desmond laughed it off. "You're right of course, you don't," he said.

Camille could tell that Desmond's mind was occupied. "Desmond is everything okay? I mean with us," she asked curiously.

"Ah… Oh I mean, yeah," he said lamely

"You don't sound so sure."

His voice was humbling. "Well that's why I'm calling. I can tell we've been moving kind of fast and well, I don't want us to make a fast mistake, if you get my meaning."

Camille held the phone in stunned disbelief.

"Hello… Hello Camille, are you still there?"

She finally found her voice. "Yes, I'm still here," she said softly. "What are you saying Desmond?"

He cleared his throat. "I just don't want to give you the wrong impression and right now I think I need a little alone time until I can sort things out."

The fight left her. She just wanted the phone call to end. "If that's what you want Desmond," she said slowly.

"Listen, I've got to go. I've got a plane to catch," he said, wishing he could look into her eyes and see that she understood him.

"Okay Desmond," Camille said, softly hanging up.

# Chapter 25

**Santa Claus...**

Two weeks past, and Camille found that if she engrossed herself in her work, she was content and thought of Desmond less.

It was after dark on a Friday when the phone on her desk rang.

"Camille, why didn't you pick up your cell phone?" Her mother's voice frantically asked. "I was stranded."

"Mom, where are you? I'm leave work right away."

"Oh, don't bother," Gabby curtly replied. "I got a ride and my old car was towed. I'm at Bingo with my friend, Grand *mere* Catherine."

Relief filled her. "Oh, that's good, you're okay. So how much do I owe Grand *mere* Catherine?"

Gabby laughed softly. "You're not going to believe my luck," she laughed. "That old clunker of mine broke down right at Montague and highway 680, and guess who just happened to be driving by at the right time?"

Camille thought for a moment. "Oh, I don't know, Santa Claus," she joked.

Gabby laughed. "Well he is my Santa Claus, anyway dear, it was Delmar. And he took me out to dinner and then he dropped me off at bingo. Isn't he wonderful?"

Camille's heart sank. Delmar's name was the last one she wanted to hear."Yes, Mom that was wonderful," she lied, as she thought about all the money she'd paid back to Delmar in the past.

Finally, her mother's voice broke through her trance. "Camille, before I go I forgot to tell you the girls and I are using Delmar's suite at the Thunder Cloud Casino this weekend."

"What?"

"Oh, close that big mouth of yours, it's not like Delmar's joining us or anything.Though if I were your age I wouldn't hesitate," she giggled. "Anyway, Grand mere Catherine brought up the whole Bingo posse in her son Louis' SUV. The bingo posse and I are sharing the room.We are going to have a great time. Whew! They are starting to call the bingo numbers, goodbye," her mother said hanging up the phone.

Camille hung up the phone and took a deep breath. She felt like her life was spiraling out of control.

# Chapter 26

**Nature of the beast**

Delmar slowly walked back to his desk carrying a lowball glass of Bourbon and studied the map. The green dot on the map represented his latest acquisition for Devereaux Industries. The property was located in Monterey and was causing him a few problems at the local permit department.

During the day, it was relatively easy for him to focus on his life. He loved his real estate empire. The building housing his office was loud with a crew of staff workers. But at home at night the huge rambling mansion he called home was lonely with silence.

Delmar's lips twisted into an off centered smile when he remembered who he'd given a lift to earlier that day.

Gabby Baptiste was upset and mad at Camille for not picking up her cell phone when her car broke down. She had told him plenty in her trusting voice. Now, he knew that Camille couldn't afford to buy her a new car and he knew she wasn't seeing anyone.

Delmar stared into his drink, realizing how much he wanted Camille. He had wanted her ever since he laid eyes on her at that business meeting with her father, Wade Baptiste, many years ago. Why, he thought, couldn't he control his beast? It was fact that sometimes he couldn't control his bodies urges. When nature called, the beast had a mind of his own. He looked down at his penis. It was the reason why Camille had become angry with him and broke things off. He shook his head. Why did Camille have to come in and catch him with that other woman, he thought? Sometimes, life wasn't fair, he said to himself.

He caressed his erection. Slowly his lips twisted into an off centered smile as he remembered who was staying the night in the Jade room. He called her

Quickly he went upstairs to her bedroom.

Tiara lay on the bed.

"Damn Tiara do you have any idea how ravishing you look stretched out there?"

She smiled. "Don't forget horny, lover," she purred. "Come over here Delmar and let he help you out of those pants.

He did as he was told and watched as Tiara fearlessly undid his zipper.

"The beast is free," she said fingering his erection.

Delmar groaned as he rolled her back onto the bed and filled her body with every inch of the sensation of him.

Hours later, Delmar woke up and stared at the ceiling as he laid in bed listening to Tiara sleep. He didn't love her. He knew that the only reason he slept with her was to quiet the loneliness within. The loneliness of knowing he loved another woman.

Carefully and quietly he got out of bed and headed for his bedroom. He took a long shower and stood silently letting the spray of water pour over him as his thoughts raced. For too long he had focused all of his energies on running Devereaux Industries. He recalled the last financial reports, he knew his financial position was strong, and there was more than enough cash on hand to breathe easily.

That wasn't always the case. Once upon a time; many years ago, when he was a lot younger, he'd gotten the worst end of a real estate deal that had gone sour. The owner of the escrow company had come to his aid and put up the money to keep his deal from falling through.

The man who'd loaned him the money was Wade Baptiste and he had the prettiest daughter Delmar had ever seen. But Wade had made it clear if Delmar was interested in his daughter, he was on his own.

Camille Baptiste had her own mind and if he wanted her heart, he'd have to win it the old-fashioned way.

"Camille…Camille… Camille," he muttered, standing alone in the shower.He put his head under the heavy spray of the water, trying to calm his thoughts. He was starting to feel he needed to put some distance between him and Tiara. Now, more than ever, he needed to focus his efforts on Camille. She was a good woman, a good woman he didn't want to lose. He smiled with his thoughts. A good woman should never be rushed.He thought of a plan as he stood there.

The door of the shower opened wide.

"Delmar," Tiara said flustered as she stepped in beside him.

"Tiara what are you doing?"

"I need a shower too. How about I wash your back?"

Delmar stared at her he could tell something was wrong. "I can handle that besides I'm finished. I was just about to get out," he said turning off the shower and reaching for a towel.

Tiara followed him out of the shower. She threw he arms around him. "Oh Delmar," she whimpered and pressed her naked body against him.

He pulled her away from him and reached for a towel and threw it at her. "Why are you acting funny? What's wrong with you?"

Tiara stifled back tears. "Don't you know I'd do anything for you? Why won't you let me be more to you Delmar?"

"Now look here Tiara, we talked about this before. There will be none of that falling in love stuff around here."

She burst into tears. She was surprised at how fast they come. "I heard you call out Camille's name a few minutes ago. And I know," she paused. "I know you dated Camille a long time ago."

His voice was hard, "So what if I did. Are you jealous?"

"Camille and I are close," the sneer in her voice seemed to reverberate off the bathroom walls.

Delmar had forgotten how close they were. His eyes ignited with a questioningly look as his brain clicked thinking. "So, what? I know that," he shook his head. "You wouldn't be up to something, now would you?"

"Not if I was paid."

"Blackmail!" He snapped.

Her slips curved up. "I want to get paid to keep quiet"

Delmar laughed helplessly. "Oh, really? How much?"

Tiara tears dried up quickly. She smiled thoughtfully; this was her chance to set upset herself up real nice for a long, long time. "You put up one hundred thousand dollars and buy me one of those new townhouses that they are building off Pacheco Pass," her voice was laced with confidence. "After that I expect you to give me another hundred thousand and then we will consider your secret safe for a lifetime."

"Is that how much you got out of Old man Duval?

"What did you say?"

"I won't repeat myself Tiara. You heard me."

Tiara looked him over carefully. "I don't know what you're talking about."

Delmar chuckled. "Oh really?  He asked but didn't wait for a response. "Well let me tell you what I know. I know that you used to do some pretty private special things with Max Duval Senior and that the old man gave you money.And I know that he hoped to keep right on doing those special things with you, even after you married his son, Max Duval Junior. How's my story coming along so far?"

Tiara bowed her head sadly; she was just about to say something but then Delmar interrupted her.

"Tell me where you really planning to marry Max Junior and continue to betray him with his father?"

There was silence.

"You don't understand nobody could," she said sadly.

He shook his head. "Oh, I know the whole story. Old man Duval wasn't Max Junior's real father and the old man never forgave his wife, Ethel for betraying him with his best friend. Max Junior never knew the truth though. But once old man Duval met you and saw what an opportunist you were.He saw the chance to get you pregnant with his grandson, who would actually be his real biological. The one he never had," he smirked. "So, tell me was the old man on top of you when Max Junior caught the two of you together or where you giving him some other special treatments?"

"Shut up you bastard!"

"You're a slut Tiara you couldn't be faithful to Max and you couldn't be faithful to me."

Rage made Tiara shudder. "You... You!"

He caught her arm just as she raised her hand. He laughed and then pulled her into his arms. He kissed her hard. "No grudges Tiara. You knew what this thing was between us from the beginning. It's all about sex, I use you and you use me. Now take your shower

and get dressed, and don't worry your secret has been safe all these years with me. He kissed her again on the lips. "Tell you what I'll give you five thousand dollars, so you can have a little shopping money. Oh, what the heck, so that there are no hard feelings, I'll make it ten."

Tiara's anger slowly subsided, she was a survivor. She smiled and turned around and started the shower.

# Chapter 27

**Camille, Eris & Tiara…**

Two weeks passed. That Saturday Eris sat on the couch and watched Camille as she played the piano. She clutched a pillow from the couch tightly against her heart and watched her best friend. She was mesmerized as she sunk back into the thoughts in her mind.

She listened attentively, as the lyrics of the song meshed with Camille's voice and became one as they floated echoing with depths of love, pain and despair, high into the air.

Eris stared back at Camille transfixed, knowing within her heart that Camille was singing that song and thinking about Tiara.

Camille's voice was sad, soulful and emotional as it sang.

*Ave Maria... Ave Maria.... Ave Maria*

*Ave Maria maiden mild!*

*Listen to a maiden's prayer!*

*Thou canst hear though from the wild…*

Slowly Camille's head bowed as she played the ending. The keys of the piano melted out an eerie presence echoing through the room.

Eris rose and retrieved a box of tissues. She carried it over and offered it to Camille.

Camille blew her nose.

Eris grabbed a tissue and did the same. "Gosh, when you sing that song like that you make me cry Camille," she said touching her best friend's shoulder.

"Eris," Camille said, reaching out to grab her hand. "Can I talk to you for a moment?"

Eris sat down beside her on the piano bench. "Talk away."

Camille exhaled. "I always thought Desmond and I had something special. I felt like he was the kind of man who only loved one woman and now I just have this nagging feeling that I've done something wrong."

Eris' face held a solemn expression. "No…No Camille, believe me, it wasn't you. I thought this matchmaker had picked right when I set you up with Desmond. I thought he was the kind of man that could only love one woman too," she breathed out. "But now I realize he's just like every other man out there, unsure of what he wants."

Camille shrugged. "Oh Eris, I feel like such a fool."

Eris touched her hand. "Camille, you weren't a fool, just a woman who fell in love. Can I ask you to do me a favor?"

"What?"

"Call him. Talk to him. Ask him what's wrong."

"I…I can't," Camille murmured choking back tears and staring down at the keyboard.

They sat silently for a moment.

Eris heard her words and understood them. She chose her words carefully. "Camille have you ever thought that maybe everything you thought you heard wasn't what you heard? I mean it just sounds to me like Desmond was saying he needed his space because maybe he was working on something top secret. You know, this is the high-tech capitol of the world. Every day some Geek is working on something he can't talk about that's top secret."

"I did call him," Camille hesitated. "And he didn't call me back."

"Give him some time Camille. Don't chase after the guy."

"You're right. I need to live my life like he does. Desmond does what he wants to. Did I tell you he said he was going to Hawaii? He told me that the last time I spoke to him."

"Maybe he's off on a business trip."

"Yeah maybe you're right," Camille said. She smiled with her thoughts and after a moment she played a few notes on the piano.

Eris tugged at her sleeve. "Oh, and another thing Camille, you haven't told Tiara right?"

"No."

Eris breathed out relieved. "Good, then don't tell her and don't go out on a double date with her or anything. You keep Tiara out of your business."

"Tiara's just a poor girl who needs her friends to love her and help support her."

"Poor girl my ass. Camille why do you always think you can save the world? Look, don't be so trusting!"

"Eris, don't you think you're being just a little brusque," Camille observed.

"It's just that I know where this conversation is going," Eris shrugged. "And I know if we don't change the subject soon and get ourselves composed. Tiara will be here and then we'll be talking about you and Desmond and you don't want Tiara in your business like that."

Camille exhaled a deep sigh and rose and walked to the window. "You know me so well. Perhaps you're right."

Eris leaned over and touched her shoulder. "Oh, and one more thing, don't tell Tiara you and Desmond aren't seeing each other."

Camille turned and looked at her. She could see the concern in her eyes.

"I know what you're thinking, but Camille you can't save the world and you really can't save Tiara from doing what comes naturally to Tiara, and that is screwing every man that crosses her path."

Camille shrugged. "But Tiara has always been a little different than us. She needs a lot more love than we do."

Annoyance etched all over Eris' face. "Uh Ah! Don't be so trusting. Tiara is a big girl. She's a big girl that knows how to jump in and out of bed with any man she wants. Besides, Tiara stood us up for dinner that night with Desmond and she's standing us up today, watch and see."

Camille gave her a quizzical look. She still hadn't told Eris the truth that Tiara wasn't the one who was expected that night. But a blind date that Desmond had set her up with. Still she thought now wasn't the time to bring that up. She quickly thought of something to make her case. "Haven't you had your heart broken before Eris? You know Tiara never got over Max Duval."

Eris' annoyed expression quickly faded. "Oh yeah, I'd forgotten she was devastated when Max called off their engagement all because he found out that she didn't come from money."

Camille looked back at Eris sharply. "Just go a little easier on Tiara, please?"

"Okay, I'll go easy on her if you agree to go out with other guys."

"Excuse me. How did we get on the subject of my going out with other guys? Besides, what if I do and then the news hits the grapevine. Then everybody knows and worst-case scenario it gets back to Desmond. He finds out that I went out with other guys and he uses it as an excuse to dump me?"

Eris' laughter broke loudly around them. "Gosh, Camille you're over analyzing this. I'm not telling you to sleep with some other guys. Who cares if the news gets back to Desmond? You're a grown ass woman, for Christ sake."

"For once I agree with Eris!" Tiara's cool voice sliced the air.

"Tiara!" Camille exclaimed. "I didn't hear your car. Goodness, it is so good to see you."

Eris' wide eyes narrowed. "And I didn't hear you knock; don't you know eavesdropping is a sin?"

Tiara's voice was gravel hard. "You would know all about all that sins, now wouldn't you Eris?"

Camille looked between her two best friends. "You two should relax."

Tiara's face was impassive. "I did knock Eris but you two were too busy talking to hear me," she said in a mulish voice. "Anyway, that's not really what you're worried about. You are worried about what I overheard."

The moment was unnerving.

Nervously Eris smiled back at Tiara. Her face was a mask. She couldn't help wondering if Tiara had overhead what she'd said about her. "Don't try and read my thoughts Tiara. Camille and I had better things to talk about than you."

"Be careful old girl, you're slipping over the edge. Pretty soon you'll start seeing conspiracies everywhere."

"Why you dirty…

"Oh hell, you both are starting to get on my nerve. Now just knock it off," Camille scolded. She could tell Tiara hadn't overheard their conversation. "You both forget the reason why we are here?"

"Nope, I remember," Tiara condescendingly said, smiling satisfied. "The three of us haven't been together in ages and Camille and I were feeling a little guilty for not spending any friend time with you Eris. So, we are both here having a guilt-trip moment and spending the day with you because, well Eris, everyone knows that the matchmaker can't get her own self a man!"

"Tiara! You didn't have to say that," Camille gasped.

The moment held an awkward pause.

"You are such a bitch Tiara!" Eris abruptly yelled. "That's why I can't stand you. You're ruining the whole day as usual."

Tiara frowned back at Eris and gave her a menacing stare.

The silence in the room was unnerving.

Eris abruptly turned. "Look Camille I promised I'd come and have lunch today with you but I'm cancelling. Yes, I said I'd apologize to Tiara too so here it goes."

She turned and stared back at Tiara. "Tiara I'm so sorry you are such a disillusion bitch!' She yelled. "Oh yeah one more thing I'm not sorry that I didn't tell you Brandon Stone asked me to give you his number months ago," she said arrogantly with a fling of her hair.

Tiara froze with a flash of vengeance. "Eris, you are a lying, thieving heifer you came between me and my chance at happiness!"

"What chance at happiness? Brandon Stone has issues, Eris yelled, turning heading for the door. "I'm out of here!"

"Oh no Eris, you promised me you wouldn't act like this today," Camille said breathlessly.

"Camille, I just can't take Tiara's crap today. I've got a lot on my mind."

# Chapter 28

**Making Amends...**

A few days later Camille met Tiara for lunch.

"Here!" Camille said thrusting the card into her hand.

"What's this?" Tiara asked before looking down at the card in her hand.

The card read.

Brandon Stone, CEO

Bruno Mega Level 1000 Entertainment Group Inc.

Films, Movies, Music

Palo Alto California

*(408)...-....*

"Oh my?" Tiara asked letting out a long sigh.

Camille grinned happy. "Eris told me to give it to you. She said he was waiting for your call. It's her way of saying she's sorry."

Tiara shook her head.

"Ah…. Eris did this for me? But why?"

"Because she knows Brandon Stone is a rich, elusive, sexy, and charismatic bachelor. And because she knows you really like him," she hesitated. "He's dying to meet you. What do you say? Do you want to give him a call?"

Tiara gazed at her with little interest.

Camille shrugged. "Also, Eris really wants you to know she's really sorry and she wants you to forgive her for her outburst the other day."

Tiara shook her head in surprise. She was at a loss for words.

"Okay after all the trouble you put me through, you're going to call him," Camille said. "I'm your best friend, I insist upon it."

"He probably doesn't even remember me," Tiara said, nervously.

Camille laughed softly. "I bet he does. So, what do you say? Dial the number."

Tiara's stomach twisted into knots as she pulled out her cell phone. She quickly dialed the number.

The phone picked up on the first ring. "Hello Brandon," Tiara nervously said.

There was a nervous pause.

"Hi Tiara, "Brandon's cool voice oozed back into the phone. "Gosh I was hoping I'd hear from you. Where are you?"

"I'm in a restaurant with Camille, having lunch and she suggested I'd give you a call. Seems there was a mix-up and I wasn't able to get your number until now."

"Where are you having lunch?" he asked.

Tiara giggled anxiously like a teenager. "Oh, we're having lunch at Milo's over on Stevens Creek," she gushed with excitement in her voice.

His voice was cool. "I'm not too far from there. Do you think I could join you?"

Tiara put her hand over her cell phone. "Holy crap Camille," she whispered. "Brandon wants to know if he can join us for lunch."

"It's okay with me," Camille grinned.

"Thanks," Tiara mouthed the words, touching her hand.

She smiled wide holding the phone. "Brandon we'd love for you to join us."

"Good," Brandon Stone said tapping Tiara on the shoulder.

Tiara twirled around and almost jumped out of her skin. "Brandon you're here?"

"Sorry for scaring you like that Tiara," he said apologetically. "I saw the two of you when I first arrived. I've been sitting at the bar trying to get my courage up to come over and talk to you. Then you called me on my cell…" he hesitated. "Well, let's just say I'm glad I didn't have to make up an excuse to come over and join you."

Camille shrugged, noticing the two only had eyes for each other. "Aren't you forgetting to say hello to me Brandon?"

"Oh, I'm sorry Camille, how are you?" He asked extending his hand.

Camille shook Brandon's hand and allowed him to help her out of her chair. "Thanks Brandon, would you care to take my seat? I was just leaving."

Brandon smiled his most dazzling smile. "I hope I'm not rushing you off Camille?"

"Oh no, I wasn't that hungry anyway. Besides, you know that old saying, twos company and threes a crowd," she said rising. "Good to see you again Brandon. Bye Tiara," Camille said with a wave of her hand and taking her leave.

Brandon Stone's sleek dark wavy hair gleamed against the sunlight as he looked questionably across at Tiara.

He signaled for the waiter. "A Cadillac Margarita with extra salt around the rim," he said.

Brandon Stone had been a local theater star in his youth. He was still the local folk hero. Even now in his mid-thirties he was still handsome to a fault. By the time he'd reached eighteen he'd traded in acting for directing and made a small fortune at doing so.

Tiara sat staring star struck. She felt like a teenager again stealing another glance at Brandon.

"Oh my God you're Brandon Stone!" a woman exclaimed walking over holding an ink pen and a napkin. "Can I have your autograph?"

"Sure," he quickly signing and waiting to the woman was out of earshot.

"My apologies Tiara for that interruption."

"No problem."

Brandon cleared his throat. "Look Tiara I know I have this reputation as being some sort of a ladies' man. But in real life I'm not what people think I am."

Shortly the waiter brought the food.

"Spinach and chicken salad with two plates," the waiter announced.

With a flushed expression Tiara exclaimed. "Oh my, I forgot Camille and I ordered the spinach salad. We were going to share. I can have the waiter bring you something else."

"Nope this is just fine," he said with a soft drawl. "That is if you don't mind sharing with me?"

"No, I don't mind sharing," she softly smiled.

Brandon laughed. "Good. You know I'm normally a steak and salad man, myself," Brandon said. "But I do occasionally eat chicken."

"So, did you learn that southern drawl when you were an actor?" Tiara asked.

"You noticed? Nope I was born with it. My mother has the heaviest Georgia drawl you ever heard. Occasionally I fall back into it without noticing, especially after I've just finished visiting with her."

A puzzled expression creeped across Tiara's face. "You visit your mother?" she hesitated.

He grinned. "Yes, I do are you surprised?"

"I didn't mean it the way it sounded. I mean you just never struck me as the visit your mother type."

Brandon laughed. "Baby, there's a lot you don't know about me."

She grinned. "I'm starting to see that. You are a very complicated man with a very heavy social calendar."

"Complicated? I don't know about that. But the social party scene is strictly for business. Underneath all that is just my mother's son. And she still expects me to stop by and pay her a visit at least once a week, if I happen to be in town."

"Once a week? How do you manage it and keep your business life going?"

"I didn't say I visited her once a week. I said she wanted me to. Don't let the illusion of my having been an actor fool you. I'm big on family. It's the number one priority in my book."

The mood shifted. Instantly Tiara grew silent.

Brandon noticed Tiara's silence. "Tell you what. How about we talk about you for a while Tiara. Tell me about yourself. I hear you are a woman with a life."

She hesitated. "I don't know what you mean?"

His expression softened. "I mean are you unhappy with your life or are you just afraid of your own secrets? Hell, everybody in life has secrets."

Tiara felt affronted. "Look, you don't know me?"

"A woman without a past is a dull woman. I know because I've dated a few. You on the other hand have been linked with some of the highest powered, successful, Geeks in Silicon Valley. Remember, I attend Eris' father's annual fund-raising event. Not to mention the Grand Isle Christmas Ball every year. I've seen you at both a few times. Never could get a dance in."

Embarrassed, Tiara shrugged, wondering what he thought of her. "It's not like you think," she said.

"Careful Tiara, I'm not passing any judgment. In fact, I think we both have a lot in common and I'm just finally glad I get to spend some time with you," he breathed out slowly. "Because you're a very beautiful woman and you don't know how much I wanted to be alone with you."

His compliment stroked Tiara's ego. It was hard for her to concentrate on her meal.

They spent the next two hours chitchatting about their life, movies they loved, and books they had read. Tiara liked talking to Brandon Stone he took her seriously and made her laugh. Her intuition wouldn't let her tell him the truth about her mother or her childhood. She sensed he guessed the part about her being poor and he didn't hold it against her.

Finally, Brandon put his hand under the table and touched her knee.

"Tiara, do you mind if we get out of here?"

"His movement caught her by complete surprise. "No."

"Good, there's a cocktail party I'm expected to put in an appearance at this evening, what say we run out and buy you a nice new dress so that you can go with me?"

Tiara exhaled softly. "I think that's a great idea."

# Chapter 29

**Camille & Eris**

Later that same day, after a grueling hour stuck in traffic on Highway 101, Camille finally arrived at the modern mansion known as the Simeon Family home.

The Simeon Family property sat on a twenty-private acre estate bordering next to a 100-acre nature conservation. The family home had a 25-yard infinity pool, eight bedrooms, twelve bathrooms, a luxurious 20-seat movie theater and enjoyed spectacular views of Silicon Valley.

Camille strode down the marble foyer heading to the rear of the mansion.

"You finally made it!" Eris declared rushing over and fervently hugging her close.

"Goodness Eris if I didn't know any better, I think you were glad to see me," Camille said gilding over and checking the food on the buffet table.

"Christ I'm starving. I didn't get to eat a single thing for lunch," Camille said picking up a plate. She filled it with several hors d'oeuvres and several jumbo prawns. She walked over and sat down at the table.

Eris quickly followed and pulled her chair in close. For several minutes she watched Camille eat.

Finally, Eris couldn't stand the silence. "Okay Camille, stop it. You're keeping me in suspense. Did you tell Tiara that I was sorry for not giving her Brandon's number? How did she take it when you gave her his business card? Did she forgive me?"

"Eris, you know the rules. No questions while I'm eating," Camille said taking a bite out of another jumbo shrimp.

"I can't wait, tell me!"

Camille took her time and poured herself a glass of water took a sip and looked back at Eris over the rim. "Yes, I gave her the card and by the way Brandon showed up at the restaurant. I left the two of them together. So, we really never got to talk about you're being sorry or her forgiving you."

"Ha! Ha!" Eris clapped her hands and threw back her head, her laughter pealing out as her eyes sparked with mischievously. "I've done it again!" she declared in earnest. "Tell me I'm not a matchmaker!"

"Eris, what are you talking about?"

"Why do you think I had this spread of food prepared for you? I knew you wouldn't get a chance to have lunch," she leaned over and gloated. "I called Brandon this morning and told him you and Tiara was meeting for lunch. He practically beg me to tell him where," Eris said waving her hand. "So, I did. Anyway, he and Tiara are having lunch right now and all is well. Soon Tiara will forgive me. Maybe she and Brandon will make a go of it. And that is the end of the matchmaker's story."

Camille shook her head. "God Eris, I forget how deviant you can be sometimes."

Eris grinned softly. "Yeah but anyway. Now I just need to concentrate on you," her eyes softened. "You need to start dating again Camille."

"Save your breath Eris. No more of your match making for me!" Camille rose, "I'm done with men."

"What's that I hear? Camille, you can't be serious?" A shrill frail voice said.

"Aunt Norella, it's so good to see you," Camille said, giving her a hug and sitting back down.

Norella Simeon-LaFluer was Eris' father's only sister. She wore a classic red Chanel Suit and graciously came and went through the Simeon mansion as if it was her own.

"Auntie I didn't know you were visiting today," Eris said standing to give her a hug.

"I spoke to your father earlier and he said you were at home," she took a seat next to Camille.

She placed her quilted vintage Chanel purse on the table and patted her well-coiffed hair. "Strictly speaking," Aunt Norella said.

"I think women have more courage than men. We never give up on finding love."

Camille sighed and sat back. "Well I have."

"I haven't Auntie," Eris added.

"Well, thank heavens for that, who'd ever want to hire a matchmaker that didn't believe in love," Aunt Norella said.

Aunt Norella reached her well-manicured fingers into her purse and pulled out a deck of cards. "Would you like for me to read your cards Camille? I don't want to get rusty," she said without waiting for a response. "Here Camille cut the cards."

Camille did as she was told.

Auntie Norella picked up one card and flipped it over and tapped it with a red lacquered fingernail. "This card means an old love will return."

Camille eyes sadden. "That can't be true."

"Pick another one, Camille," Aunt Norella demanded.

Annoyed Camille flipped over another card.

"Camille you're a hot mess," Aunt Norella giggled. "That card there says there is another man who is very much in love with you."

Camille's eyes flashed furiously. "There's something wrong with your deck of cards Aunt Norella."

"Ha!" Aunt Norella grunted annoyed. "The cards don't lie! And don't look at me like I'm crazy," she sighed heavily. "Okay I'll pick another card," she said reaching for another one. "There you see it is the romance card again, it is never wrong, it's the same as the other one, that means it's the same man who is very much in love with you."

At that moment Camille gazed at the cards and felt a splitting headache coming on. She lifted her gaze and stared at Aunt Norella for a moment longer, and then she said, "I'm sorry but I need to be going."

"Ha! Ha! Ha! Ha! You can't run Camille. Love will find you," Aunt Norella laughed out.

# Chapter 30

**Blame it on the alcohol...**

Brandon had been right the cocktail party wasn't anything but a business meeting, Tiara thought as she surveyed the room of people. She smiled with her thoughts. Brandon had no problem introducing her to his friends. He made her feel special.

The luxurious penthouse was filled with the most affluent Geeky bankers, stockbrokers, engineers, wheelers and dealers in Silicon Valley that Tiara had ever seen.

Tiara checked her watched it was half past midnight. When she looked up Brandon was standing in front of her.

"Tired?"

"Just a little," she said.

"If you like, I have a suite a couple floors below and we could go there so that you could get some rest, unless you'd like for me to drive you home?"

"That would be fine."

As they got off the elevator he said. "Don't worry its safe I have two bedrooms in my suite."

Tiara didn't remember much after he said that, as they entered his suite, she was amazed at how the room didn't resemble a hotel at all. The extravaganza of the suite was an understatement.

"Gosh this place looks regal, like a king live here."

"One does," he smiled. "And he's admiring his queen," he said.

Tiara looked back at him and all she could think of was how great it must feel making love to him in a room like this.

Brandon reached out taking her in his arms and kissed her on the lips. "I want to make love to you, please."

Tiara looked back at him and nodded.

Instantly Brandon placed his hands on the bodice of the shimmery silk gold cocktail dress, he'd brought her earlier that day. He tore the dress off her.

"Brandon!"

"You have a beautiful body and I wanted to see it. I'll buy you another dress. In fact, I'll buy you a whole wardrobe of silk dresses that I can tear off you."

Brandon got out of his expensive suit and kissed her tenderly at first, then with a fiery passion.

The next thing Tiara knew she lay naked on the floor as Brandon climbed on top of her and began ramming her like a wild animal. She listened to his groaning before he shuddered out his climax. Then she remembered neither one of them had mentioned having a condom.

Hours later that night, Tiara and Brandon ended up sharing a bed. He cuddled her in his arms as she softly slept. Finally, he nudged her awake. "Listen babe, I'm sorry about how rough I treated you earlier the excitement of finally being alone with you, and the fact that I had too much to drink is my excuse."

Tiara saw the expression on his face. He was embarrassed. "That's okay?"

Brandon had a big grin on his face. "It's just that a girl shouldn't be left with only that as a memory from spending the night with me."

"Oh?"

He kissed her softly. "I'm going to make it up to you," he said as his mouth danced over her shoulders. He kissed his way down moving to her abdomen and then to her sweet spot.

Tiara moaned and pulled his face harder against her, spreading her legs wider for him. She shuddered and trembled feeling his tongue working its magic against her skin.Brandon Stone had been well worth the wait, she thought as her body shuddered and climaxed.

# Chapter 31

**Maui Hawaii**

"Look Desmond our Cattleya hybrid species is a success!" Fredrick Chiu exclaimed.

The two men admired the newly blooming orchid. The flower's petal segments were broad, well formed with a light pink color and a vivid deep magenta lip with a center speck of yellow.

Desmond nodded. "Well Fredrick it looks like you were right about spending that extra time perfecting the germination flasking process."

"Yes, but you were the initiator who laid the basis for the possibility of this new species. All I did was to keep updating the notes that you started," Fredrick said with a smile.

Both men happily grinned at the new creation.

All at once Fredrick breathed out. "Well Desmond, we can't stand here all day just grinning at it. We must give your orchid a name."

Desmond rubbed his brow. "You're right, what do you suggest?"

Fredrick turned to face him. "Earlier when I heard you call it Camille, I thought that name was fitting."

"What are you talking about?"

"Don't get me wrong. I wasn't spying on you Desmond. It's just that for the last couple of weeks you've been talking to that plant when you thought I wasn't looking," he shrugged. "Well, more like you just kept calling it Camille so I just figure it was an appropriate name to give the orchid."

Desmond thought about it only for a second. "You're right Fredrick.

We'll call the orchid *Camille's Truth.*"

Fredrick nodded as he walked over to the computer and started typing. "Excellent, I'll record it in today's report and then we'd better head to my house for dinner. My wife said I had better not arrive home a minute past seven for dinner," he said. "By the way, thanks again for bringing the Krispy Kreme Donuts when you arrived. They made a very good impression with her. She still bragging about your gift."

Fredrick Chiu's wife, Thelma, was thin and attractive. She was an art dealer who specialized in supplying native antiques to the discreet and very wealthy.

"Here Desmond try this," Thelma said invitingly as she placed a drink in his hand.

"What's in it?"

"Pineapple juice, vodka, and orange liqueur, together they have a very magical taste," Thelma said.

Desmond stared at her. Just like Fredrick, Thelma's voice always oozed sincerity. He took a sip. She was right it tasted delicious and quenched his thirst. He took a big gulp.

"Good thing I made a couple of gallons of it," she grinned placing her hand on his arm. "Come I want to introduce you to everyone. Only one guest hasn't arrived yet," Thelma said leading him over to the small group and making introductions.

She introduced him to the small dinner party of the night, Saul Adkins, Arthur Antes, Stuart and Carol Hall, Curtis and Sue Wong.

For fifteen minutes more, the group chitchatted about nothing. At the end of the conversation Desmond learned Saul and Arthur were very special friends.

"Excuse me everyone, but I'd better check on dinner," Thelma said.

Arthur's eyes perked up with interest. "Thelma I'll help you."

Saul did a slicing motion with his hand. "And that's my cue to help or else," he said following behind them heading for the kitchen.

Fredrick escorted Desmond over to the bar. "Let me pour you

another drink. I don't think the married couples will miss our leaving the conversation."

Desmond nodded. "On, that we can agree," he said, taking a sip.

Minutes later, the two ignored the doorbell ringing, chatting easily.

Desmond was deep in conversation with Fredrick when a young woman walked over and didn't move. His eyes shot up. She looked familiar. He turned back to resume his conversation with Fredrick and then looked back at her again.

The woman standing before him smiled softly.

Fredrick saw Desmond take a second look. "Desmond this is Lily Lo-Evans, Lily Lo-Evans this is Desmond Garcia."

"Hello," Lily said extending a small delicate hand and shook his.

Desmond held her gaze.

Lily Lo-Evans had full lips, a golden-brown complexion and kinky jet-black hair. It was apparent she was half Asian and half African American.

"Would you both excuse me for a moment," Fredrick said.

Desmond nodded not listening. He was mesmerized by Lily's exotic slanted eyes and full red lips.

Her eyes flickered with desire.

It took a second for the expression to penetrate Desmond's brain that she wanted him.

Lily was aware of the effect she was having on Desmond. "So, I finally get to meet you. I've heard so much about you? You know you're practically a God here in Maui," her voice teased with invitation. "Ever since you gave Thelma ten dozen of Krispy Kreme Donuts, I wanted to meet the man," she laughed. "And it's an honor to meet you."

Desmond found his voice. "I feel the same."

Lily leaned in close and whispered. "Well if that's the case then my next question is what would you like? That is for me to do to satisfy you?"

"Excuse me?"

"You heard me Desmond; I asked what you would like?" she whispered.

At that moment Thelma summoned everyone to dinner. "Oh Lily, I could I have word with you," Thelma's soft voice sung out.

"Excuse me Desmond but it looks like my hostess needs my help," Lily said, swaying her hips as she walked away.

Fredrick cleared his throat and touched Desmond's arm. "Desmond, Lily is easy on the eyes and in bed," he hesitated.If I was a single man, I'd take advantage of her while you're here in Maui. It will take your minds off the one that got away."

Desmond listened in silence.

"Uh Desmond, a word of caution," Fredrick looked around, as if worried he'd might have been watched. "Lily doesn't have a faithful bone in her body."

Later that same night, before midnight, Desmond returned back to his hotel suite and stood watching, the moon's silvery rays in the distance as they danced magically on the waves of the ocean. The ocean view from his hotel suite was the reason he enjoyed staying at the famous hotel. The view was like a little piece of heaven and it made him feel lonely and frustrated. He only had himself to blame. He missed Camille. He took full responsibility for having broken things off with her. It was a dumb move and he regretted it fiercely.

"Desmond, you still haven't told me what you would like for me to do," Lily said walking up and kissing him.

He allowed her to lead him back inside. He knew it was because he felt overwhelmed with his frustration. "I need to get up early."

Lily smothered his neck with kisses. "I promise not to stay to long, just until I pleasure you."

She smothered his mouth with kisses and eagerly unzipped his pants. She slipped her hands around his erect cock. "It's feeling hard already."

Desmond couldn't deny how good it felt; he was horny. He moaned.

"Feel good huh? Do you want more?" she teased.

"Yes."

Her mouth found his again.

She kissed his mouth again and then she slipped down his body moving lower until her tongue found the spot. Her ministrations to his body eclipsed him and he gave into the sexual gratification that brought him to a point of orgasm where he was sure he would die.

After an hour of intense raw sex, he lay dizzy with relief panting with joy mixed with regret. For the first time in his life he felt something new. He felt ashamed of his behavior toward Camille.

A humming noise carried on the air.

"What's that?" Desmond asked.

"Oh, it's nothing, just my cell phone humming."

# Chapter 32

**Admitting you've been wrong...**

A week later, back in California, Eris was running late. She'd spent that Saturday morning shopping with Camille and trying to cheer her up since Desmond had vanished from the scene. The two had such a great time that she'd completely forgotten about the promise she'd made to meet her father, E.J. Simeon, for dinner.

Eris moved softly down the dark corridor leading to private dining room of *The London.* The restaurant was her father's favorite.

A mirror hung on the wall just before the door. Eris stood in front of it and checked her appearance. She let out a soft breath; glad she'd donned her favorite black cocktail dress and took her time piling her hair elegantly on top of her head. Her makeup looked flawless.

Pushing back a dark brown curl of hair she walked to the door and turned the knob. The door swung open.

For some reason the door gave, and Eris found herself flung into the arms of a hard-solid body.

"Careful," a man's voice said, reaching to steady her.

For a brief unguarded moment, Eris relaxed in his arms.

"It's you!" she said breaking out of his grip.

"Eris, finally you're here. Now we can all sit down and enjoy our dinner. I see you've met Ethan Armand," her father E.J. Simeon called from across the room. "He's our guest of honor tonight. Come take your seat."

"What?" A confused daze expression crossed Eris' face, as she took the seat her father held for her.

"Good evening Eris," four voices greeted her.

She looked up as four pairs of eyes stared back at her.

The eyes belonged to her father's oldest friends Sheldon Richmond, Craig Eden, Russell Manning and Robert Chandler. All four of them were boring, old gray-haired men, with even duller conversations.

"Hello gentleman," Eris said.

Ethan sat down beside her. "Eris, you look like you could use a drink. I'll pour you a drink."

Eris took the glass of wine he poured and sipped it briefly.

She glanced up and noticed her father chitchatting with Sheldon Richmond. The others joined in the conversation. They talked in a predetermined order based upon a hierarchy that had been set years ago, with her father at the center like a supreme being.

For a moment Eris sat quietly and sipped her wine. She knew the men could chitchat about the weather or some business deal and completely ignore her unless she made her way into the conversation. Something she didn't feel like doing at the moment.

Eris looked out of the side of her eye and caught a glimpse of Ethan Armand. She studied him a minute longer under the guise of sipping her wine. Gosh, the man was handsome. Her heart raced.

"So, are their meetings usually this exciting?" Ethan casually asked.

She blushed. "If you mean boring then yes, they are," she hesitated. "I'm a bit confused. What are you doing here?"

His warm and speculative gaze swept over her. "I guess you're owed an explanation.I just finished writing an exclusive for *Silicon Valley Real magazine* on your father's *Platinum Men's* group donation for the new youth facility that they built over off of Alameda Street."

Shock raced across Eris' face. "Really, I didn't know you write articles?"

Ethan nodded. "I only write for causes I think are worthy. And your father's Platinum Men's group does a lot of good in the community."

"Impressive!" Eris nodded. "I now see you are a more complicated man than I first thought. And you have a good heart."

She sat silently with her thoughts studying him. *Maybe I was wrong about you,* she said to herself.

"A lot of young kids will be helped by the programs at the youth center," Ethan said with a nod of his head. "Did you know one of the biggest computer companies in the valley donated five hundred computers for their after-school program?"

She smiled. "I didn't know it was that many. It makes me really proud of the way my father and his friends give back to the community. Giving the youth of today a brighter future has been my father's and his friend's mission for many years."

Ethan nodded. "On that we can agree."

"Ethan," Eris said softly. "May… Maybe I have been wrong about you."

"Excuse me?"

She leaned over and looked into his eyes with calm serenity. "You heard me right the first time. I want to apologize for the rude way I acted toward you since we first met."

Ethan warmly smiled.

# Chapter 33

**Old familiar feeling...**

That Wednesday evening, Camille was working late again. She found that if she put in longer hours she thought less of Desmond Garcia. She checked the reports on her desk and then checked her appointment calendar for the next day, her calendar was clear.

Good she thought. *Maybe it was time to treat herself to some spa therapy. Where should she go?* She wondered.She typed in *luxury day spas* on her computer. She got so wrapped up in what she was doing she didn't hear the door to her office open. The creak of the floor finally caught her attention.

Camille looked up nervously her voice carried an edge. "Bob, are you working late?"

Bob Madden was the owner of Lipton Escrow. He often worked late.

"No Camille, Bob left for the night. In fact, he let me in as he was leaving," he said walking further into the room.

Caught by surprise Camille whirled around in her chair and rose quickly. "Delmar, you almost scared me half to death."

Delmar closed the door as he entered. He thought back to the moment Tiara had let it slip that Desmond and Camille had broken up. He smiled with his thoughts and closed the distance between them he took her hand and pulled her close kissing her on the cheek as close to her lips as he could. With any other woman he could have kissed her on the lips until she was breathless with desire for him.

With Camille he knew he had to take things slow.

Her voice jarred him back to the present.

She pulled out of his embrace. "You're a long way from Monterey what are you doing in San Jose?"

"Oh, I was just in town to see a man about a car."

She looked up at him. "Oh, adding another car to your collection?"

Yes, and no," he said placing his hand under her chin, lifting her head to look at him. He studied her face. There were dark shadows under her eyes. "How are things Camille? You look like you have been working too hard."

She hesitated and gave a nervous laugh and stepped away. "Things are okay.Why are you here?"

He rubbed his hands together having enjoyed the sensation of her touch. "A friend of mine has a bit of a problem," he began. "And I thought you and I could help her out. You see, this friend can be very persuasive and if I don't help her there's no telling what she might do."

"A friend of yours huh?" Camille asked trying to hide her smile. She knew instantly who their mutual friend was. She gave him a sassy look. "You wouldn't want to use the word annoying when you talk about our mutual friend, my mother, now would you?"

They both burst into laughing.

Delmar stared back at her attentively. "God it's so good to hear you laugh," he hesitated.

There was a long silence between them.

"When... I meant to say Gabby told me she suspected you and that Geeky guy Desmond had parted ways I was worried about you."

Hearing the words from Delmar somehow made breaking up with Desmond a reality. Silently she thought back on their relationship and how Desmond had broken things off with her. Tiara had always said a man with money could make a woman feel worthless when he broke things off with her. Now she understood what she had meant. She felt worthless and betrayed

Delmar studied her. "You're a million miles away Camille do you want to talk about it?"

"I didn't broadcast Desmond and my relationship to begin with, so I certainly wasn't telling anyone we broke up."

His voice was low and calm. "You don't have to explain anything. I'm here for you if you need me," he said watching her with a deep tenderness.

Camille looked up. Maybe it was loneliness, but she could feel that old pull. "Oh, Delmar I feel like such a stupid desperate fool!"

"Don't say that," he said taking her in his arms.

She snuggled in close just as her stomach rumbled loudly.

"Someone hasn't eaten," Delmar said. "And I'm guessing you're here working late to earn extra money to take care of Gabby and her car situation?"

Camille pushed back and looked up at him nodding. Suddenly the phone on her desk rang. She checked the number. It was her mother. "Excuse me, Delmar I have to take this."

"Hey baby girl! "Gabby's excited voice said.

"Hi Mom, you sound happy."

"I am and Camille you won't believe my new car! It handles like a dream and it's the top of the line, fully loaded with leather seats and everything."

Nervously Camille laughed. "Mom what are you talking about?"

Gabby breathed out long. "Camille, hasn't Delmar told you? He bought me a brand-new Honda."

"Delmar brought you what?" she asked too shocked to get into an argument with her mother in front of Delmar. She knew that no matter what, she loved her mother and if she thought long and hard enough, she'd figure out some way to come up with the money to pay Delmar back.

Then Gabby's laughter sliced through the phone. "Camille baby, momma is so happy with her new car. You've got to thank Delmar for buying it for me baby."

Camille tilted her head and gave Delmar the stare.

Gabby chuckled. "Well Camille, mommy has to run."

"Look Mom. I'm just about to leave work. How about you stop by my work and give me a ride home in your new car?"

Gabby sighed heavily into the phone. "I'm sorry Camille, didn't I tell you. The bingo crew and I are headed to Reno for the weekend.  I'm on my way to pick up Myrtle and Grand *mere* Catherine right now."

"Oh, okay you guys have a fun time," Camille said.

"We will, goodbye," Gabby said, hanging up.

Camille stared back at the phone in her hand as her thoughts raced, trying to figure out how much the new car must have cost.

Angrily she turned away from him. "Delmar, you shouldn't have brought my mother that car! We don't need any favors from you!"

"Hold on Camille that's why I came here I realized I should have talked to you first. I came here to tell you and to apologize but I never got the chance," he said apologetically.

"You don't understand Delmar I don't have a new car for Gabby in my budget right now. That's why I was working late."

"I know," he said taking her hand. His eyes filled with concern. "This is crazy Camille. I can easily afford that car! You don't understand I wanted to do this for your mother? I needed to do this for her," he hesitated. "Gabby and Wade were like parents to me. I couldn't live with myself if something happened to Gabby in that old clunker of hers."

Camille pulled back out of his embrace and stared back at him. Something flashed as she looked back at him. The expression in his dark eyes told her he wanted her. She hadn't realized how bad her self-esteem suffered when Desmond broke things off with her. She had to admit it. She felt excited knowing Delmar desired her.

He pulled her close. "Please just accept the car, no strings attached."

Camille was silent for a moment. Delmar was right. She'd forgotten how well Delmar and her father Wade had gotten along. Just like her father, Delmar was always looking out for them.She felt like she owed him. He was hugging her so tight she could smell his cologne. "Look Delmar, I'm deeply grateful to you for buying my mother the car, and yes we both know I'm no match for you when it comes to the money thing. But I have a proposition for you. I still have those shares in Devereaux Industries that you gave to my father Wade," her stomach's rumbling interrupted her.

"Right now, your stomach is rumbling too loud for me to consider any propositions you want to make with me, but I will suggest that you have dinner."

"Dinner? When would you like to go out to dinner?"

"I'm thinking, by the sound of that rumbling in your tummy, right now would be a good time."

"But Delmar it's so late…"

"Come on Camille my limousine is just outside," he said grabbing her hand and leading the way.

Camille had just enough time to grab her purse as they exited through the door.

Outside on the sidewalk Delmar rushed Camille to his waiting limousine pushed her inside.

"Hold on a minute," she said as her purse caught in the door. She jerked hard and bummed several glasses in the limousine bar.

Delmar smiled back at her. "Is everything okay Camille?"

She thought she heard something hit the floor. The limo was dark. She hoped she hadn't knocked over anything. "Yes, I'm fine. I think I knocked something over."

"Oh, don't worry about anything Camille you're in a limo everything is fine," Delmar hoarsely laughed.

Then the limousine pulled away from the curb.

# Chapter 34

**Loyalty**

*Days later...*

Since his stay in Hawaii Desmond realized that time had become like a tesseract to him, where day and night blended into one. He quickly dialed Camille's number.

The phone rang. It picked up.

"Hello Camille, did I wake you? It's a couple hours difference here in Maui," Desmond said urgently.

"Camille ain't home," Gabby answered.

"Isn't it awful early there? Where is she?"

"I don't know she's out. She doesn't tell me everything," she paused, and got nosy. "Boy I wish I was in Maui. Are you having a good time in Maui? I hear there are a lot of nice beaches there, with pretty girls wearing bikinis?"

Desmond said quietly. "I wouldn't know I've been busy working in a laboratory. When do you expect Camille home?"

"Like I said earlier. I don't know Camille doesn't tell me everything."

"When you see her will you tell her I called? Oh, by the way. Do you know if she has a new cell phone number?"

"I ain't sure if she got a new cell phone number. Like I said Camille doesn't tell me everything, "she said exhaling. "And I guess I can tell her that you called. Okay, goodbye," she said before hanging up abruptly.

Gabby stared back at the telephone as she hung up the receiver.

Desmond sounded desperate she hadn't heard Camille talk about him in weeks. She may not have been the world's best mother, but she wasn't about to start blabbing to Desmond on the whereabouts of her Camille. Besides, she wasn't sure herself. She assumed Camille was just working late. Besides Camille rarely told her where she was going, still if she needed her, she knew she was just a cell phone call away. Still she knew one thing for sure no matter what was going on between her daughter and Desmond she did know one thing for sure she owed Camille her loyalty.

Anxiously Desmond stared back at the phone after he hung up and his thoughts raced. He had met many women in life who used sex to manipulate men. Camille wasn't one of them. She had always been honest with him. Now more than ever he'd wished he hadn't just left her so abruptly but sat down and talked to her.

# Chapter 35

**The Schemer ...**

Days later, when Delmar arrived at his office, he was surprised to see his driver Marshall. "Marshall, I thought you said you were taking the limousine in for service today?"

The driver closed the office door behind him. "Yes, I did but I found this," he said, thrusting the cell phone on his desk. "I found the cell phone in the car when I dropped it off for service this morning," his driver Marshall explained."I thought maybe it belong to the young lady you took out days ago."

Delmar kept his thoughts to himself, but his lips curved up at edges. He checked the cell phone the batteries were dead, but he was sure it was Camille's.

"Marshall, thank you for your trouble" he said hastily. "Oh, and I'll makes sure there's something extra, in your pay envelope, for your finding it."

"Thanks Mr. Delmar."

Delmar looked up as Marshall made his exit and the closed the door. He opened his desk drawer and removed a miniature coaxial universal interface connector kit and then quickly removed the back of Camille's cell phone. He easily connected the cell phone to his computer. He keyed in a command into his computer and watched. The screen showed the list of calls Camille's phone had received.

Delmar lean over and smiled as he scanned the list of numbers. His fingers typed in more commands and he watched while the computer's screen loaded in the information. The list of contacts appeared, and he scanned down. He found what he was looking for and smiled.

171

# Chapter 36

**A Friendly voice...**

The afternoon of that same day, Camille sat at her desk at work. Her phone rang, and she checked the caller ID. It was Eris' number. They hadn't spoken in over two weeks.

"Eris old friend long-time no hear," she said.

"Camille I've been calling your cell phone for days. Why haven't you called me back?"

"Oh, that's because I seemed to have misplaced my cell phone."

"Yeah, that sounds like you," Eris chuckled. "You probably dropped it under your bed again like the last time. Anyway, have I got some news for you?"

"What?" Camille responded. "Don't hold me in suspense.

"I've been dating Ethan Armand."

"You mean the Ethan Armand the guy that has his own television show?"

"Yes! Isn't it great? He's a real gentleman and everything."

Camille's voice was cool. "Are we talking about the same Ethan Armand that you said was a pompous jerk when we watched his show together that time?"

"Yeah, but forget about what I said then," Eris said patiently. "I didn't really know him well like I do now. Since I've been staying with him, I've got to know him better."

"Staying with him!" Camille yelled. "What has this guy done to you? You never stay overnight with anyone. It sounds like this guy put a whammy on you. I need to come and get you. Where are you Eris?"

"Ethan hasn't put a whammy on me Camille. But I think his family's home has," she said with a deep sigh gazing out the window as the sunshine sparkled on the low range of hills covered in vineyards as far as the eye could see.

"Sounds like you need a chaperone."

"Are you kidding Ethan lives with his mother and she keeps tabs on me like a Captain in the Army. I've got bigger problems than needing a chaperone for a man, to deal with."

"The guy lives with his mother?"

Eris giggled. "Calm down Camille and let me explain, I'm staying at the Armand family home in Sonoma. I was invited by Ethan's mother Adria Armand to help her with her charity event. You've heard me speak of the Armand Foundation Charity Faire? The one they give every October."

"Yes, I have," Camille said with shocked surprised. "You sound like you got no problems are worries."

"Camille as usually you fail to see my problem," Eris replied.

"Problem? Eris, you have no problem," Camille responded. "Ethan Armand is drop dead handsome; his family is rich, and he lives in Sonoma."

'I know but that's not my problem, Ethan is a man and I know he's attracted to me. My problem is his mother. She is so accomplished, intelligent and successful." Eris said anxiously.

"Okay I'm listening Eris what are you really worried about?"

"Well for starters Adria said she has complete faith that I can bring something new and fresh to the Armand Foundation Charity Faire event, that is why she invited me to stay here. And I don't know how I could ever live up to her expectations," Eris voice trailed off.

"Oh my God you think that's the only reason why Ethan's mother only asked you to stay? "

"Yeah, I know it is Camille. Adria Armand asked me to help her put together this year's event. She wants it to be something over the top and unique. And I've just been racking my brain and nothing I can think of is any good."Eris paused for a moment; Adria Armand is the kind of woman I wish I could grow up and be. She's a mother, a businesswoman, and a great cook. She is so… So successful and accomplished I feel intimidated by the woman."

Camille listened intently. "Stop feeling sorry for yourself Eris," she said. "It sounds to me like you've been having a pity party. I know how smart you are Eris. You've got way more skills at putting on events than you're letting on," she said. "I've seen the work you have done in the past. Adria Armand is right. You are totally capable of bringing something fresh and new to their Charity Faire. You and I both know it."

"You are so right Camille," Eris responded cheerfully. "I just needed to hear my best friend say it. And I just thought of a fresh idea, while you were talking."

"See I knew you'd come up with something," Camille answered.

"Camille just as soon as invitation for this event is ready. Yours will be the first one I put in the mail."

"You promise?" Camille asked. "Oh, and don't forget Tiara's"

Eris sucked in a deep breath. "Speaking of Tiara, can you do me a big favor?"

"Yeah I already know. You don't want me to breathe a word about Ethan Armand to her, right?"

"Camille, you know me so well."

Later that same night, when Camille arrived home, she found her mother Gabby dressed to leave.

"Hi Mom," Camille said. "You're not wearing your lucky bingo attire."

"No bingo tonight dear and you look tired. You should get some rest," Gabby nodded. "I'm off to play cards tonight at Grand mere Catherine's house. If you need me call me on my cell," she said giving her a quick kiss on the check and leaving.

Camille watched her mother leave and closed the door. She hurried to her room and took a shower and then went into the kitchen and got something to eat.

The phone ring just as she finished her sandwich.

"Hello?"

"Hi Camille, it's me Delmar"

Camille knew why she just didn't hang up the phone at the sound of his voice. She was lonely, and she needed someone to talk to.

The two of them chitchatted easily that night for hours. Delmar knew just what to say to ease her loneliness.

# Chapter 37

**Feels like old times...**

For the next two weeks, Camille and Delmar went out to lunch every day. He was the perfect gentleman. With Delmar filling up her free time she thought about Desmond less.

They had arranged to get up early that Saturday morning and spend the day together in San Francisco. After taking in the Palace of Fine Arts, and having a long leisurely stroll down Fisherman's wharf, Delmar's limousine navigated smoothly through the crowded streets of San Francisco and kept them from worrying about parking.

"So far, I've really enjoyed myself Delmar," Camille grinned, walking back over to him, as they strolled leisurely through the San Francisco Botanical Gardens. "Today I really got to see the city like a tourist, and believe it or not, I'm not exhausted."

Delmar took her hand in his, leaned in real close, and then he drew back. "That's thanks to me and my limousine."

She saw him step forward and then stop himself. She knew he was doing his best to act like a gentleman with her today. His efforts weren't lost on her. "Actually, to tell you the truth I'm enjoying that too," she leaned, and brushed her lips softly against his. "Thanks for acting like a perfect gentleman today Delmar," she said with a glance at her watch. "It's getting late, I hope you don't mind if I fall asleep on the drive home."

He kissed her hand. "It feels just like old times huh Camille, right?"

"Yes," she nodded. "It truly does."

Delmar grinned. "I've got one other place I want to show you."

An hour later, Camille looked out into the distance, the breathtaking bay views of the Golden Gate Bridge sparkled in the moonlight. The twinkling lights stretched past the bridge into Sausalito.

Camille stared, overwhelmed at the awe-inspiring view and said to herself. "God it's so beautiful."

"But it's not as beautiful as you."

Camille turned and stared back into the luxurious penthouse. It was lavish and spacious.

"Delmar? Where are you?"

Delmar appeared suddenly by her side and handed her a drink. "Here, I was making up some drinks. Try this; it's a Passion Fruit Collins?"

They touched glasses.

"Mmmm, this is yummy," she said.

Delmar experienced a rush of feelings at the sound of her voice. She didn't know what kind of effect she was having on him. He wanted her, but he couldn't express his desire. He watched her enjoy her drink.

"Excuse me for just a moment," he said turning and strolling down the hallway.

Moments later, soft psychedelic trance-music filled the air.

Camille started to sway to the techno throbbing beat as she finished her drink. Then she remembered Delmar had left the room.

"Delmar, where are you? I want to dance," she called out.

His voice filled the air. "Follow the curved glass wall down the hallway."

She did as she was told. It led straight into what she could only describe as his gigantic master suite bathroom. She stood awestruck, overwhelmed by the sight of Delmar's glistening naked body as he stood staring back at her like a predator. She felt weak in the knees. She knew she was no match for Delmar, and she owed him too much.

"You see the view from her Camille?" he asked pointing his hand past her.

She was too overwhelmed by the sight of the naked man walking toward her to look where he pointed.

"You're naked," she giggled, as she stared back at him. The soft lights from the ceiling lights made his body glow. She smiled as her inhibitions left.

Delmar had a hungry look in his eye. She felt like she was looking at him for the first time.

Camille moved in closer and touched his bare wet skin. All at once she felt like she should take her clothes off.

Delmar looked at her with predatory eyes wandering over her face. "Oh, Camille baby, you are all I think about all the time."

Her mind seemed to float out of her body. "I… I'm real lonely."

"Shhhhh," he interrupted her.

At that moment all that Camille could think of was that she didn't want to be alone.

"Gosh you smell good," she said leaning her head against his shoulder.

"I'm supposed to tell you that," he said smiling a secret grin of half joy and half pain.

He quickly helped her out of her clothes, and she let him. He stood there looking at her naked. e didn't "Camille I've spent the last few years of my life trying to get you out of my mind, and it hasn't worked," he hesitated. "I'll do anything for you and Gabby, you know this," he said pulling her against his body.

His erect penis rubbed up against her as he kissed her hard and then he lifted her and carried her to the bed.

Then he kissed her neck, moaning. "Tell me what I want to hear."

She wrapped her arms around his neck. "I want you… I want you inside me Delmar," she said feeling his hard erection between her legs.

Hours later, Camille slowly stirred in and out of consciences, as a list of questions swirled around her head. Why had she been so weak and given in to Delmar, she wondered. What had happened to the educated, ambitious woman that she was? How did I get here? Her thoughts raced as she laid there. She knew the answer. It was because Desmond had left her and now the loneliness had brought her to this place. A place that brought out the pure animal need within her to be wanted and desired, she thought drifting off to sleep.

The atmosphere in the room felt changed.

Sleepily Camille opened her eye as she felt something. She watched with deep fascination as dust, mist and vapor glowed, and swirled before taking form.

The mist and vapor spoke out. *"Camille can you see me darling?"*

For a moment Camille felt a deep pang of loss and the opened her mouth. "Nana, it's you."

*"Be careful Camille… Be careful,"* Nana's voice chilling warned before she faded away.

A chill seeped through the air.

Camille tried to speak again and felt her voice frozen in her throat. She woke with a start, feeling someone nudging her.

"Camille… Camille wake up it looks like you were having a bad dream," Delmar said.

At that moment the only thing Camille could think of was where was Desmond. Why wasn't he here with her and then the thought occurred to her. What if he was sleeping with someone else too? She looked back at Delmar and wanted to cry.

"Oh, Delmar please hold me. Just hold me."

He kissed her face tenderly and whispered. "You know I will."

A couple of weeks passed since Camille had spent the day with Delmar in San Francisco and made the mistake of ending up sleeping with him. Since that night, he'd shown up at work almost daily to take her out for lunch, and she was certain that he was hoping for a repeat of that night they'd slept together. But she knew her heart was not in forming a relationship with Delmar. She'd only slept with him out of loneliness for Desmond.

Camille stopped what she was doing and turned her thoughts to Desmond. She found herself agonizing daily on why he had not called her or returned any of her calls. Still she missed Desmond; he was all that she thought about.

She shook out her thoughts just as the phone by her desk rang.

"Hello Camille, Are you busy for lunch today?"

"Hello Delmar."

"I was hoping the two of us could go to lunch," he said.

"Oh… Sure, there's something I want to talk about."

# Chapter 38

**Heart Manners...**

Since he'd been in Maui Desmond had arrived at work every day promptly at eight o'clock every morning. Each day he worked until late that night. He spent his mornings of each day in the propagation house inspecting the long tables of new growing specimens and charting the progress.

He' always loved to watch things grow.Gardening and farming were his passion. It was rooted deep within his blood.

He walked over to the side and quickly dialed the number. The telephone line just rang and rang. Annoyed he hung up his cell phone. His calls to Camille were going unanswered. He couldn't even leave a message he didn't understand it. He'd try her cell phone, home and work and nothing.

He walked down the corridor through a set of glass doors and walked into the conservatory. He ran his hand across his face and felt the beard that had grown from weeks of not shaving. Camille wouldn't recognize him right now, he thought.

Just at that moment Fredrick Chui walked into the laboratory and cleared his throat loudly.

"Desmond, how are you today?" He asked walking over and plopped down in his favorite chair. "You know Desmond, I was thinking you and I should hit the party scene and go where the party people go. Have some fun," he grinned. "You know Lily Lo Evans knows where to find the hot crowd."

Desmond stared back at him in silence.

"You can't help me fix my life, Fredrick."

"Yes, I know this now, "Fredrick said hesitantly, "When you arrived here in Maui over a month ago with that sad look in your eye, I knew it was because of a woman and I figured another woman would take your mind off of her. A woman like Lily Lo-Evans provides that shall we say, professional touch."

"Yeah, it goes without saying that Lily does give off a certain aura of I'll screw you if you're rich enough, any day of the week, just call me," Desmond said shaking his head. "Sorry Fredrick, but I like my women to have some lot more human qualities. You know the kind of qualities that separates us from the lower beasts."

Fredrick chuckled at his remarks. "Yes, I must say, Lily does lack such qualities. But she does know how to give pleasure."

"Yes, I know that, her cell phone hummed regularly about every ten minutes that night we were tighter, from all her admiring fans I'm sure."

"Lily does love her fans."

The two men laughed.

Fredrick's voice was conciliatory. "But now I see an easy woman in bed is not what you need. You need a wife up in your premises."

"Oh, when did you start listening to rap music?" Desmond grinned.

They both laughed again.

Fredrick stopped laughing. "You need to go home Desmond and find your happiness.  No matter how much you wish something to happen, it won't happen until you put it into action.  Go home Desmond, don't learn a harsh lesson about losing true love. Go back to California and find your Camille. I believe she is your truth and your happiness."

Desmond rubbed his beard, and listened Fredrick was making a lot of sense to him.

# Chapter 39

**Eyes wide open...**

Tiara thought that she had hit the jackpot with Brandon Stone. He was generous, and kind. And he made sure he'd introduce her to all his friends.

Still she thought, a girl should be made love to by a man that knew how to please a woman in bed, every now and then. She smiled with her thoughts; Delmar could be an expert at pleasing a woman when he wanted to be. Brandon on the other hand, got his first, and maybe thought to include you when the mood hit him.

Tonight, she told herself it was going to be different. She was going to teach Brandon how to make love to her right, and to take his time to please her first. She'd even cooked his favorite.

She heard Brandon's keys in the door before it opened.

She put a big smile on her face and wafted gracefully towards him, trying to look as seductively as possible, in her new negligee'.

"Hey Babe, what's that I smell?"

Tiara cupped his face with her hands and kissed him. "Roasted beef tenderloin with Chanterelles mushrooms. I had it catered."

"Mmmm it smells like *Le Chef Restaurant*," he said kissing her again.

Tiara nodded. "Yes, I knew it was your favorite."

"Thanks, my girl, but before we eat, I need a quickie, he said walking past her heading for the master bedroom.

Tiara's smile faded. Things weren't going as planned. She quickly went after him. "Brandon, we should eat first while it's still hot."

"No," he grunted while walking into the bathroom, and without bothering to close the door, he urinated loudly.

"I'll take a quick shower first," he said without a glance toward her.

A few minutes later, Brandon walked out of the shower and sat down on the bed. "Tiara, where are you?"

Tiara rushed in and went to lie down on the bed.

"No, I need a blow," he ordered.

Tiara slipped off the bed and did as she was told. She grabbed his limp penis and squeezed, and stroked it, watching it come to life. Soon her lips and her tongue brought Brandon's penis to life.

"Good it's hard now," he said quickly pulling her off the floor and onto the bed, as he lowered himself on top of her.

He pushed her legs wide and grabbed his erect penis and thrust it inside of her.

While Brandon stroked in and out grunting, Tiara fantasized about what she was going to do. The first thing she knew was to find a man who knew how to make love to her. Her thoughts raced, Delmar. At least he was good for that.

All at once Brandon groaned loudly and rolled off of her.

Tiara just laid there and felt disappointed.

Brandon leaned over and kissed her lips and then lowered his mouth and sucked her nipple. "Damn, I wish I had time to do more tonight to you babe, but we've got to get dressed," he said rolling out of bed.

"What?"

"I promised that we would show up at a party at the Fairmont in downtown San Jose tonight. There's a limousine waiting downstairs to take us. Don't worry about the dinner you fixed. I'll have one of the maids come in and clean it up," he hesitated. "Oh, and I do care about you Tiara, in fact, maybe too much. Let me show you just how much."

He got out of bed and walked over to his jacket. "Here, I picked this up for you, but don't get hysterical because I'm thinking this little box here just means we're exclusive" he said thrusting the tiny box at her.

Tiara's breath caught in her throat. The box was from Tiffany's. She opened the box and her eyes flashed wide open.

A two-carat cushion cut diamond ring stared back at her.

"You've got to be kidding me," she exclaimed excitedly. "I wonder what you give a girl when you really do propose."

"Babe once we hit that mile marker the rock will be so huge you can't hold your hand up."

# Chapter 40

**I'm taking it out on you...**

That Saturday Camille was sitting in her office determined to wait until it was almost ten o'clock before dialing the number. She quickly dialed Tiara's cell phone to confirm their get together. The phone rang.

"Tiara, it's me Camille."

"Oh, darn Camille! I meant to give you a call. Brandon and I went out late. We didn't get in until almost three o'clock this morning."

"Sounds like you had a great time, Tiara."

Tiara sighed loudly. "I guess parts of it were okay, but you know Brandon…" her voice trailed off.

Camille took a deep breath. "Your life is still way better than mine right now."

Tiara breathed out slowly "Camille I'm so tired."

"Gosh Tiara, I was hoping we could talk."

"Why don't you call Eris?"

The line went silent.

"Camille! Camille are you still there?" Tiara asked. "You sound upset," Tiara said giving Camille her full attention.

"Yes, I'm still here," Camille said in a low voice. "And I can't talk to Eris because Eris is seeing someone."

"Eris is seeing someone?" Tiara repeated. "Who? Is it anyone we know?"

"I don't know," Camille's voice was low. "Look I thought we were talking about me. My life is the one falling apart."

Tiara spit out a laugh. "Yeah right, Miss I'm madly in love with Desmond Garcia. How can your life be falling apart right now?"

Camille sighed. "I didn't want to tell you over the telephone, but Desmond and I broke up several weeks ago and…"

"What, you broke things off with Desmond?" Tiara asked but didn't wait for a response. "You let a man like that get away? Girl are you crazy?"

"No Tiara, I'm not and in fact, Desmond broke things off with me."

"Oh, this I've got to hear," Tiara said sitting up on the side of the bed."Where are you anyway Camille?"

"I'm at work," Camille answered.

Tiara paused. "It figures. Why did I ask?" she answered. "I'm going to get dressed. Do you want to go and get some lunch and talk?"

Camille laughed out. "Oh yes."

"How about we meet at that Burger restaurant you love on Market and First Street in say an hour and a half?"

"The Burger Machine sounds great to me," Camille said with a smile in her voice.

The Burger Machine had the best burgers in all of San Jose. The restaurant had been around since before Camille and Tiara could remember.

Camille ordered a double big bacon cheeseburger with onions and sweet grilled peppers with an order of onion rings on the side and a large root beer float.

Tiara ordered a regular bacon cheeseburger with coleslaw and her favorite triple pineapple banana split with a vanilla shake.

Camille filled Tiara in on her breakup with Desmond, while they waited for their food.She took a deep breath and burst out in a cry. "And the next thing I knew Desmond told me he needed his space and I haven't heard from him since. I don't think he ever loved me."

Tiara listened silently for a moment. "Damn, Desmond didn't look like an asshole. But what man has. By the way, it's like I always say you just don't really know a person."

The waiter brought over their drinks.

Camille composed herself and took a sip of her root beer float. "You're right about that," she answered dabbing her eyes with a tissue. "I just wish I wasn't the one having an emotional breakdown right now," she sipped her float. "Thank God for whoever invented the root beer float. Talk about therapy in a glass."

Camille looked around the restaurant and spotted several happy couples together. "Just look at that woman over there," she nodded toward the couple. "She thinks he's the perfect man just like I did with Desmond. I thought I had found the perfect guy to spend the rest of my life with too," she sighed. "Desmond was better than all the rest. He was everything you could wish a guy to be. Strong, intelligent and he knew how to build up my confidence."

"Better than the rest, amazing," Tiara nodded taking a big sip on her vanilla shake. "That should have raised the red flag of warning right there. That's the type you've got to watch out for. Some men get off on just building up your confidence so that they can just tear you down."

Camille gave her a long look. "Well, I'm off love and relationships, "she paused. "And men for at least the next, I don't know, forever."

"You cannot let that stupid notion of love, named Desmond Garcia, ruin your life forever. You're too beautiful to just be stuck on a shelf. You never let Delmar stop…" Tiara stopped herself in mid-sentence. Delmar, she knew wasn't a saint and neither was she.

"For the record Tiara, Delmar never built up my self-confidence like Desmond did."

"Look Camille, all I'm saying is don't be a cry baby loser, sitting around feeling sorry for yourself just because Desmond is gone. So, get that crazy notion of never dating again out of your head. Too bad you didn't listen to me in the first place and get some money or jewelry out of dead-beat Desmond from the beginning. Now the rich bastard is history and you don't have a damn thing to show for the relationship," she said waving her diamond laced hand. "At least I've got a ring of consideration for my efforts with Brandon," she said modeling her ring. "I bet you feel like a fool now."

"I resent that, as usual you take my kindness for weakness. There's a word that they have for a woman who sells her affections for money and diamonds Tiara, and it starts with a "W," and you know what it ends with," Camille said becoming defensive. "I've never judged you on how ridiculous any of your past relationships were, or ended, or the way you behaved while you were in them. No matter how close you came to look like a …!"

Camille stopped herself from saying the word. She regained her composure.

"Look Tiara, I'm sorry…"

"No, I'm sorry. If I hadn't been rude and judgmental, we wouldn't both be at each other's throats," Tiara said. "No matter what, we've always been friends. Forgive me?"

"I'm sorry too," Camille smiled.

Tiara shrugged. "I guess I'm just not all that happy in my relationship with Brandon and I'm taking it out on you. Brandon can be kind of selfish, as I'm sure you know, since you warned me about him from the start."

"Do you need to talk," Camille asked with concern in her voice.

Tiara gave her a weak smile. "No… No, it's nothing I can't handle. Besides, today is all about you. So, tell me, what do you think we should do to get you back into the dating game? Should we hire Eris the matchmaker to hook you up with your next wealthy man," she hesitated and then laughed. "Scratch the wealthy part."

"Scratch the matchmaker part," Camille laughed out.

"Oh, I have just the thing. Brandon's friend is having this way cool cocktail party at the Wicked Widow's Den, and you should be there."

The waiter brought their order.

Tiara stared at Camille as she lifted the oversized burger and took a bite. She watched as she took another bite.

"Mmmm this is so good," Camille said, stuffing her mouth.

"Camille girl it's so amazing watching you handled that king size burger. You never let anything fall out?"

"It's a gift," Camille said, as she chewed a mouth full of burger.

Tiara scooped up a big chunk of pineapple and ice cream. It went smooth down her throat. "Now old friend, we've got to figure out how we can get Eris to reveal who the man is that she's seeing."

Camille choked back a laugh. "Tiara, that's why I love hanging out with you.You always know how to cheer me up and make me laugh."

"Oh, goodness, that vanilla shake went right through me, I've got use the restroom," Tiara said rising quickly and making her way around down the aisle.

"Excuse me Miss.  Aren't you Camille?  Camille Baptiste?" A woman's soft voice asked.

"Yes," Camille answered, trying to place the face of the woman. "Where do I know you from?"

"I'm Nona Allen, the older woman said. "Desmond "Garcia is my employer."

The recognition caused silence between them.

Camille nodded her head. "Oh!"

"I hope you don't think I'm being rude. But when I saw your friend go to the lady's room I just had to come over. I hope you don't mind if I sit down? In fact, I've got something I need to get off of my chest," Nona said, not waiting for a response and taking Tiara's chair and moving it close. "I know that it is none of my business, but I just have one question I'd like to ask you."

Camille stared noting the resentment in her voice. "I'm listening," she said calmly.

Nona took a breath.  "I thought you had more class Camille.  I thought you were the kind of woman who'd put up the good fight," she stated outraged. "Desmond has called the office every day since he left over a month ago, inquiring if you've called. Why haven't you returned any of his calls?"

"What are you talking about?" Camille asked curiously.

The moment was tense.

Nona looked back at Camille and studied her face, determined to have her say. "Camille, I know you're young and beautiful now, but just remember youth and beauty don't last forever! Love is the only thing that lasts. Sometimes love isn't what it looks like. Sometimes it rude and doesn't know what it wants."

Camille watched her intently as she spoke. She realized that Nona Allen was serious. She was fighting for Desmond. "You really care about him, don't you Nona?"

"Yes, he's like a son to me and he's a decent guy," Nona hesitated. "A decent guy, who sometimes does stupid things."

Camille reached out and touched her hand. Out of the corner of her eye she saw Tiara returning. "Thanks for telling me Nona, but my friend Tiara is coming back right now, and I don't want her to be rude to you. You understand?"

Nona's eyes followed Camille's gaze. "Yes, I understand," she said. "Oh Camille, no hard feelings, she said rising to take her leave.

Just then Tiara walked in close. "Who was that?"

"Who her?" Camille answered. "That was Mrs. Allen, an old client of mine."

# Chapter 41

**Wicked Widow's Den...**

A week later, Saturday night, the crowd in the Wicked Widow's Den was thick with throngs of people. The music was jamming from the minute Camille, Tiara and Brandon arrived and stepped through the doors. It was the most popular place in town for live band action.

Camille laughed and danced and flirted and couldn't remember the last time she had so much fun out, as she danced with a tall guy that pulled her close every chance he got. The DJ changed the tempo of the music and a slow song filled the air.

"Thank you for the dance," Camille said, determined not to let the guy feel her up doing a slow dance.

The tall man reached out and touched her bare shoulder with a sweaty hand. "How about we get to know each other better? Say, let's go somewhere where we can talk?"

"Sorry, no," she said.

"The name is Chad. Chad Harper and your girl Tiara thinks the two of us would get along quite well," he said looking over at the VIP section where Tiara sat with Brandon.

Camille turned and stared. She watched as Tiara laughed at something Brandon was saying. She thought about how much trouble Tiara must have gone through, trying to play the matchmaker. She knew why she'd done it. She was trying to play the part that Eris always played with her. She always knew Tiara had a heart. She signed deeply, ready to give in and to and talk with Chad in private when his voice stung her like a bee.

"Look, give a guy a break. I'm here to help you. Why don't you act like the two of us are getting along so we both can have what we want? You know what I mean?"

Camille leaned back in her heels and looked him in the eye.

"You know what Chad? You sound like a straight shooter to me. Why don't you tell me what you're talking about?"

"Well, I mean we both can help each other reach our goals," Chad nodded.

"And what's your goal Chad?

"Well, I got a chance to have a small part in a film Brandon's company is making," he said.

"Huh, this may sound dumb to you Chad, but you wouldn't happen to know what my goal is now would you?"

His eyes gave her body the once over. "Oh, you know you're spending the night with me, locked in a warm embrace, and you know the two of us doing the love making thing," he paused licking his lips. "Your friend said you needed a man really bad."

Camille was devastated. She was sure he was too busy devouring her body with his eyes to realize what he'd said. "Tell you what Mr. Want-to-be-an actor guy, Chad," she hissed. "I'll promise not to tell my friend you humiliated me tonight, if you use those great acting skills of yours and leave the premises right now with a big smile on your face, like I'm going to leave out of here and meet you somewhere."

"You are?"

"No, I'm not, I'm being sarcastic! But if you don't leave, I'm going to see to it that you never get that part in Brandon's movie, because I'm going to start screaming my head off like you tried to steal something."

"Okay, I'm leaving," he said, making his exit.

Camille took a deep breath and forced herself to smile as she crossed the room heading for Tiara. She leaned in close and whispered in her ear. "Tiara, you wouldn't mind if I escape... I mean left early. I've got to be at work early," she lied.

Tiara sat there thinking of her own chance to escape early. She nodded. "No Camille not at all."

Just after two o'clock that morning, Tiara closed the door of Brandon Stone's limousine and walked over and got into her car. She watched the limousine driver drive out of view before pulling her car into traffic. She drove her car down East Santa Clara Street stopping for a traffic light. She glanced quickly at herself in the mirror. She smiled softly with her thoughts. She knew that she looked calm, cool, collected, and horny.

The light changed, and she moved down the street slowly and turned into the darkened street. A car flashed its lights.

Tiara parked her car got out and walked over to the parked car.

"Delmar what kind of car is this?"

"This is a 1950 fully restored Silver *Dawn*," he said, starting the car engine and driving down a short distance into the entrance of an exclusive parking garage off Market Street. A private garage elevator door opened, and he drove the car forward. He pressed a remote control and the car rode up. The elevator stopped, and he drove the car forward and stopped in front of tall windows that looked out on the city views.

Delmar descended from the car and started stripping. Within minutes he was naked."Get out of the car and strip Tiara. I need a quickie."

"Who doesn't?" Tiara hissed, walking around the car. "But I'm not doing it on some cold floor. "Wow, take a look at that view."

The San Jose Skyline spread for miles in full view.

Delmar hoisted up her dress, lifted her up on the hood of his car. "Look at the skyline for all I care! Just spread your legs wide and invite me in. I'll do the rest," he said pushing his way in and feeling her heat.

Tiara gasped out a moan of pleasure.

Delmar established his rhythm and drove in and out of her.

"Oh… Oh…," she moaned.

He poured into her turning up the heat. "You still want me?"

"Yes, I do-o-o-o…" she pleaded.

"Then do that thing you do and make me moan," he said, his lovemaking was ferocious and savage as he dug into her.

# Chapter 42

**Making a choice...**

Camille lay in bed wide awake and stared at her alarm clock. It read six o'clock. Instantly the digital clock's piercing electrifying hum filled the room and she reached over and silenced it. She got out a bed and headed for the shower.

When ten minutes to eight o'clock rolled around that morning she was standing waiting outside of Desmond's locked office in downtown San Jose wondering why the office wasn't yet opened. The wait was killing her.

Nora Allen arrived promptly at eight o'clock with her key in hand. She was surprised to see Camille standing in front of the large glass windows enjoying the view.

"Ms. Camille what are you doing here?" Nona inquired.

Camille was nervous when she turned and looked back at Nona Allen. "Hello Mrs. Allen. You don't know it yet, but I'm your first appointment this morning," she rambled nervously reaching inside her purse and pulling out her cell phone. "I've been awake half the night, hoping you'd talk to me and help me understand what's going on. Take a look, I don't have a single call from Desmond on my cell phone."

Nona put her hand on Camille's arm and lead her inside. "Come inside, I'll make a pot of coffee and we'll talk."

Half hour later, Nona listened attentively to Camille. Camille had pulled out her cell phone and showed her it didn't register a single call from Desmond.

"There you see Mrs. Allen. There are no incoming calls on my cell phone from Desmond. I'm not making anything up. Desmond hasn't called me not once on my cell phone. And my mother would have told me if he'd called the house and I wasn't there."

"Yes, I see. You definitely had no calls from Desmond since he left," Nona frowned faintly. "It just doesn't make sense. I know I am a little biased when it comes to Desmond. He's like a son to me. Desmond is a wonderful person. He'd never lie to me about calling you when he hadn't, and I can vouch for his character. I've worked for him for years. He is as honest as the day is long," she paused in deep thought. "And you said he called you abruptly that morning before he left?"

"Yes, it was just like I said earlier. It all just happened rather suddenly," Camille hesitated. "Desmond called me early that morning and just told me he needed his space. He didn't try to explain anything. I... I wish I had a chance to talk face to face with him to get him to tell me what was wrong."

Nona sat there frowning, debating with herself. Finally, when she spoke, she choose her words carefully. "You know in many ways Camille; Desmond is really like a little boy. Oh, don't get me wrong. I'm not saying he's not a man. He is a real man. Desmond is just a little different. You know the Geeky, brilliant scientist type but with a natural flair for business. But when it comes to his emotions..." her voice trailed off.

"Believe me, I understand the type. My family has an old acquaintance with the same trait," Camille said, as she slowly sipped her second cup of coffee. "You know Mrs. Allen, when I try to put myself in Desmond's shoes and think like he might think, all that seems to keep flashing back is the night before Desmond called. It has a connection somehow. Anyway, that night my mother got a lift from an old Geeky family acquaintance, and he kept acting strange that night too," she nervously laughed. "When he left that night, it was just after midnight and I felt like someone was watching me as I stood at the door showing him out. It's funny…"

Nona's face contorted into a strange expression as she stared back at Camille. She was silent for a few moments.

"Mrs. Allen a strange look came over your face just now," Camille said caringly, as she studied her, she realized Nona knew something. "Is anything wrong?

She looked back at her. "I was thinking back to the night before Desmond broke things off."

Frustrated Camille stared into space. "Yes, why?"

"Camille don't you think it was strange you thought someone was watching you?"

"No, I don't know what you mean?"

"I feel disloyal talking about it," Nona said calmly.

"Why don't you just tell me?"

Nona voice was low. "Well, I remember that night because Desmond worked late. I remember it clearly because he had one of the most beautiful Orchid plants, I'd ever seen sitting on his desk all that day. When I finally jokingly asked him who the plant was for, it was already late. When he told me, it was for you I suggested that I dial your number for him so that he could tell you he was dropping it by. He told me he didn't want to call you because he wanted to surprise you."

Camille thought about that night Delmar left their house just after midnight and she'd felt like someone was watching her. Suddenly a light went off inside her head. Desmond must have seen Delmar leaving and thought the two of them were seeing each other.

"Nona, I hope I'm not keeping you from anything urgent."

"No and I'm glad you're back to calling me by my first name," Nona smiled. "Besides, after listening to your story and seeing your cell phone contact list, I'm convinced it's been tampered with."

"Yeah, it looks like it to me too. The only problem is, I don't know how it could have happened."

"I'm sure if you thought about it, you'd probably remember leaving it unattended somewhere," Nona suggested.

"You could be right. Goodness take a look at the time. I must be leaving."

Nona nodded and noticed the clock and thought about the time difference."Oh, can you just wait a moment?I just remembered I need to check something," she said reaching and pressing a button on the phone.

The speaker phone's ring filled the room. Nona's eyes brightened as she picked up the phone.

"Hello Nona, how are you?" Desmond's voice sounded through the receiver.

"I'm fine," she hesitated. "Desmond there is someone here who needs to speak with you."

Nona turned and handed Camille the receiver. "Camille, I believe this phone call is for you."

There was a pregnant pause as Camille reached for the phone. "Hello Desmond, Nona told me you've been calling me. Is that true?"

At the sound of Camille's voice, Desmond let out a sigh of guilt. He needed to release his guilt and make her understand how stupid he'd been. "Yes Camille, I'm so thankful I finally got hold of you," Desmond's voice choked finding the words. "God, I've been so stupid. I messed up big time telling you I needed space."

Tears of desperation and frustration ran down her face. "You don't have to explain anything to me Desmond, I'm a big girl."

"Yes, I do, please hear me out. I was such a fool," he said. "You are all I think about! I've got you so deep in my soul that I don't know what to do. If I must spend the rest of my life getting you to believe just how sorry I am for what I did, I'll do it. I can't tell you how sorry I am for hurting you."

The pain in his voice ripped through her heart and sent the time they'd spent apart scattering. Camille tried to remember some reason from the past to make her hate him, but she couldn't. She sucked in a deep breath. "Desmond… Desmond, you hurt me bad," her voice shook, laying on the guilt trip.

"You've got a right to be angry at me, but please let me tell you how I feel. You don't know how sorry I am for hurting you like I did. You're the only woman I ever felt this way about and my instinct told me this crazy notion that maybe you didn't love me as hard as I loved you and I got scared and I ran...," he said his voice shaking. "Like a foolish man trying to stick a steel door into my life to shut you out, I ran... Please forgive me Camille and give me a second chance.I love you like you wouldn't believe."

His voice was serious. And at the sound of his confession she knew everything was different this time. She felt it deep within that he was telling her the truth, and everything was going to be fine this time. After a long pause she muttered. "I don't know why I'm saying this, but okay."

# Chapter 43

**Sorry I'm just not into you...**

Even before she visited Nona at Desmond's office Camille had made the decision. She felt guilty for leading Delmar on. She didn't have the kind of feeling for him that he had for her. In fact, she was sure she had just been on a rebound from her loneliness when she started seeing him again.

Before she walked into the restaurant to meet Delmar, she smoothed out her dress and took a deep breath. She saw him sitting at the bar and walked over.

"Hello Delmar, I'm so glad you agreed to meet with me on such short notice," she said sitting beside him.

Delmar rose quickly. "Camille let me get us a table."

"Oh no Delmar, this is fine."

He kissed her gently before he sat back down. He picked up his drink sipped and put it back down. He slipped his arm around her and kissed her again.

She broke out of his embrace. "Look Delmar, I just don't want you to get the wrong impression. I can't go out with you anymore. It wouldn't be right."

"What are you talking about?" he demanded.

Camille looked back at him and felt the need to explain. "I'm sorry Delmar. It's difficult to explain. But it was a mistake my sleeping with you that one time that I went out with you. I told you then that I was feeling lonely. Anyway, it shouldn't have happened."

"No, you don't mean that Camille. You're just upset. I haven't been patient with you enough," he said, his eyes filling with pain.

"No," Camille forced herself to say it. "Delmar, its' over. It was over a long time ago between us."

His eyes flashed coldly. "Then I'll need the money for your mother's car back," he hissed out, not masking his bitterness. He was sure his actions would have her rethinking her decision. "I'll take my twenty-five thousand dollars in a lump sum, right now."

Camille stared back at him. "What? Twenty-five thousand dollars?"

He sneered. "Yes, I assumed if I wasn't dating you. You'd pay it back. Or if you prefer the old barter system."

It was the old Delmar rearing its ugly head Camille thought; just like all those years ago when she'd first become aware that he always did everything with an ulterior motive connected to it.

Calmly she reached into her purse and pulled out a fat envelope. "Here Delmar!  I'd thought you spent more!  You are a cheap car negotiator that's for sure. I bet you didn't pay the sales guy a profit over the invoice," she said pushing the envelope into his hands. "There are ten thousand in one hundred-dollar bills and a cashier's check for seventeen thousand dollars. I expect you to mail me the difference overnight express if you don't mind, and if you don't, I'm charging you one hundred percent interest," she said turning to make her exit. She stopped abruptly and looked back at him. "Oh, and Delmar, don't you ever call me again. And if you see me in public I wouldn't chance trying to speak."

# Chapter 44

**That Thing you do...**

After the disastrous break, up with Camille that previous Saturday Delmar sat in his office wondering why he was having such a bad week.

He checked his phone and quickly dialed the number.

Miles away in San Jose, Tiara was happy and content. She had arrived home early from work showered and changed and packed a small suitcase with a pair of jeans, a couple of blouses, her little black dress, some sexy lingerie, and her black negligee. She'd planned to spend the weekend with Brandon.

The day had been unnaturally warm for that time of the year.

She studied herself in her full-length mirror. The shimmering panels of the buttery soft metallic leather dress accented the curves of her body to perfection. It was the perfect evening dress. She haphazardly looked though her jewelry box for her pair of gold teardrop cascading earrings.

The telephone's loud ringing interrupted her task. She cradled the phone to her ear.

"Hello."

"I've been trying to reach you for the last few days."

"Delmar!"

"Yes, it's me, Delmar. Were you expecting someone else?" he asked but didn't wait for an answer.

Tiara swallowed hard and sat down on the bed. She quickly thought of something. "Are you still at work? I mean it's early. Shouldn't you still be at work?"

"Yes, I'm working from home. I'm still in Monterey. But I have an idea. Why don't we get together, and you and I can do that thing that we love to do?"

Tiara felt her throat fill with cold fury.

Delmar cleared his throat. "Look Tiara let's say we meet at my home in say about an hour?"

"No Delmar. I mean sorry I can't. I …"

"Oh, you need me to send a car for you. No problem. I can have my driver pick you up."

"No, I can't meet you because I have to return to the office," she lied. "We're just so busy right now. You understand?"

Delmar's voice became insistent. "Sure, I understand but I haven't seen you in a while."

Tiara shifted the phone in her hand. "Things are just so hectic, at work Delmar. I only came home early because I left a report here that I forgot to take to work with me this morning," she mumbled her words together hoping he couldn't see though her lie.

Delmar's tone was ingratiating. "Working hard for the money? Do you need some money? I could help you out in any way that could free up your time; maybe I could tempt you with a shopping spree?"

There was something about his tone that she found distasteful. "What did you say?"

"I said I could give you some money to free up your time so that you can do that thing you do for me," he said.

"Look Delmar I've really got to get back to work. I'll talk to you later," Tiara said hanging up abruptly.

# Chapter 45

**I'm so sorry...**

On the plane ride back to San Jose, all Desmond could think about was Camille. She was the only woman he'd ever seriously considered settling down with.His desire was so great that he didn't even have a word for it.

Getting off the plane Desmond followed the crowd of people heading for baggage claims. As soon as he saw her, he experienced a rush of feelings for her. He wanted to never leave her again. He was going to ask her to marry him and spend the rest of her life with him, he thought to himself.

Camille stood at the bottom of the escalator at the baggage claims terminal of the San Jose International Airport and waited patiently. The moment seemed to stretch into infinity.

When she saw Desmond come into view her heart skipped a beat.

Quickly Desmond made his way around several people and threw his arms around her.

His eyes were filled with pain. "Camille… Camille…I'm so sorry for being so stupid my love. There is no explanation for what I did. I was just so stupid…Stupid," he whispered. "Can you ever forgive me?"

The sad apologetic expression on his face told her all she needed to know.

"Shhhhh," she said touching his face. "I've missed you too Desmond," her heart slammed against her chest feeling the warmth of his skin.

He pulled her into his arms and kissed her long and lingeringly.

When he pulled apart, he said, "Let's get married today if you want too."

A burst of laughter escaped her. "Is that a proposal?"

"Yes, you know it is," he said kissing her again.

A slight frown crossed her brow. "We can't get married today, and I'm sure tomorrow is out of the question too."

"What?"

She laughed tenderly deciding to end his misery. "We'll have to wait until I can get a hold of Eris and Tiara. You know they'll both be upset if they're not included in the wedding."

"Well then, that is the only reason I will wait," he said. "But at least let me take you home with me and cook your dinner."

Hours later, just past midnight Camille and Desmond finished dining on huge porter-house steaks, tender asparagus, and risotto.

Desmond had given Consuelo the night off.

The two of them sat quietly at the grand piano as Camille toyed fingering a soft melody. She stopped abruptly nervously and said. "Desmond I'm so sorry about our misunderstanding. If I had known, you drove by the house that night and saw Delmar leaving I would have explained."

Desmond took her hand. "Shhhhh," he silenced her. "The past is over and done with. From this point on we move forward into the future."

"I thought you would never forgive me," she said.

"Well, you thought wrong."

There was a flash of something that looked like desire in Desmond's eyes.

She looked back at the dining room table. "We should clean up those dishes."

Suddenly he took Camille's face in his hands and drew her close. "Let's leave the clean up until Consuelo gets back, she'd hate it if I didn't leave anything for her to complain about," he smiled dangerously as he kissed her lips.

He stopped abruptly. "But for the record Camille, I don't want you seeing anyone but me, agreed?

"Agreed."

This time he kissed her, and his hands fumbled with the zipper of her dress.

Quickly his clothes joined hers on the floor. He lifted her and placed her on the top of the piano. He spread her legs and enjoyed the slippery wetness between her thighs. Camille felt her muscles tense and her back arch as she threw back her head with a moan as she felt her body tremble and explode with a climax.

# Chapter 46

**Baby wait for me. . .**

Tiara sat at the vanity table and thought as she slipped on her panty hose and slipped into the exquisitely sexy black cocktail dress. She looked back into the mirror and admired that it clung to her body perfectly just the way he liked it. She smiled to herself running her hands down her body as her thoughts traveled back. You couldn't fake it when you were having sex, you were either good or bad, and he was good especially when he wanted to be.

"Oh Christ," she whispered, under her breath, shocked at her own thoughts. She was thinking of having sex with Delmar and not Brandon.

Panicked, Tiara closed her eyes and stood in front of the mirror silently.

"Babe, it's almost nine o'clock. We really need to get going," Brandon said.

He kissed her on the cheek, and she could smell the booze, and then she noticed the glass in his hand.

"Oh, pretend you don't see this," he said lifting his glass. "I'm going to need a couple of more glasses to get me through tonight. I call it courage," he smiled back at her in the mirror. "Oh, by the way, did I tell you I have to go out of town for a week, possibly longer?"

"What?"

"Yeah, we've got to check the location for the movie, and I have those meetings lined up with that director. Remember, I told you about them before?"

She tilted her head and looked at him calmly and stated. "Yes, but I didn't think you'd be leaving right after tonight's party."

He paused. "I guess when I told you about it, it wasn't important enough for you to listen. Any way we are on our way to a tiny little island off the coast of Peru in South America."

Nervously Tiara giggled, ignoring him.

"I have to catch the red-eye tonight or rather the first plane out," he said kissing her cheek. "Here this is a little token of my affection. It should keep you happy until I get back," he said, securing a diamond necklace round her neck.

Tiara stared back in the mirror and watched the pride on his face. "Brandon! It's beautiful!"

"Just like you Tiara, anyway the jeweler let me name that necklace and do you know what I called it?"

"No, "she smiled brightly shaking her head.

Her chuckled softly. "I call it *baby wait for me*."

"Brandon, you are so crazy," she said revealing a big smile.

"Crazy in love, and I'm spoiling you so that you know what you have to wait for," he hesitated and looked at her seriously. "Tiara, when I get back, let's say we look at what we both think about that great institution called marriage.We both have a lot in common. We both aren't hung up on some unattainable perfection in another person."

Tiara turned and gave him her undivided attention. "Ah you serious? Are you proposing…?"

Brandon interrupted her and placed his finger on her lips. "Shhh," he silenced her. "This is not a proposal, I just meant we'll talk about it more when I get back, agreed?"

She nodded her head.

He kissed the top of her head. "Let's get going, we've got a party to attend."

# Chapter 47

**Can't help myself...**

With Brandon flying out that early morning, Tiara felt alone and anxious being left alone in his huge suite. Quickly she packed her things back into her suitcase and set out for home. She headed north along Montague Expressway heading toward the north foothills and her thoughts preyed upon her. Brandon's skills in bed left her hungry for good sex. She felt like a caffeine addict addicted to coffee. She needed it and she needed it bad.

She had to admit Delmar was good for sex and his call the day before kept running through her mind. She thought of something to say as she dialed his number. His cell phone rang and quickly went to take a message. "Hello Delmar, it's me Tiara, call me," she said before hanging up.

Tiara hung up and headed for home. She was turning into the parking lot of her apartment unit complex when her cell phone rang out.

"Hello," she said.

"You called me," Delmar said.

"Don't sound so romantic lover. I was just checking to see if your offer was still good?"

Delmar immediately bursts into laughter. He knew Tiara was the one woman who had a sexual appetite as great as his. "You mean you're interested in having sex with me? Let me guess. You're tired of putting in those extra hours at work, with that actor fellow what's his name?" he asked but didn't wait for an answer. "We both know you can get more enjoyment sexually and monetarily from the generous donator of good sex and good money, me Delmar."

"Sure, if you're saying you are going to be generous both money wise and sexually with Mr. Big Salami, if you know what I mean. Are you up for the challenge," her voice teased?

He laughed again. "You know I am. Do you need a ride? I can send my driver."

"Good, I'm at home and I do need to pack a bag," she lied looking through her rear-view mirror.

"Pack more than one and considering staying at least a week or two. I'm horny," his laughter burst out.

"Sounds perfect," Tiara answered.

Delmar paused for a moment and got serious. "I need you here with me right now Tiara. Don't you worry about a thing, I'll take care of anything you need money wise," he said with urgency.

Hours later with her eyes closed Tiara lay back against the bed and felt Delmar moving rhythmically up and down on top of her. She couldn't believe she let Delmar talk her into doing this without a condom. She was just about to open her mouth and say something when she heard him moan.

"I need you Tiara, I need you…" Delmar moaned into her ear. "We are two of a kind."

She always wanted this moment. She knew Delmar didn't love her, but he needed her. In Tiara's mind it was the closest thing to being the real thing. They understood each other.

She wrapped her legs tighter around him as she listened as he made groaning noises, and then she felt her body surging up as Delmar's face contorted with passion and they climaxed together.

That afternoon, just after three o'clock, Tiara sat quietly alone enjoying the view sitting on Delmar's patio. In the distance the coastal outline of Monterey Bay sparkled under the bright afternoon sun. She was about to rethink her plans for staying the week with Delmar when her cell phone rang. She checked the number. It was from Brandon.

Tiara grabbed it anxiously and looked around nervously. She exhaled speaking softly. "Hey baby, it's so good to hear from you."

"Tiara, I'm sorry I haven't phoned you before now," he apologized. "But I've been busy from the moment I stepped off the plane."

Her voice was gentle and sweet. "I understand."

"Tiara darling I'm afraid my stay is going to be longer than a couple of weeks. We began shooting a few scenes for the move and it's going to take at least eight weeks, maybe longer. But it will mean that this movie will get off on the right start."

"Oh Brandon, I already miss you so much already," she cooed into the phone softly hoping she was giving off the right effect.

"I miss you too," he told her. "You know I'll make it up to you when I get back."

"I don't know if I can go so long without you, Brandon baby."

Brandon chuckled. "Tell you what, just as soon as I've got everything under control, I'll send you a round trip plane ticket, agreed?"

"All right," Tiara smiled smugly into the phone.

"Look Tiara, I have to go, I'll call you soon, I promise," he said hanging up.

Tiara played with her hair and hung up with a triumphant smile.

Her triumphant smile was short lived as her phone rang out again.

It was Camille.

"Hello Camille," Tiara said, still checking making sure it was safe to talk.

"Hi Tiara, I was calling to say I was sorry for missing the party the other night," Camille answered.

"That's okay," Tiara paused and got nosy. "Well, I figured you had to work. I know you've been working a lot of long hours to earn money to buy Gabby a new car."

"Yeah that's old news, didn't my mother tell you? She's been driving her new car around a couple of weeks."

Tiara chuckled. "Good for Gabby, you know Camille I've been so busy I haven't had a chance to speak to your mother in a while," she took a deep breath. "So why did you miss the party the other night?"

"Brace yourself. That's why I'm calling. I've gotten back with Desmond," Camille responded, excitedly.

"Damn, I thought things were over between you and Desmond!" Tiara blurted.

"Tiara you sound like you're in a really bad mood. Don't get so excited."

Tiara realized Camille had been right. She checked around her to make sure she was still alone. She lowered her voice. "Camille I'm not in a bad mood. Are you sure you want to do that?"

Camille laughed it off. "What do you mean by that? Can't a girl change her mind and work things out with the man she loves?"

"Oh, I guess she can, especially if the man is good in bed," Tiara added with a laugh. "I hear it in your voice Camille. You guys are having a lot of make-up sex and you sound satisfied. In fact, you sound positively happy."

"Oh, Tiara I am," Camille's voice bubbled over with joy. "And ditto on the makeup sex thing we are having a lot of it. We've even played a few sex games, if you know what I mean. But I'm sure it's nothing like the sex-play Brandon has to offer you."

Tiara cleared her throat to hide the lie that rolled off her tongue. "Obviously, you got that right."

"By the way are you and Brandon out of town for the weekend?" Camille asked.

Tiara instantly tried to think of a response. "As a matter of fact, we are," she lied and was glad Camille was on the other end of the phone. "Look Camille I was sort of in the middle of something. Can you call me back later?"

"Yes… Yes… of course."

Tiara hung up the phone with Camille and thought she'd have a moment with her thoughts when Delmar's voice carried on the air.

"Tiara, where are you?"

Seconds later he emerged through the bushes onto the patio.

Tiara steeled herself to make her voice calm. "Delmar were you looking for me? I've been sitting right here all this time."

"Yes, I see, anyway you know Carmel has some wonderful shopping. I thought you might like to visit there today Tiara," Delmar said

Tiara took a long deep breath and studied him. He didn't act like he overhead her conversation. She faintly smiled. "Lets' go."

# Chapter 48

**Delmar Devereaux**

That Saturday evening, after returning home from taking Tiara on a shopping spree, Delmar stood at his bedroom window and loosened the top buttons of his shirt collar. He loved the view of the Pacific Ocean his bedroom afforded him. He saw the reflection of his face in the plate of glass and saw the dark shadows underneath his eyes.

Was Camille sleeping with Desmond Garcia? It was a thought he'd wished he didn't have.

He stood at the blind and tried to clear his thoughts. He squinted as he watched the car approach. There was no time to ponder about Camille Baptiste. His dinner guest had arrived. He quickly changed his shirt.

A half hour later, Delmar chitchatted over nothing with his guest as they dined on huge porterhouse steaks, garlic roasted mash potatoes, asparagus, and California Cabernet.

"Goodness, you must really love porterhouse steak Mr. Browning," Tiara said looking into his face with calm serenity.

For a moment Adam was paralyzed by her undivided attention. She was beautiful he thought, looking longingly at the swell of her breasts.

"I do, it's my favorite," he took a sip of his wine. "Tiara, I asked you to please call me Adam."

"Well Adam, if you desire anything more," she hesitated.

"I'm sure we can find plenty more where that came from."

Adam choked on his wine. She had no idea the affects her words were having on him. He stammered out. "Ah… Thank you Tiara."

Finally looking up from the report in his hand, Delmar broke the ice and broached the subject.

"Adam, how soon can you review the reports and finalize those permits?"

Adam Browning never took his eyes off Tiara. He stared at her like she was sex on a plate.

When he kept ignoring him Delmar loudly cleared his throat. "Tiara, I believe Adam may like for you to past the bread."

Tiara picked up the basket of bread and handed it to him. "Here Adam."

Adam tried to get his bearing. "Uh Huh? Thank you."

Tiara looked at him calmly and said. "Do you need me to pass you anything else?" she asked helpfully.

"No, this is fine," Adam answered.

Delmar took in Adam's long gaze at Tiara he'd noticed the man couldn't keep his eyes off her. He grinned to himself and tried to probe Adam for more answers.

"Adam I'm confused. Page three of your report clearly stated that the samples were thoroughly tested and contained no sign of contamination. Therefore, I see no reason why the permits cannot be finalized."

Adam quickly shook out his thoughts and entered the conversation with Delmar. He began stressing his point.

Tiara saw her chance to escape as the two men were eagerly talking business. "Would you two gentlemen please excuse me?"

"Of course," Adam said rising.

Tiara quickly made her exit.

A long silence ensued as Adam Browning sat back down and carefully folded the report back to page 3. "Here on this page it clearly states that if the result is inconclusive more samples must be taken to ensure there is no contamination."

Delmar watched his face. He knew Adam was up to something.

"Here, let me read this section to you," Adam Browning suggested.

"Never mind," Delmar protested. "I've read that report almost a hundred times."

"Look Delmar, I know you need those permits to resume construction. But you know the county's position has always been firm on soil conditions and your geological reports were incomplete," he stressed. "You have to follow procedure.The county takes these matters very seriously."

Delmar shrugged. "Okay Adam, we both know you have a lot of pull when it comes to handling certain county officials."

Adam laughed and shook his head. "I don't know what you are talking about."

Delmar blinked and clasped his hands together. "What's it going to take to make this happen?"

A frown came across Adam's face. "You know Delmar, for a minute I thought you were on the right track to having the permits approved when you invited me here to dinner today."

Delmar watched Adam for a second longer. "What do you want now?" he asked but didn't wait for an answer. "I suppose you want me to send another payment to that so-called external consulting company you employ?"

"Oh no, that's not what I meant," Adam eyes darted around the room. He cleared his throat and tried different approach. "I hope I'm not out of line. But months ago," he hesitated. "When I first saw with the young lady. I got the impress that you weren't in love with her. You said something then that stuck in my mind. And well, earlier today when I saw you with the young woman again, you said it again."

Delmar shrugged. "Oh, I can't seem to remember. What did I say?"

Adam took a sip of water. "It was the way you said it too, that gave me the impression and I consider myself to be fairly good at studying behavior."

"Well cut to the chase. What did I say?"

Adam felt his chest tighten. "You said that the young lady was available, if I was interested."

Delmar put down his drink as a light went off in his brain. Now he understood why Adam had agreed to have dinner at his home so suddenly. Finally, he'd found Adam's weakness.

Adam Browning began to slowly smile. "Why do you think I brought up the subject of making sure that dinner invitation you'd offered was for today? When you suggested we dine at your home I thought you understood?"

Delmar begin to smile. "So, what are you saying Adam?"

Adam got up and walked closer and pulled his chair in closer. He looked around before he leaned over and said, "I think you know what I'm saying, but if you need me to spell it out. Adam's voice grew softer. "I'm interested in having sex with that young woman, Tiara, but only if she doesn't mean anything to you, if you know what I mean."

The covers of Delmar's lips sneered up. "Don't worry. She doesn't mean anything to me," he said giving him a malicious grin. What a bastard he thought. Here he'd been worried about how much money he'd have to pay to get those permits approved on a contaminated building site. Now he had the official who was willing to look the other way. His problems were solved.

A fleeting expression crossed Adam's face. "Oh, but I don't want to cause any trouble for the young lady, if she's not the willing type."

"Don't worry about Tiara. Let me just get this straight. So, what I'm hearing is you want a favor in order to do me a favor."

Adam folded his hands. "I'm willing to pay of course if the young lady likes a little something for services rendered, jewelry or money you know what I mean?"

"No need to pay Adam, you get me with I need, and I'll throw Tiara in for free." He rose. "Come to my study Adam I have a very old private reserve there I'm sure you will love and then I'll go and see about your room," he looked back at him. "You do want to stay the night don't you Adam?"

"Yes of course," Adam knowingly nodded.

A half hour later Delmar knocked on Tiara's door. She opened it and he walked in carrying a tray loaded with a pitcher of mango juice, a bottle of vodka, glasses, and a gold foiled wrapped shoe box wrapped like a present with a bow on top.

"A present for me Delmar, you shouldn't have."

Tiara was curious about the box.

Delmar waited a moment before answering. He put the tray down on the table.

"I have a favor to ask of you."

Tiara started to speak and curiously looked at the box. "First, who's the gift for?"

"Open it," he smiled.

Excitedly she did as she was told.

Several neat bundles of one hundred-dollar bills greeted her.

"Money!" Tiara exclaimed, doing the money dance. "How much is here?"

"There's fifty-thousand dollars there. Enough to put down on that townhouse you asked me about months ago," he hesitated. "Now put the money down Tiara, it's not yours yet. You look like the lioness let loose in the hen house," Delmar jokingly said.

Tiara smiled softly. She could tell from the look on his face Delmar needed her and she knew better than to take a drink from him until she laid all her cards out on the table and had everything she wanted.

"Okay if I'm the lioness in the hen house then you're the predator who eats rabbits for dinner and I'm guessing you got Adam Browning bagged as your next rabbit," she joked.

Delmar stood there grinning back at her.

Tiara knew he was up to something. "Jesus, you and I are two damaged people Delmar," she said smoothly. "What do you need Adam for?"

"Who says I need Adam? Maybe Adam needs me."

Tiara looked him over. She knew he was lying. She gave him her best seductive smile and ran her hands over her body. "Looks like I've got the good stuff that men like you and Adam can't get enough of."

Delmar laughed. "You're speaking the truth. Are you going to help me?"

"First tell me what you want me to do for all this money."

"Let's have a drink first," he said handing her a glass.

"No Delmar let's talk more money first," she brazenly smiled. "That money isn't even a five percent down payment on the townhouse I was looking at."

Silence fell.

Delmar turned his head, so she could not read his emotions.

"You see, you're a man with power and money and yet you want a woman to do the hard work for nothing."

Tiara could see his brain working. She knew she needed to press her case. "You want me to screw that old weasel looking goat Adam and make him feel happy.Happy enough so that you can get what you want and then you're going to make a lot of money, millions I bet."

He pretended to ignore her as he walked over and stared out the window.Through the window he could see the light in his study where he'd left Adam drinking. He took a deep breath; he was so close to having what he wanted.

Her thoughts raced as she stared back at him. She heard the voice inside her head say. *"But you are not willing to pay me what I am worth."*

Delmar turned and looked back at her and snickered out. "Do you want the money or not?"

Tiara looked at him and thought she saw dollar signs flash behind his eyes. Her instincts told her how anxious he was. Delmar was a crooked wheeler and dealer that was used to writing large checks to get what he wanted. She saw her chance to get him to spread some of his wealth her way. "You don't care anything about how doing things like screwing that old goat would make me feel," she said laying the guilt trip on him heavy.

"This is all the cash I have," he rattled off, shaking his head.

She quickly saw a way to end the debate and make him make a decision. "Maybe I'm thinking I'm about ready to head back home to San Jose for the night."

Delmar's voice softened. "It looks like I was holding out on you here's a cashier's check for two-hundred thousand dollars. This will buy you that townhouse you said you wanted," he oozed with charm and sex appeal. "Just so you know I expect to be invited over for the housewarming."

"Just so you know Delmar. I expect you to leave. If I've got to do Adam, I want privacy," Tiara demanded. "I've got some pride you know?"

At just past eleven o'clock that night, Tiara enjoyed herself in the dimly lit atrium styled enclosed pool area at Delmar's house. The temperature-controlled pool felt like bliss against her naked skin as she swam.

She heard the sliding patio door open and looked up as Adam Browning walked in.He was wearing a pair of swimming trunks.

"You don't want to get those wet," Tiara laughed as she swam over and got out of the pool.

"Damn you naked," Adam said staring back at her with predatory eyes.

"Yes, I am Adam. Do you like my birthday suit?" Tiara asked not waiting for a response.

"Of course, I like it. What's not to like. You're a very beautiful woman," Adam said.

Tiara offered him her hand and he took it. She led him over to the round canopy enclosed bed at the far end of the pool area.

They stood their facing each other.

She could tell he'd drunk the spike drink Delmar had given him, but Tiara didn't care. She was operating on greed as her eyes looked over his body. "So, what do you think Adam? Do you want to play around with me?"

"Sure, I do," he nodded.

"Do you know what I want Adam?" she asked but didn't wait for an answer, as she yanked at his swimming trunks. "I want to see you naked," she giggled uncontrollably.

She took his swim trunks off him and gave him a condom.

"Here tiger put this on," she giggled handing him a condom before she leaped onto the bed.

Adam was a man who had no restraint when it came to a naked beautiful woman.His breath quickened as he did what she had instructed. He felt his erection tighten against the condom as he put it on.

Tiara's eyes grew wide as she laid there and watched Adam's male organ inflate enormously. Who knew, she thought, a man that looked like an accountant was as well hung as this.

Quickly Adam crawled up on the bed after her and one of his huge hands caressed her breast. The nipple got hard. His other hand stoked her erogenous zone.

Tiara loved the way he was pawing her. Adam Browning had skills that spoke to the nymphomaniac within her. She started giggling. She knew she was a twisted person.

"Thank you, Christ," he said before his mouth began to move slowly down her naked body.

# Chapter 49

**Can't get enough of your love baby...**

The next two weeks Camille and Desmond had no worries as they stayed at the cute beach bungalow off the coast of San Simeon.

Earlier that day, it was so beautiful that they took the early tour of Hearst Castle. Now the two headed back along the same path up the slope back to their bungalow she called a little piece of heaven.

Forty minutes later she watched the contours of Desmond's strong muscular body as he put another log on the fire. Camille thought about the months they had been apart. Only weeks ago, she was determined to shut Desmond out of her life for good, yet now, with him back in her life, she felt like time seemed to fall away as if it had never existed. Yet she knew one thing was for sure. She was not Desmond's puppet to be manipulated at his will.

Desmond watched the flame roar up as he put another log on the fire. His sex throbbed just like as the flame roared higher in the fireplace, he thought. Never in his life had he wanted a woman as much as he wanted Camille.

He poured them both a glass of wine and walked over and handed Camille her glass.

Camille took her glass and sipped slowly. Feeling of anxiety ripped through her mind as she thought back on the month's past. All the joy of the morning seemed to slip away from her and she said it out loud without realizing it. "I can't believe you've managed to change my mind about you in just two weeks. I hated you so much all those months you were gone from me Desmond. I hated you for ruining my life," she paused, and stared back at him. "I bet you didn't even know I was ready to move away from San Jose and start all over again?"

Desmond's face contorted with agony. "Babe…"

She lifted her hand silencing him. "But now I understand it wasn't until later when I found out that you had driven by the house the night before you left and seen Delmar there with me," she stopped abruptly nervously and said. "Desmond I'm the one who should be sorry about our misunderstanding."

"Hush, sweetness! I want to be with you for the rest of my life. You know I can't get enough of your love Camille. It must be because of that big forgiving heart of yours." Desmond joked, trying to hold himself back. "Besides, you've never been one to hold grudges."

She nodded. "No, I don't, and you're right I can't get enough of your love either," she grinned.

His appetite for her was growing; it was insatiable as he felt his erection. His eyes locked with hers and spoke to her.

Camille's grin died instantly as she watched his eyes making love to her without touching her. She knew why she was in love with this man. She could feel his passion for her deep within. She gulped down the last of her wine and put the glass down. "Just don't ever do that to me again," she commanded in a low voice.

Desmond's eyes roamed with a hungry need over her body. His hand reached out and caressed her breast. "I want to be with you."

For a brief moment she smiled and then grabbed his head between her hands and brought his lips to hers kissing him with pent up urgency. Then her fingers fluttered delicately along the strong lines of his body and unzipped his pants. She found his bulging erection and her fingers began to stroke him.

Within minutes their clothes littered the floor as Desmond groaned and swept her up into his arms and carried her to the bed. He lowered her beneath him as he felt her slippery hot wetness as he entered her.

Camille groaned and gasped with pleasure, aware of nothing but the powerful sensation as he satisfied her completely.

# Chapter 50

**One more thing...**

It was almost ten o'clock that morning, when Delmar looked at his watch. He left the five-star hotel in downtown San Jose almost an hour ago. He sighed and rested his head on the steering wheel of his mint condition fully restored 1934 black convertible Pierce Arrow.

He watched as the white Honda accord pulled into the drive way. He got out of the car and walked over.

"Good morning, my future Mother-In-Law."

Gabby turned at the sound of his voice and reached up and gave him a hug. "Poor Delmar, you've lost the battle," she murmured. "Well I guess you haven't heard the news?"

Delmar frowned. "What news?"

"Come inside Delmar I'll make you a cup of coffee."

"No, I want the truth right now," he said, his voice laced with pain.

Gabby shrugged. "Suit yourself. It's probably good I don't invite you in what with Camille and Desmond getting married and all."

"What? You're lying," Delmar said as his lips quivered, as the muscles in his face worked silently.

Gabby nodded. "Yes, it looks like they are planning a big wedding."

Delmar's lips turned up into a sneer. "This is ridiculous. I want to speak to Camille."

"No Delmar, I don't think that would be a good idea."

"What do you mean it wouldn't be a good thing?"

"It seems that fiancé of hers has not only been doing the wooing part to get my daughter back and marry him, but the man has also been doing some spying on you," she softly said. "Did you know Delmar that the private investigator Desmond hired learned somehow that you were responsible for tampering with Camille's cell phone?"

"What I… That's a lie," he blurted.

Gabby's mouth firmed into a hard line. She took a deep breath and knew she must not tell Delmar what other information Desmond's investigator had found, no matter what. Now more than ever she was grateful Camille had chosen Desmond Garcia over Delmar. Desmond had shown Gabby the investigator report and she knew Delmar and Tiara had been having a torment affair. Desmond had even asked Gabby if she should tell Camille. And they both had agreed not to. Gabby felt sorry for Tiara. She knew the kind of childhood she had growing up.Tiara would always be like a daughter to her.

"Don't lie to me Delmar all the evidence that investigator found was traced back to you. I can't believe you would do something so underhanded to Camille," she shook her head staring back at him."

Delmar's stricken face changed expressions. "All I need to do is talk to Camille and sort this thing out. Tell me where she is? Gabby, I need to talk to her. Look, I'm prepared to give you some bingo money," he pulled out a wad of one hundred-dollar bills and thrust them at her.

Gabby stared back at him as her thoughts raced. *"He's trying to pauperize me with blackmail money."*

She cleared her throat. "I don't know where Camille is right at this minute. But she's been staying with Desmond since he got back." She softly chucked. "You know Delmar life can be funny sometimes. Who knew that Desmond, *the Orchid Lover* would figure out who was your secret *Mistress of Desire?*"

"What?" Delmar asked looking miserably back at her.

"Don't worry Delmar, your secret is safe with me," Gabby said coldly, before reaching into her purse and pulling out her keys. "Delmar, just in case you didn't know, Desmond was watching out for me and Camille all along, while he was gone. He gave Camille the money to pay you back for my car. So, it looks like you didn't buy me my new car after all."

For the first time Delmar's face cloudy over with understanding, as Gabby's words set in. He couldn't believe what he had been hearing. Desmond had outsmarted him and taken his rightful place beside Camille.

Gabby opened the door and paused. "Oh yeah, one more thing Delmar, I don't think it would be a good thing if you came around again. Desmond wouldn't like to hear that you were coming around," she said, as she slammed the door behind her.

# Chapter 51

**You Idiot!**

Three weeks later, Tiara had plunged herself into her work while waiting for Brandon Stone to return from shooting his movie. Now she sat at her desk at work and smiled looking back at her bank statement on the computer. She had been worried the check Delmar had gave her wouldn't clear the bank. But nothing had gone wrong. She was now a very wealthy woman. If Brandon didn't return, she didn't care. She could go on with her life with the balance in her bank account.

Her eyes scanned over the Tuscany property development brochures. She let out a big sigh as her stomach did flip flops. The first thing she needed to do was to get some lunch.

A wave of nausea swept Tiara at lunch and she ended lunch abruptly and hurried home and took a relaxing shower. She stood in front of the bathroom mirror and examined herself. She knew she was pregnant. She almost cursed herself for wondering how she had let it happen and then her mind thought back. She checked to see when her period was due. She was late. She thought back. The only man she let sleep with her without protection was Delmar.She remembered she had let him talk her out of using precaution that whole time she spent with him.

She buried her face in her hands and started crying. "What a mess I've made."

That night as she tossed and turned trying to sleep, suddenly a thought hit her as she found herself drifting soundly off to sleep.

When Tiara awakened that morning, she knew what she had to do. She turned her car into the driveway arriving at Delmar's home. It was Sunday. She knew he was at home.

Tiara got out of her car and pressed the doorbell until someone answered.

Delmar finally opened the door and looked at her curiously. "Tiara, what the hell are you doing here at this time of the morning?"

"I've got news that can't wait Delmar," she said walking into the foyer. "Shall we go to your office?"

A few minutes later Delmar poured himself another glass of brandy, sipped, and turned and looked at her. "What's this news that can't wait Tiara?"

She bit her lip. "I'm pregnant Delmar!"

"What? Why should I care?"

"Because it's your baby Delmar!"

The color suddenly drained from his face. "No… No, I'm sure that little bastard ain't mine."

Tiara slapped his face.

Delmar's hand whipped out and slapped her back.

The moment was tense.

"You're going to pay for that Delmar! I've got a mind to call the police and have them arrest you for beating the mother of your child."

"Then I'll have them arrest you for being a thief and a slut, and I will tell them you hit me first."

"I'm not a thief you idiot," she said rubbing her face.

"Well that's original, now I'm an idiot. Are you going to call your child that?" He laughed out. "I can see it now, you, living in that townhouse that you made me buy calling your child an idiot! And what will the child protective people say? Better yet, I can just see them taking that poor kid away from you. I'll make sure of that."

"Shut up Delmar. You and I are just alike. Like you said so before.

Only I'm trying to change and you. Well you can't help yourself. You know this is your child you bastard."

He sneered back at her. "I'm not going to play some twisted mind game with you right now Tiara about who your baby daddy is. I know you've been sleeping with that Brandon Stone guy. Why the hell don't you pin that brat on him. It's probably his baby. Hell, it's probably some other stupid bastard's brat for all I know. Who knows who your nymphomaniac ass has been sleeping with," he said taking a gulp of his brandy?

Tiara ignored him and walked over to pour herself a drink.

"Uh! Uh! Uh! Naughty…Naughty, you can't drink this stuff anymore. You're pregnant, remember?"

"Oh Delmar, you do care about me."

He smiled and patted her head. "No darling, haven't I taught you anything? I'm still pretty much the guiltless, scoundrel, bastard you've always known me to be."

She read the seriousness in his eyes. She could tell Delmar's mind was calculating up a plan. "What are you thinking of?

A slow smile came to his lips. "Suppose you sit on the couch and listen to me for a while Tiara."

He grinned. "What's the one thing I'm always telling you Tiara?"

"I know that you never feel guilty about anything that you do in this world Delmar and knowing you, you're looking at this baby thing from an advantage point to get something you want."

"Correction, something we both want," he said.

You came here today hoping to get a lot of money out of me for that baby you're carrying. But what if I came up with a solution that could get you what you want and me what I want?"

There was a silent pause.

"What… What do you mean?" She rubbed her face. "Why should I help you Delmar?"

"There's a rational solution here, and you really want a rich daddy for your baby."

Tiara walked over to the couch and sat down. "I'm listening."

233

# Chapter 52

**Reno Nevada...**

Tiara waited for Camille outside of the lady's restroom at the Reno International Airport. It was just past nine o'clock that night.

Her cell phone rang.  The number was from Delmar.  He was checking to see if they had made it.

"Hi", she answered softly.

"Did Camille join you?" Delmar asked her.

"Yes, we made it."

"Good job well done.  I booked you two at the Peppermill.  I put you up in the Palace Suite and it looks like everything is going as planned," he hesitated. "Oh, and Tiara, only call me if it's an emergency. Otherwise I'll see you at our set time."

"Will do," Tiara said.

As soon as she hung up Tiara spotted Camille coming out of the restroom.

"Camille, there's a limousine waiting to take us to the hotel."

Camille nodded and followed her. "I'll call Desmond from the limo and see if he's made it in."

After Desmond had checked in, showered and changed.  He spoke with Camille and arranged to meet Hugh London in the sports bar in the hotel lobby where he was staying.

Desmond checked his watch again. He knew he was acting nervous. Hugh London wasn't late, he was early. But it was the first time he'd been asked to act as best man and he wanted to get it right.

A man walked up to him. "Let me guess, you're Desmond Garcia, right?"

Desmond smiled "And you are Hugh London. You look just like Camille described. So, tell me what gave me away to you. This tuxedo," he joked

Hugh gave him a wide grin. "Well that, and the fact that I could tell your tuxedo wasn't a rental like mine."

The waiter walked over.

"Waiter, I'll have a martini," Hugh said. "Desmond, let me buy you a drink before we get this wedding underway."

"Sure, I'll have a martini as well."

"For some reason Desmond, I've started back to drinking, martinis, as well as other hard liquor. I don't know why," Hugh said. "I guess this marriage stuff gives me the nervous Willies."

Desmond nodded. "You could have something there. So, Hugh, what kind of drink do you regularly drink?"

"I've always been a beer drinker," he took a breath. "Now marriage, that's a road, that will make a man drink hard liquor every day."

"I take it you've been married before?"

Before Hugh could answer the waiter brought their drinks.

Hugh paid for their drinks and tipped the waiter generously.

"Thank you," the waiter said.

When the waiter was out of earshot, Hugh said. "The answer to your question Desmond is no. I haven't been married before. And I never intended to be. Being in the movie business I'm already married to the craziest bitch that ever lived."

Desmond laughed hard and held up his drink in a toast. "Thanks for the drink and the best joke I've heard in ages."

Hugh threw back his drink. "Whoa man that takes the edge off," he said looking nervously around. "You know Desmond, I get the feeling you're not taking me seriously. Marriage is not for the faint hearted and I believe we should put our heads together and talk Brandon out of it," he said reaching into his jacket pocket pulling out a flask. He tipped the flask into the martini glass.

"Oh, I am taking you seriously Hugh," Desmond said, glancing at his watch and then downing his martini. "But we're not ones getting married. Brandon is. If Brandon hasn't figured out yet that marriage is a dangerous game filled with dangerous people playing dirty tricks, well then who are we to tell him?"

With that Hugh laughed out and then held out his flask and filled Desmond's glass.

"We'd better finish here and head over to the chapel. We don't want Brandon Stone looking for us," Desmond said reaching into his pocket and pulling out an envelope. He made a show of flipping the envelope over in his hand examining it carefully before he then put it back into his pocket.

Hugh eyed the envelope with interest and rubbed his chin with an unsettling sense of déjà vu. He'd been paid a lot of money for what he had to do. "Come along Desmond the chapel is waiting."

# Chapter 53

**Final Acts, The Cat & The Ladies...**

Camille stood at the altar holding Tiara's bouquet and felt a warm sleepy feeling creep over her.  She was sure she was still standing because Tiara was standing beside her propping her up. Slowly she tilted her head. 'Tiara, how much longer will this take?"

"Everything will be over in a moment. Just be patient. Here take another sip of your iced coffee, this should keep you awake."

Tiara looked up and watched as Hugh London helped Desmond Garcia through the chapel door. It was obvious some drug was racing euphorically through Desmond's veins.

The next thing Tiara remembered was hearing a man's voice say.

"Is this the bride to be? He hesitated. "Oh, I see there are two brides just as there are two grooms. I see...I see," he repeated

"Yes. Yes...Go ahead and say the vows."

The minister said robustly.  "Dearly beloved, we are gathered together here in the sight of God – and in the face of this company – to join together this man and this woman in holy matrimony..."

Camille giggled. "Someone is getting married."

"Hush Camille," Tiara scolded, feeling her chest tighten.

The minister continued, "Marriage is the union of husband and wife in heart, body and mind. It is intended for their mutual joy – and for the help and comfort given on another in prosperity and adversity."

At that moment Tiara looked back at Desmond Garcia, the man she was here to marry. Desmond had no clue she was the one he was marrying today. He was too drugged out to know anything.

She looked up at the man standing next to him. Hugh London had done his job well. Little did Desmond know Hugh was nothing but an actor, who had lied to him about being a friend of Brandon Stone and that Brandon had wanted the two of them to be the best men at his wedding.

Tiara leaned over and whispered. "Delmar, I can't believe it your plan is working."

"Shhhhh, the minister isn't finished yet."

For once in her life Tiara was confused as she looked back at Camille playing with the wedding bouquet like a toy and rambling like a two-year-old.Tiara Blake, the girl who had never needed anyone, was about to hurt the only true friend she'd ever had in her life.How could this be happening she thought?She loved Camille like a sister. She was the only true friend Tiara had.

Then she looked back at Delmar Devereaux. The man who had cleverly devised this scheme to get himself married to the woman he truly loved. Camille Baptiste.

"Do you take this woman ...."

"I do! I do!" Delmar shouted.

And all that Tiara could think of was that she would forever be alone, friendless in a loveless marriage being hated by her best friend for stealing her man.

It was a strange world she lived in. Nothing made sense to her anymore, but one thing Tiara knew for sure, she had to make things right. She couldn't just stand there and do nothing.

"Stop! Stop! This wedding is a sham!" Tiara screamed at the top of her lungs. "Camille! Camille wake up Delmar made me spike your tea and your coffee!"

Delmar tore Tiara's hands from Camille's arm. "Shut up Tiara before you ruin everything!"

Tiara immediate turned her attention she clutched Desmond's arm. "Oh, Desmond you've got to wake up and help me! Camille loves you wake up and fight for her! Somebody call 911. Delmar is a crazy drug dealer!"

The loud meowing of a cat carried across the air.

Tiara's shrill scream died in mid-air as she turned and looked up at three women standing before her.

"Who are you?"

"You called 911 and we answered," one of the three ladies said."

Tiara shook her head. "I don't get that, what?"

A Brazilian looking woman took a step forward. "I am Consuelo, Desmond's housekeeper."

"And I am Nona Desmond's secretary," another woman said.

The woman holding the cat stared back and said. "And I am Glenda D'Goodwrench dear. And this is my cat "Pinky", she said.

The cat called pinky jumped out of Glenda's arms and glided over to Tiara. Tiara panicked and went sprawling to the floor.

"Come ladies Glenda commanded. "My muffins are needed here."

"Tiara, get up off that floor!  You can help Consuelo," Glenda bellowed.

Instantly Tiara did as she was told.

Quickly Consuelo brought over a chair and helped Tiara eased Camille down into it.

"Mister your name is Hugh London, right?" Desmond's secretary Nona asked tapping him on the shoulder. "Help me get Desmond into a chair."

Glenda D'Goodwrench looked around the room. "Oh, minister did you know it is a crime for a person to marry someone when they are legally married to someone else?"

"No one here is married to anyone else," Tiara stated puzzled. "Right Delmar?"

Delmar locked gazes with Tiara for a fraction of a second and then averted his eyes.

The minster cleared his throat. "Look Miss," he shook his head. "I ask that question in several ways on the marriage application, and no one has ever pulled a fast one on me before."

Glenda glanced up. "Delmar don't you have something to tell the minister?"

The minister turned and held a steady gaze on Delmar. "Mister you ain't trying to pull a fast one on me here?"

Delmar gave a goofy confused smile. "Sir you see, these ladies are just trying to sabotage my wedding."

"Delmar Devereaux you are still married to me and you know it," announced a loud woman's voice.

"Oh shit!" Delmar blurted, as his goofy smile faded.

The woman entered the room. She had lots of dyed blonde hair piled high on top of her head. She had a great figure and was wearing a bright pink, tight dress, that accent her voluptuous hips. The woman played up the sensual effects of her hips as she walked provocatively into the room.

The woman walked straight up to Delmar and stood in front of him. Her fingernails were painted the same hot pink of her dress. She reached out a hot pink lacquered fingernail and tapped his chin.

"Hey Delmar sugar, remember me Mrs. Delmar Devereaux?" the woman said coquettishly tilting her head to one side. "It seems you forgot to pay me that final payment to make sure our divorce was final," her lips curled up into a sinister smile. "Looks like ain't nobody getting married today!"

"Raven Channing what the hell are you doing here?"

Squaring her shoulders Raven walked over in front of Desmond and studied him."That is Raven Devereaux, but I prefer Mrs. Devereaux and the question of the day Delmar, is what have you done to that Orchid lover, Desmond Garcia?"

"Damn Raven don't come here butting your nose in other people's business and stop keep pretending you are my wife."

Raven laughed out. "I ain't pretending sugar! I'm the real thing! And Delmar you know I love it when you call me Mrs. Devereaux."

Tiara was stunned as she took in the situation. "Delmar, you never told me you were married?"

"Shut up Tiara!" Delmar blurted nervously rubbing his brow. Things weren't going as he had planned.

Then Mrs. Delmar Devereaux favored Tiara with a big smile, as her gaze journeyed from Tiara to the young woman Tiara was fanning. The woman looked like she had fainted.

"Oh, hello Tiara, I guess you are Delmar's latest *Mistress of Desire*?"

Tiara was stung. "I'm not Delmar's Mistress of Desire!"

"Honey, oh yes you are," Mrs. Devereaux said, letting the word slide off tongue. "Maybe you can tell me what is wrong what the Orchid Lover, Desmond Garcia and your friend, which you are fanning?"

Tiara shrugged. "I… You have to ask Delmar."

Raven shrugged. "I don't have to ask Delmar to know that it looks like there on one of his little spike drink trips. Let me give you a word of advice Tiara, never drink anything Delmar gives you," she hesitated. "Oh, and never become one of Delmar's Mistresses of

Desire. It doesn't pay well and believe me, I know. He pays more when you are his wife."

Glenda D'Goodwrench watched the encounter between the two women and laughed. "Whew, what a mess this is," she breathed out. "Hey minister, why don't you go and brew us a pot of strong black coffee?" Glenda D'Goodwrench stated. "It's going to be a long night. Where are my muffins?"

# Epilogue

Three months later…

"Take the road, south when you head back home tonight Camille," Glenda said.

"What? But San Jose is north of here," Camille said. "I was heading home."

"Glenda D'Goodwrench knows the way to San Jose Miss Camille Baptiste. I don't need you to tell me that," she said nodding her head while walking Camille to her car.

She looked up at the sky and Camille's gaze followed hers.

"It is almost morning," Glenda said. "Now you listen to me. You came here last night to tell me your story and I listened attentively. I did not interrupt you. Not one moment, right?"

Camille's eyes looked at her questionably and nodded.

"Okay now I tell you what to do and you will listen to me and take the road, heading south, okay?" Glenda pointed and closed Camille's car door.

Glenda stepped away from the curb and watched Camille's car as long as she could.

"You drive safe Miss Camille," she whispered to the wind.

Moments later, Camille took the old south road, leading out of the old town of San Juan Bautista.

When she saw the Jaguar with its trunk up parked on the side of the road with a flat tire, she almost passed it by. And then she saw the man when he turned, and her car lights hit him.

She came to an abrupt stop and got out.

The moment seemed to stretch out into infinity as she stood there staring back at him.

Finally, she whispered out in disbelieve. "Desmond, is that you?"

"Camille! Oh Camille. Oh, thank God that I found you," he said, closing the gap between them.

Her heart pounded hard in her chest and she swayed as Desmond drew near. He grasped her by the arms and pulled her into his embrace.

"Oh Desmond…Desmond," she cried. "I thought you were dead!"

He held her close. "Oh Camille, I love you," he said kissing her. "I have always loved you. You are everything to me. Everything I ever dreamed of. Please tell me that you still love me?"

He kissed her again.

She gasped in delighted surprise. She loved him so much. A flood of tears ran down her face. "You don't have to ask. Of course, I love you more than anything else in the world," Baffled she stared curiously at him. "But Consuelo… I never knew if you were alive or…"

"I've been back among the land of the living for a while now. But Consuelo wouldn't let me out of the house. Finally, I escaped from her this morning determined to drive to San Jose and find you. But then Consuelo caught me before I could get my car out of the driveway and she told me you spent the night in San Juan Bautista, at Glenda's home. I was trying to get there we you found just now."

Their eyes held.

And then he stepped back away from her and fumbled in his pockets and pulled out a ring. "I've waited long enough and I'm not going to wait any longer," he said staring back at her with sincere eyes. "Camille, please say you'll marry me. Be my wife."

"Yes, Desmond. Yes!"

Desmond smiled relieved. He pulled her closed and kissed her passionately.

She hugged him for what seemed like hours. Finally, she raised her head. "Oh, Desmond you know I love you, don't you? But look at the sky," she said checking her watch. "I have to get back to San Jose today. I've promised Tiara I would be there for her."

He pulled away from her. "Why?"

She smiled. "Because Tiara is pregnant, and I promised to drop by her and be there with her when she has her ultrasound. You see Desmond in about six months I'm going to be a God-mother," Camille explained.

He cupped her chin in his hand gazing down at her. "His face filled with a brilliant expression of fierce love. "Six months gives us plenty of time to get married, before Tiara's baby come. In the meantime, let's call triple A and have the tow one of these cars home. I'm riding shotgun with you today Camille. For some reason I can't explain I just want to be close to you today. That is if you don't mine?"

Camille laughed out. "Oh, Desmond baby I would never mind."

# Books By J. A. Jackson

**A Geek an Angel Series...**
**The Deceiver**
**The Proposition**
**The Grand Hotel**
**Lovers, Players, & The Seducer**
**Lovers, Players, Revenge (Book II)**


**The Mistress of Desire**
**& The Orchid Lover Book I**
**Mistress of Desire**
**& The Orchid Lover Book II**


**The Deceiver's Secret**

**When A Taker Dreams**


Diamond at Midnight

(Release 2019)

# About the Author

J.A. Jackson is the pseudonym for an author, who loves to write deliciously sultry adult romantic, suspenseful, entertaining novels with a unique twist. She lives in an enchanted little house she calls home in the Northern California foothills.

She spent over ten years working in the non-profit sector where she wrote grants, press releases and contributed many stories to their newsletter. She was their Newsletter editor for over ten years. She loves growing roses, a good pot of hot tea, chocolate, magical stories, suspense stories, ghost stories, and reading Jane Austen again and again in her past time.

**You can connect with me on:**

http://jerreeceannjackson.blogspot.com

https://twitter.com/jerreece

https://www.facebook.com/JerreeceJackson/?ref=bookmarks

https://www.goodreads.com/author/show/7515379.J_A_Jackson/blog

**Subscribe to my newsletter:**

https://www.linkedin.com/in/jerreece-jackson-1657853

# Also by J. A. Jackson

The Series - A Geek, An Angel)Starting this series is ~ The Grand Hotel, next - Lovers, Players, & The Seducer (Book I) and Lovers, Players, Revenge (Book II).

Second Series ~The Mistress of Desire & The Orchid Lover Book I Mistress of Desire

& The Orchid Lover Book II.

~Stand alone books are: The Deceiver's Secret,When A Taker Dreams, Diamond at Midnight and The Proposition.

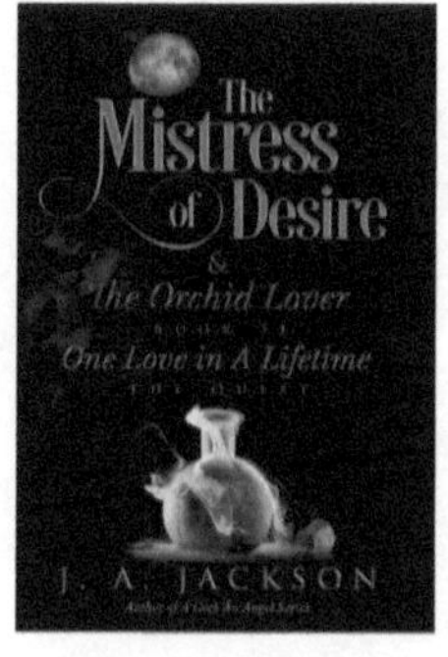

**Mistress of Desire & The Orchid Lover Book II!**

Neither Tiara Blake or Delmar Devereaux have a past to be proud of. With a joint history packed with dishonesty, blackmail—and a juicy, torrid love affair—the pair didn't expect their paths would cross again.

**Lovers, Players & The Seducer, Book I**

Lust and passion fueled star-crossed lovers Lacey & Kienan. Their love was packed with angst and heartbreak from the start.

Add in brother Nicholas and his addiction to playing deceitful games. And you have a slam-bang roller-coaster ride of scandal and excitement!

**When A Taker Dreams**

Sometimes life is not that simple. Love can be complicated. Especially when Lust is a powerful emotion!

Cierra Cantrell is insecure, tortured by her past life experience with men. After accepting the help of a matchmaker. Cierra soon discovers that old vendettas from the past could stop her chance at happiness and put her in danger!

**The Deceiver's Secret**

Prepare to lose yourself in a fascinating world of romance, intrigue and sultry secrets, a world of decadence, adventure and excitement, a world you'll never want to leave!

Enter the world of Eve Lafoy- a world filled with decadent parties, sultry encounters, and a fabulous nightlife. A world inhabited by jealousy and betrayal.